THE LONESOME TRIALS OF JOHNNY RILES

THE LONESOME TRIALS OF JOHNNY RILES

GREGORY HILL

Leapfrog Press
Fredonia, New York

Published in 2015 in the United States by
Leapfrog Press LLC
PO Box 505
Fredonia, NY 14063
www.leapfrogpress.com

Printed in the United States of America

Distributed in the United States by
Consortium Book Sales and Distribution
St. Paul, Minnesota 55114
www.cbsd.com

Map courtesy of Kevin Rontel

"Horse with no Name" by Dewey Bunnell. © 1971
Alfred Music Publishing. Used by permission.

First Edition

Library of Congress Cataloging-in-Publication Data

Hill, Gregory W., 1972-
The lonesome trials of Johnny Riles / Gregory Hill. -- First edition.
pages ; cm
ISBN 978-1-935248-67-5 (softcover)
1. Country life--Fiction. I. Title.
PS3608.I4293L66 2015
813'.6--dc23
2014044516

Maureen, I think you're the bee's knees.

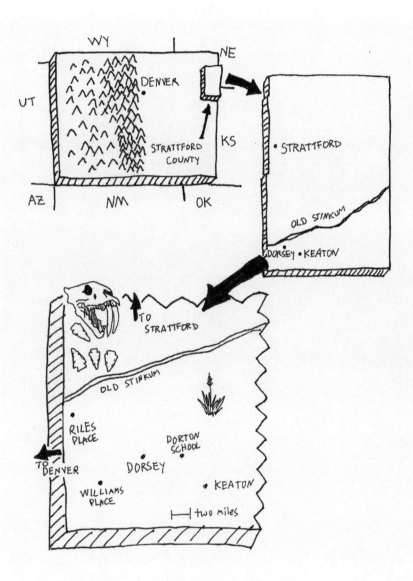

PART I

A HORSE WITH NO NAME

CHAPTER 1

OCTOBER

One day, the wind blew. It lifted the dust and took it away. The next day was Thursday, the day my little brother played his very first professional basketball game, so I climbed on my horse and rode north toward the riverbed in search of arrowheads. It was October twenty-third, nineteen seventy-five. There's nothing to worry about in October.

Trotting across the grasslands, my grey mare took me up a hill and down the other side, right to where the river used to run.

There's no flow in Old Stinkum anymore. Hasn't been since the flood of '35, when the water ran so deep and fast that it drowned five hundred head of cattle and left their carcasses rotting in the mud. The flood took away the river's will. Now Old Stinkum is just a stripe of moist sand with half-dead cotton-wood trees lingering on either side. I sometimes hear stories of a mountain lion that lurks amongst those trees. I find those claims to be dubious.

I don't look for arrowheads in the riverbed itself. That'd be foolish. But just on the other bank, on the north side, there's a flat, dead prairie that gets swept clean every time the wind blows. Nobody else knows about that place.

After the horse and I crossed the river, I hooked my elbow over the horn of the saddle, leaned sideways, and started scanning the landscape. The ground was bare and packed hard. I let the mare choose her way. We wound about, moving generally away from the river. I saw a couple of flint chips, nothing worth climbing down for.

I find it relaxing to ride in this manner, leaning and bobbing off the saddle. Staring at the ground as it passes underneath, I often consider various aspects of life. Whether it's worth living, mainly. Previous contemplations of this sort had always ended inconclusively and, on this particular occasion, I was having even less success than was customary. I was stuck, in particular, on the manner in which a slam-dunk could be deemed a greater achievement than that of raising a healthy calf, and how a man can be paid good money for playing a game, but not for holding down a ranch in a half-desert that hardly exists.

The horse lurched backward. I hung onto the saddle horn with both hands, one foot kicking for a stirrup. I spoke some cuss words. The horse eased up enough to put four feet on the ground.

I looked this way and that. No mountain lions. No rattlesnakes. The horse pranced in a nervous circle. I walked her back a few steps. Her breaths pushed her ribs against my knees.

I said, "You're okay."

I climbed off and told her to stay put. I peered about, looking for anything that'd frighten a half-ton mammal of reasonable intelligence. I found it, directly ahead and half buried in the hard-packed sand. A skull of some sort. Not a human skull, not anything I'd ever seen before. It was black, and roughly the size of a football. Bigger, even. The size of a pillow. Monstrous, if you get right down to it.

The mare stood watching me out of one dopey eye. I told her she didn't have anything to worry about. Then I squatted and began digging the skull out of the ground. I have a good knife. I found it under a rock when I was fifteen years old. You don't come across many rocks in this country and there's damned few knives hidden under the ones that you do. The handle had rotted off. The blade was as long as my right hand, rusty but not altogether pitted up. It had once been a good knife. I brought it home and showed my brother, Kitch. He's eight years younger than me but ever since he could talk he's had an opinion on everything. He took a look at the knife and said, "That deal's older than you or me put together. It's probably fifty years old."

I ground the rust off, polished the blade, and made a new handle out of a block of cherry wood. I honed that knife until it could cut a fly's wing. Then I found some old leather hanging in the barn and made a holster, which I tried to emboss with the name Excalibur but there wasn't enough room. So it's just Excal.

The skull was stuck. Sand had settled into it hard, almost like stone. One side was exposed and I could clearly see an eye socket and some chewing teeth, pure black, just like the skull. The skull had a curve to it that reminded me of a cat. But it was way too big for a cat. I supposed it was a mountain lion.

I began to scrape away the dirt. The process required patience. First, I squatted, and then I sat on my haunch. Eventually, I was lying on my belly, soaking up the sun-heat of the earth. My breath came quick when I got to the front tooth on the right side. The tooth was thick and round and black like obsidian. As I chipped away, it just kept on going. It ended up being longer than my knife blade. This was not a mountain lion.

For an hour, I scraped dirt. Every so often, the mare would snort just to remind me that she was still alive.

When I had pretty much loosed the skull from the ground, except for one stubborn knob of bone next to the spinal hole, I stood up and walked to the mare and untied my canteen from where it hung on her saddle.

I wiped my forehead with my forearm and sipped some water. Then I removed my flask of whiskey from my front shirt pocket and sipped some of that. I returned the flask to my pocket and brought the canteen back to my excavation. I poured water over the skull, hoping to loosen the bone from the earth. As I waited for the water to soak in, a cloud slid in front of the sun. It was a little cloud, trailed by big clouds. The wind picked up. It was October. Nothing to worry about.

I gave the skull a gentle tug. Working it easy, I loosed the bone knob and pulled it out of the ground. The thing weighed fifteen pounds, easy. Who needs arrowheads when you've got a saber-tooth tiger skull? This was better than a wheelbarrow full of arrowheads.

Talking nice and carrying the skull behind my back, I eased my way up to the horse. She didn't appear worried exactly, but she did keep looking at me. I patted her ham until she turned her attention to a clump of grama grass. The skull was too big to fit in the saddlebags. I took ahold of one of the leathers that was dangling off the saddle and began tying it in place for the ride home.

The horse started walking sideways, away from me.

I said, "Be a good girl." Her tail switched back and forth.

Quick, I ran the leather around the skull and tied a good knot so it could hang off the saddle without bouncing too much. I let the skull rest gently against the mare's flank. I was wearing a flannel over my shirt. I considered taking it off and covering the skull with it, except the temperature had begun to drop and I didn't want to get shivery. The clouds had covered half the sky.

I patted the horse on her neck. "We'll go home now."

I took another sip from my whiskey flask. As I braced to climb into the saddle, the horse's eye skipped off me and went to the skull. The eye waited a minute, then looked at me and then back at the skull.

She made up her mind that she didn't want that skull tied to her. She reared up, balanced on her back legs like something from the cinema, and then took off. I watched as she bounded away north, in the opposite direction of home, with the skull bouncing up and down against her flank.

I jogged after her. The ground in that country is mostly flat. I was able to keep a watch on her for the first mile or so. But then she galloped down a slope and out of sight. I slowed to a walk and followed her tracks. I walked an hour, and then another. North of the river, that's empty country.

The sky was completely grey now with the sun a pale disc hovering behind the clouds. A steady wind pressed my clothes against my skin. I was tempted to walk home and wait for the mare to show up on her own. A smart person would have done just that. But it was late afternoon and I was in the wasteland. It'd be dark before I could walk halfway home and by then it'd be cold and my flannel shirt would be worthless. I had a pair of gloves, a canteen, and various other items stowed in the saddlebags. I needed my horse, so I followed her.

I counted fifty steps and then whistled. Every fifty steps, stop and whistle. My lips started to hurt. I sipped from my flask. I wanted my canteen.

The wind stepped up. I pushed my hat tight on my head. The sun peeked beneath the cloud line and shone for a few moments before dropping into the horizon. My shadow grew long and then got eaten up by twilight. I stuck my hands in my armpits. I had to squint to see the horse tracks. Her steps were close together. She was walking now, no longer scared. I'd find her.

A flake floated at my face. Then another. Then it was snowing. I wasn't worried. It did that in October sometimes. I'd find my horse. God damn. I could have wrapped the skull in my flannel. She wouldn't have seen it and I'd be home getting drunk right now.

The flakes grew fat and wet. The hoof prints would soon be covered with snow. Not that it mattered. With the clouds there was no moon, no stars, no light to see by.

I began to think that I might have to spend the night outside. That wasn't an option. I began to run, chasing a horse that I couldn't see.

There was no direction. Just darkness and a pounding of snow. The flakes fell on my shoulders and face and hair. Running kept me warm.

The ground began to slope down so I followed that slope. The wind was at my back. If I was a horse, I'd go downhill with the wind at my back. If I was a horse, I wouldn't be scared of the skull of some animal that died a million years ago.

At least the wind wasn't blowing awful bad. A strong wind will numb your fingers in the time it takes to take off your glove and light a cigarette. I had neither gloves nor cigarettes. I had it rough. Running blind in the snow in the night. There were no ranches for miles. Not even any fences. Give me a tree. Just one cottonwood tree.

I hollered for the horse. "Here you! Here you!" Except my throat hurt so it sounded like "Airooo! Airooo!"

I stopped a moment to breathe. It was so dark I couldn't see myself blink. I listened for the horse. The sound of the night was pretty. The soft thump of all those millions of flakes settling to the ground.

I could curl up. Curl up on the ground and die. An Indian once told me he came across a frozen body in the mountains. The fellow, the dead man, was naked, hugging a tree with his arms and legs. They had to chop down the tree so they could bring him home.

The only thing to hug out here would be a prickly pear cactus.

If I could find my horse, I'd have gloves and a canteen full of water. God damn that selfish beast.

The wind kept calm. The snow kept falling. I kept walking.

I heard a snort, to my left. I yelled, "Airoo!" The snort happened again. It sounded like my horse. She snorted again. I tried to follow the sound. The snow and the dark played with my directions.

She kept snorting and I kept walking towards the sound. I said, "It's okay, girl." The snow was up to my ankles. I'd make it. When I found her, I'd rip that skull off the saddle. Smash it. Save a tooth, maybe. And then she'd bring me home. A horse knows where home is. When I got home, I wouldn't tell anyone about this, not even my brother.

Then a yelp. A horse yelp. I heard hooves thud. Another thud. A loud thump, like something collapsing into snow. My horse screamed. I'd never heard a horse make a noise like this before.

There's pain and then there's fright. My grey mare was frightened as bad as anything ever had been. She screamed and screamed.

I ran toward the sound. But it was further away than I thought. And it shifted to my left. The snow was tricking my ears. I spun circles. The scream turned into *hiiii hiiii* sounds, then a gurgle, and then it was done. I stopped and listened. But there was no other sound. A tugging noise, maybe.

I didn't feel cold. I didn't feel scared. I felt abandoned. Everywhere I walked was the wrong direction. I decided that if everything was backwards, I'd go backwards. I'd walk backwards until

I bounced into something warm or until I died. I counted my steps, figuring these would be the last ones I ever took.

With my thirty-seventh step, my right foot landed in something wet. It made a little squish. I took another step. My left foot landed on something slick, like a water balloon coated with grease. The balloon squirted out from under. My ankle twisted in my boot and I fell to my hands and knees.

A blessed warmth soaked into my jeans and covered my hands. I twitched my fingers in the puddle. They were pressed into something soft. I took a breath and the smell was sweet and rank and fresh. And then rotten. A puke and shit smell. I reached very carefully and groped the empty air. A few inches to the left, a few to the right. It was so dark, it felt like my eyes had been plucked out.

I reached as far as my arm could stretch. My fingers touched hide. I brought them back quick. I reached again and my fingers touched the hide again. There wasn't any movement. I patted it. Short hair. I crawled forward, my knees and boots sucking in the puddle below. I patted, ran my hand along until I felt the mane, until I came to her ear, her eyelashes, her face, her nose, her lips, her teeth. I held my hand in front of her nostrils, feeling for breath. My horse's guts were soaking into my jeans and I was checking to see if she was still alive.

CHAPTER 2

I pushed myself up, walked ahead a few steps, and bent down to scrub my hands in the snow. I kicked my feet around, hoping to wipe my boots clean. There was no cleaning my jeans.

I stood, listening. All I heard was the hiss of snowflakes melting as they landed on my horse's insides. Whatever had done this, it had to be nearby.

I considered my options. I could wait and see if the thing that tore apart my horse did the same to me. I could run scared and freeze to death. Or I could look for my saddlebags.

The saddlebags contained a pair of calfskin gloves, a canteen, a box of matches, and a pack of cigarettes. I wanted those cigarettes.

I shuffled back to the swamp of my horse. I moved my boots until they bumped against her head. Then I crouched and felt around. The mare was on her side. As I worked my way down her mane and to her back, I bumped into the saddle. It was lying just off her with the cinch split apart. I reached into one of the saddlebags and groped until I found my gloves. They were cold and stiff, but I slipped them on. My fingers were moving okay for now. They wouldn't for long. A cigarette could wait.

I took my knife out of the holster and cut the bags away from the saddle and draped them over my shoulder. I peeled the saddle blanket away, rolled it up, and tucked it under my arm. The canteen had been hanging on the saddle horn by a leather loop. It was gone. I kicked around the snow but my toes did not find it. No matter. The water inside was probably frozen anyway.

That cinch had me worried. A cinch is thick, woven from

mohair. It straps a saddle to a horse and it doesn't split easily, or naturally.

I would best hurry up and get away from this place. I'd have to leave the saddle. I started walking. Before I'd gone three steps, I turned back. I cut off the horse's tail, stuffed it into my shirt, and marched into the dark.

I needed a fire. There were trees all about the riverbed, but that was miles away and I didn't know which way was which. I'd die before I found the river.

I was still on the slight downward incline that I'd more or less followed to the horse. Maybe it led to a ravine. A ravine is a place where water flows occasionally. Might be trees. Might be mountain lions. Whatever killed my horse would likely stay with the corpse and let me go. Compared to a fresh-killed horse, I wasn't worth the trouble. This is assuming the thing had a lick of common sense.

I walked down the incline, directly into a patch of yucca plants. The frozen horse blood on my jeans kept the leaves from poking into my shins. When I could no longer smell the horse, I stopped, stomped a flat spot in the snow, and laid my things down. Working blind, I took the horse's tail out of my shirt and pulled it into two halves. I sat down, took off my right boot, stuffed half the hair into it, and slid my foot in. I did the same with my left boot. It would make for lumpy walking, but it'd keep my feet warmer.

Next, I unrolled the saddle blanket, cut a slit in the center, and put it over my head like a poncho. I undid my belt and cinched it around the poncho at my waist.

I poked thru the saddlebags until I found the matches and the pack of cigarettes. I shook one out, stuck it in my mouth, and struck a match against the side of the box. The flame shook in the wind. It was the brightest thing I'd ever seen. All around me was swirling snow. The fire made the cigarette crackle. I inhaled half of it with one breath. I held the smoke until I got dizzy and then let it out in a burst. I took another sip from the whiskey flask.

Numb toes, dead horse, cold, dark, snow, and now a new

touch of the wind. I watched the cherry on the cigarette. I might survive, as long as nothing came after me.

I finished the cigarette in three more drags. Then I pitched it into the night.

I walked down the incline with the saddlebags over my shoulder and my handkerchief tied over my mouth. I stuffed my hands down the front of my britches. There's warmth in there.

Step careful, listen to the wind, breathe deep. Step again. Fear helped me move. I didn't want my guts spilled.

I counted five hundred steps and took a rest. I stood in the pitch black, sipped more whiskey, and smoked another cigarette. By the time I'd pitched the butt into the dark, the wind had picked up another notch and the snow was falling thick, moving sideways. I pushed my hat on as tight as possible, dropped the hankie over my mouth, stuck my hands down the front of my pants, and resumed the march.

I'd go a few steps and the wind would almost shove me over. The snow was deep some places, absent in others. My toes got sore from the cold. I kept on downhill.

After another five hundred steps, I stopped to light a cigarette. But this time, when I took my hands out of my britches and took the glove off my right hand, the cold hit my fingers. I couldn't strike a match. I was able hold the whiskey, though. I poured the final drops into my throat. The flask slipped from my grip as I tried to put it back into my shirt pocket. I left it where it fell.

I commenced to marching again. The snow came harder, landing in my ears. I tipped my hat over my eyes to keep the snow away. I couldn't see anything anyway. I took step after step. I couldn't feel my toes anymore. My nose got cold and then I couldn't feel it anymore. My ears. I forgot I had ears. Even my guts were shivering.

I followed the incline. I hoped I was following it. With the wind, it was hard to tell. My lips dried up. My tongue dried up. Self-pity arrived. My parents, they wouldn't miss me. Two years ago, they'd left. It was my fault. I shot my dad.

It was an accident. We were hunting pheasants and I shot him with a four-ten shotgun. It was just a few pellet holes sprinkled along his right leg. But one of the pellets hit a nerve. He lost feeling in that leg. After that, he kept falling over, busting his nose, bruising his ribs. Ranching became difficult. I picked up the slack.

Dad had always tinkered with watches. He'd honestly never cared for cattle. The shotgun pellets were a blessing. He and Mom left me and Kitch on the ranch and moved an hour east to Saint Francis, the first proper town across the Kansas border. He started a watch shop on Lorraine Street.

I was twenty-five when they moved. My brother, Kitch, was seventeen. I raised him for his senior year of high school. Put away the basketball. Do your homework. Pancakes for supper. Be home by twelve-thirty.

I wondered what Kitch was doing while I stomped the snow with horse hair in my boots. Playing his game, mugging for applause.

I wondered about the animals. The chickens would be fine. They had a coop and plenty of feathers. The feeder cattle could huddle up. This wasn't a bad snow, not for cattle. The milk cows, though, were another story. I was more worried about their udders than about the cold. They were in the barn, warm. But I'd missed their evening milking. It looked like I'd miss tomorrow morning's milking as well. They'd be sore and angry, but they'd be all right, as long as I made it back eventually.

The wind pushed me in the chest. It was a gust and then it stayed like that, a gust that didn't stop. I leaned forward. The wind slid to the side and then it lifted my hat off. I ran after it for few steps but it was no good. My hat went tumbling in the dark. After the storm ended, some lucky turd might find it stuck in a barbed wire fence ten miles away.

I knew what they said about hats, about how most of your heat escapes from your head. I felt like a chimney, shooting all my remaining warmth out the top of my skull.

Every direction seemed uphill except when the wind was at my back. But the wind swirled so much I got dizzy trying to keep in front of it.

My handkerchief was crusting up with frozen snot. I pulled it down for a moment so I could breathe, and inhaled a lungful of snowflakes that felt like tiny crumbs of glass. I coughed until my lips tasted blood.

Every snowflake became a rat's kiss. Thousands of rats in the dark, kissing me over and over.

If I didn't make it home, that would be okay. Maybe someday someone would find my skull and tie it to a horse's saddle and have better luck.

There's a song I enjoy. It goes like this.

I went thru the desert on a horse with no name.
It felt good to be out of the rain.
In the desert, you can't remember your name
'Cause there ain't no one for to give you no pain.

It comes on the radio a couple times a week. My favorite part is in the last verse: *The ocean is a desert with its life underground.*

Kitch thinks it's corny. Kitch thinks everything I like is corny. But I love that song. *La la la la la la la.*

The ocean is a desert with its life underground. A blizzard is a snowstorm with its knife on your throat. A son of a bitch is a man with a hound for a mom. A boat is a bottle with a bastard aboard. A horse carries burdens 'til it loses its guts. Horses are grey, violets are blue. My nose fell off and froze in the snow. If I'd of pulled out the liver, I'd have a new hat. River of livers. Rivets in jeans burn cold into hips. Loose hips sink. Whiskey burns. Shot glasses make good spectacles. Hangovers make good neighbors. I deserve a dessert. An apple pie is a dessert with its life under crust. Saber-tooth tigers climb out of the earth. They grow wings and leap to the sky, eat everything in their path. Clouds, mostly. Clouds and hooves. And entrails. Trails. Rails. What ails you? I'll see you off. S. O. S. The iron horse. Iron. I run. Run. Am I moving?

My face was touching the planet. My back was loaded with snow. My nose was pressed sideways. Something was holding my foot. I had fallen.

I yanked hard to pull my foot free. It slipped out the boot, which was caught in something. I crawled to it, patting. I could hardly feel my hands. I knocked with my knuckles. It was hard, this thing that wedged my boot. A root. I pulled the boot free and tugged it back on. I was at the base of a tree. I stood and patted the trunk. A big one. I couldn't wrap my arms around it. I groped and found twigs. I held the twigs to my cheek to feel their size. I gathered more and placed them at the base of the trunk. I would make a good pile before I tried to light them.

I needed to block the wind. I read that story, the one about the man and the dog in Alaska. He fouled up on two accounts. He lit his fire wrong and he didn't check the branches above for snow. His was an evergreen, mine was a bare cottonwood. My tree wouldn't have hardly any snow on the branches. I would survive.

I crawled ahead. I required a large branch, something to hold a flame, to make me warm. This tree was old. Branches would have fallen off. I crawled for twenty paces. No branch. I turned around and headed back to the tree. I crawled forty paces. No tree.

Snow blew down the collar of my shirt. Heat poured out of my skull. I had lost my tree.

I stood against the wind and walked in a spiral. The wind pushed and pulled. I was going to die.

CHAPTER 3

I bumped into a solid thing. It made a thump. I knocked it with my fingers, felt it up and down, walked sideways to the edge. It was a car. A pickup. The panels were rounded. This was an old truck, left to die.

I touched the door. It still had a window, rolled up. I found the door handle. My fingers wouldn't grip. I forced my right hand with my left hand. Together, they pressed the button, held the handle, and tugged and pulled. The door squealed open. I crawled inside and shut the dark behind me. The wind couldn't push me around in here.

I faced backward. My knees were on the floor board, my elbows on the seat springs. I rested a moment and then I shook off the saddlebags and pulled my gloves off and felt for stuffing. There was plenty. I breathed into my hands. I pulled the matches from my pocket and struck them until one lit. I held it just above the floor, searching. Right in the corner was a mouse nest. I set it alight. It burned quickly. I put stuffing from the chair on the fire. The stuffing didn't take the flame. I needed fuel.

When I unlatched the door, the wind pushed it open. I reached underneath the truck. I found a mess of dried tumbleweeds and stuffed those into the cab. I stepped out, hugging the truck. I felt in the bed and found snow. Under the snow were sticks. Small sticks, big sticks. I brought a handful back to the cab, shut the door, and built a fire.

I worked the vent windows open so I wouldn't get smoked out. I made a fire on the seat. I held my hands right on top of the flames. My hands hurt like murder. My left middle finger got a piece of burning ash stuck to it. I blew it out, tapped out the ash. The truck smelled like burnt finger. My feet hurt. My nose hurt.

I fed sticks into the fire. Snot drip dripped from my nose. As my britches thawed, the horse blood melted. It stunk and it made me hungry. When the fire got low, I went back out and brought in more branches.

As I warmed up, my skin hurt like worms were crawling underneath. I know it was just drops of blood trying to slide thru shrunken vessels. It felt like worms. My fingers, feet, ears, nose. It went on and on.

CHAPTER 4

The sun came up, the wind died, and the clouds disappeared. I didn't even see it happen. I closed my eyes to blink and when I opened them, the day was real. My life had been saved by a 1948 Ford pickup. Ice-melt dripped down the windows and the hood. The seat was blackened springs. My fingers were sooted. The rearview mirror held a cracked up version of my face.

The truck was parked within a patch of cottonwoods. I don't know how I had managed not to walk straight into any of those trees. Birds sang and chased from branch to branch. Directly before me and thru the trees, I could see a winding stripe of land covered by snow. This was the riverbed. I'd made it back to Old Stinkum, the creek that didn't flow.

I won't grant that divine intervention brought me here. It was wind that brought me, and now it was time to go home. I knew right where I was, a few miles north of the ranch, and a few more miles up the river. I'd be warm by noon.

I kicked open the door of the truck, stepped out, draped the saddlebags over my shoulder, and walked home.

The feeder cattle were mad at me. Huddled in the pasture next to the barn, they glared, slit-eyed, suspicious of me in my saddle blanket poncho. When I approached, the old bull turned away and splashed out a half-gallon of shit on the snowy ground.

I shook out of the saddlebags and the saddle blanket and hung them over the fence. Then I climbed into the corral and approached the stock tank. It had iced over. The surface was dusted with snow and decorated with little bird footprints. An axe was leaning against the tank. I picked it up and swung it several times into the ice. With their water freed up, the cattle seemed less upset.

I went to the barn to milk the cows. We owned two dairy cows, by the breed of Jersey. A Jersey is a beautiful animal, the color of sand. As with all Jerseys, our two girls looked similar to one another. They had different dispositions, though, one being generally polite and the other being generally otherwise. This morning, after a night with swollen udders, they were both otherwise.

The milking didn't go easy. My fingers wouldn't move right. My left middle finger was the worst. It was blistered, numb, and stiff. I did the milking with my right hand.

When I finished, I went outside the barn and poured the milk out on the ground, as always. I don't care for the taste of milk.

I went back to the barn, where I climbed to the loft and tossed a couple of hay bales out to the feeder cattle in the corral. I dropped another bale down the climb-hole, went back down, and put a few flakes in the trough for the girls.

On my way out the barn, I held my breath as I walked past the stall where my horse used to sleep.

I looked in on the chickens. They hadn't missed me. They clucked around in their coop, warm and dumb. I poured seed into their feeder and they gathered around. I'd get the eggs later.

The sun was bright. It was close to noon. I walked to the house, where I sat on the concrete of the front step and pulled my boots off. Grey horse hair strung out and stuck to my socks. I peeled the socks off, wadded them up, and tossed them as far as I could.

My toes looked bad. They never had been pretty, but some of them, mostly on my right foot, were black. I figured I knew what that meant.

I stepped into the house. The furnace was on. I'd forgot what warm was. I limped my way to the bathroom and started running water in the tub.

I went to the kitchen, located a clean glass, and pulled out the fifth of whiskey I kept in the cabinet above the sink. I screwed the cap off the bottle and poured until most of the air was out of the glass. Before I could take a drink, the phone rang.

"Johnny?"

It was my brother. I said, "Uh huh."

"I been trying to reach you."

"I've been out."

"I guess you're back now."

There were echoey conversations in the background. I said, "Are you in an airport?"

"Hotel lobby. We're in Virginia. We played our first game last night, remember? I scored."

"How much?"

"Let me put it this way. We won by six points. If it hadn't been for me, we only would have won by five."

"Well, you scored."

"That's how I see it."

"Get any rebounds?"

"These fellows are big. It's not like at Pueblo."

"I suppose not." My glass of whiskey was staring at me. I could hear the water running into the bathtub.

"There was a fellow for San Antonio who was almost seven foot. We got a buck who's seven-two. Their giant and our giant did all the rebounding. It's a sight. Believe it or not, I'm short compared to most of these fellows. It's just my first game. Coach says I'll get used to it. Afterwards, we got on our bus. Normally, we'd fly, but it's not a long trip so we rode on the bus and—"

"Kitch. I can't stay on the phone."

"Why? You got a girlfriend?"

"I'm awful busy."

"I just played my first game as a pro."

"I can't wait to hear all about it. But we had a blizzard last night and the cattle got anxious and they pushed against the fence on the corral. It's about to bust wide open. If I don't fix it—"

Kitch sighed. "If you don't fix it, the world will go to hell. Well, let me just say it was a wild night. I'll tell you about it some-day. We're heading to Indianapolis tonight for a game tomorrow. I'll call you afterwards."

"Tomorrow."

"And we'll be in Denver in about three weeks. I'll make sure you get a ticket."

"Do good tomorrow."

We hung up. I drank half the glass of whiskey in my first sip. I limped to the bathroom, took off my clothes, climbed in the bath, and drank the rest.

By the time I got out of the tub, it was clear that I wasn't going to be able to keep all my fingers and toes. The left middle finger was the worst. The skin was sloughing in some parts and swollen with infection in others. A couple toes were in trouble as well.

After I'd dried off and dressed, I drank another glass of whiskey. It made me warm and dopey. Even so, pulling on my boots hurt something awful. And then I stubbed into the kitchen table as I walked to the front door. It hurt so bad I picked up a coffee cup and threw it. I don't normally lose my temper. I left the broken cup on the floor and walked outside. The sun had already begun to melt the snow.

My pickup was parked in front of the house. I squelched thru the slush and climbed in. I started the engine, then waited for the heater to warm up. I held my hands in front of the vent. The middle finger looked awful bad. I had my knife in the holster on my belt. I wondered if I could cut off the finger myself. A hatchet would be best. The challenge would be to get drunk enough to not feel the pain and remain sober enough not to chop off my entire hand. I was plenty drunk at the moment. Not drunk enough to chop off my own finger. Leave it to the professionals.

I drove to the hospital in Strattford, thirty-seven miles north.

According to Doctor Shepard, if my finger hadn't been infected, he would have left it alone. As it was, the frostbite had killed the flesh and the burn from the fire had allowed some sort of bacteria into my blood. The finger was, as he said, a liability.

The Doctor injected a numbness into my palm. He laid my hand on his exam table and told me to look the other way. There was a crunching sound and then a plop of my finger being deposited in a trash can.

After he'd stitched me up and wrapped the stump, Doctor Shepard said, "You picked a good finger. The pinkie, now, that's a bad one to lose. If you want to grip anything, you need that pin-kie." He made pinching shapes with his hands. "As long as you have a pinky and a thumb, you're officially human. Let's look at those toes."

I removed my boots and socks.

He picked up a pen and poked the two sloughy toes on my right foot. "Feel that?"

"No."

"Keep an eye on 'em. They might get to stinking. As long as they don't get infected, I'm not worried. They'll shrivel up and be worthless, but I hate to chop off anything unless it's neces-sary. If they do get infected, or if they even start to stink, get here immediately so I can take them off."

I nodded. "Will do."

He gave me a crutch, which I laid it over my knees. He took out his pad. "I'm writing a prescription for antibiotics. Take them with food, twice a day. You might get the runs. Also, the anesthetic on your hand will wear off in a couple of hours. You'll know it. I expect you'll want some pain pills."

"I don't need pain pills."

"It's going to hurt."

"I can take it."

"Stay easy on the whiskey."

"I don't drink, hardly."

"Keep it that way."

"Don't worry."

"How's your brother doing?"

"He had his first game last night. He scored a point."

"The first of many, I expect." The doctor handed me the pre-scription. "Call if anything gets stinky or swollen or infected. Keep the bandages on. Stay out of manure."

I picked up the antibiotics at the drug store on the way out of town. The whiskey was wearing off, as was the anesthetic. It's not easy to drive with one hand bundled up, especially when you're becoming sober.

When I got home, I hobbled out to the barn and gave the cows their evening milking, all with one hand. My forearm was sore by the time I finished. It was over forty degrees outside, which meant I didn't have to smash any ice in the stock tank. I tossed hay to the bovines, fed the chickens, and went to the house. I cracked four eggs into a glass and swallowed them down. Then I got undressed, crawled into bed, and drank a quantity of whiskey sufficient to put me to sleep without any lingering thoughts as to the murder of my horse.

CHAPTER 5

At five a.m. I pulled on yesterday's clothes and crutched myself outside to take care of the animals in the morning dark.

I finished my chores and was back in bed before the sun had come up. I woke again at noon and the first thing I wondered was if it'd be sensible to kill myself. Lying in bed with my head too heavy to lift, my left finger missing, and with two black toes, I asked the question over and over, and offered myself no reply.

My tongue was crusted. I needed water. I crutched to the bathroom. I slurped water out of the faucet, then sent a bright yellow stream into the toilet.

To the kitchen. The thermometer outside the window said sixty degrees, but it was in the sun. The actual temperature remained closer to forty. Already, the snow had melted, except on the north of the buildings.

I took an antibiotic, drank a glass of whiskey, and then crutched back to bed.

• • •

Three years ago, the day before Thanksgiving of 1972, Dad and Kitch and I came home from a long day fixing fence and found mom asleep on the Davenport. She liked to take naps after she'd been drinking. Mom normally drank very little. By that, I mean she confined her drinking to what could fit in a shot glass. Nine of them every day. She had her reasons.

Dad shook her awake. "We've been working, we're hungry, and you're asleep."

She rolled over and pointed at her rear end.

I remember the way her slacks were worn thru so you could see the outline of her drawers. Kitch giggled. He was only sixteen, when everything is either funny or stupid. At twenty-four, I was grown up enough to know that Mom was making a mistake.

Mom turned to face us and pulled up her shirt so we could see her stomach. "See what you've done, you men? Two babies and I'm stretched out and tired and I've a right to rest. So let me rest, dummy."

Dad stepped forward, calm. With two hands, he leaned forward and shoved her hard in her baggy stomach. There was a *whoof* as the air left her lungs. She curled up on the couch and didn't move until we'd all left the room.

The next day, everything was normal again. Mom cooked the turkey, Dad carved it, we all ate it. The shot glasses got filled and Mom got drunk. Me and Kitch watched carefully, but the day was no different from any other Thanksgiving.

After dinner, Dad, Kitch, and I hiked north for our annual pheasant hunt. We walked the prairie in a line, thirty yards between us, shotguns perched on our shoulders. The rule was, if a pheasant scared up to your right, you could shoot it; if one scared up to your left, the person on your left could shoot it, unless you were the person on the far left, in which case you had a green light to shoot pretty much anything you saw. Be safe, stay in line, never shoot behind, only forward. I was in the center with Kitch to my left and Dad to my right.

As we marched, a pheasant rooster popped up and glided just above the grass, his head a metallic green in the late afternoon. The bird was to my right and just ahead, firmly in my jurisdiction. I aimed and fired. *Ba-boom!* The bird dropped to the ground and, at the same time, my dad started hollering.

Kitch and I ran to him. He was on his back, clutching his leg, looking mad. Dad had gotten in front of where he should have been. It was an accident.

He ended up with a numb leg and an inability to look me in the eye. As the scabs healed, he spent less time outside and more time in the house, tinkering with his watches, grunting at Mom. I did his portion of the chores while Kitch tossed a basketball thru the hoop nailed to the light pole.

Spending that time in the house, my parents began to change. Mom drank less and Dad grunted less. It was remarkable, really. Me and Kitch outside, them in the house. Dad started doing dishes. Mom filled fewer shot glasses. For the first time since I'd known them, my parents acted as if they were fond of one another.

Things changed so much that, a few months later, on a day in which all by myself I'd helped a cow deliver twins, the parents informed Kitch and me of their intention to move to Saint Francis so Dad could start a watch repair shop. That June, they drove away with a trailer full of belongings.

Kitch stayed with me. He only had one more year left in school and Mom and Dad didn't want to mess with hauling him to a new town. It might affect him, they said.

We knew they just wanted to be alone with each other, someplace far from us.

At that point, Kitch stood six-seven, a foot taller than me. But he was as awkward as a brand-new foal. Even in my cowboy boots, I could dribble around him and leave him scratching his butt while I scooped in a layup. Every morning, before the school bus came for him, we'd play one-on-one, with me winning every single game.

It was just after Thanksgiving of 1973 that he beat me for the first time. He was seventeen, I was twenty-five. When his winning shot went up, we both stood and watched as the ball slipped thru the net and bounced to a stop in the dirt. This was impossible. He accused me of throwing the game. I reluctantly agreed that that had been the case. For a couple of weeks I regained my dominance, working harder and harder to stay one point ahead of him. While he was at school, I'd practice until the wind made my fingers numb. But Kitch's shot improved, he learned to dribble, his shoulders filled out, and eventually he started beating me, then toying with me, then embarrassing me. I found reasons not to play him, but he insisted. We went a week where I didn't score a single point.

Our last game turned sour. I tried my skyhook, the one shot he couldn't defend. He leapt like he was on springs and swatted the ball into the corral, where it splashed into a mound of fresh shit. That was it. I had nothing left for him. I shoved him in the stomach as hard as I could. As his big brother, it was my right to do this. He grabbed me by the scruff of the neck and put me on the ground and sat on my back until I apologized. He'd earned the right, I suppose.

We stopped playing basketball after that. No great loss for Kitch. He was busy leading the Dorton Rangers' varsity squad in points, rebounds, and bad grades.

In the spring of '73, he took the Rangers to the state tournament in Colorado Springs. Mom and Dad came to the championship game and sat quietly in the back of the bleachers. Kitch scored forty-seven points and won.

Afterward, his picture made the papers. He had girlfriends. The whole deal.

A few four-year colleges contacted him but they all lost interest once they took a look at his grade. He only had the one, D in everything. After he graduated high school, he went to the junior college in Pueblo for a year, where he immediately became the team's starting center. He'd play great one game (thirty-five points, seventeen rebounds), lousy the next (fouled out in the first half, two points, zero rebounds). He grew another inch that year, topping out at six-eight. Thirteen inches taller than me. He averaged sixteen points and nine rebounds a game.

After his year at Pueblo, he declared himself ready for the draft. There are two professional basketball leagues, the National Basketball Association and the American Basketball Association. The NBA has been around forever. That's the real league, with the Celtics, the Lakers, the Warriors, all the big boys. The NBA didn't pay Kitch any mind. They don't trust nineteen-year-old kids. But the ABA, they're the wild league with the red-white-and-blue ball, where shots can count for three-points, and even a hick from Strattford County deserves a chance. Kitch was hoping for the ABA all along, with the Denver Nuggets being his destination of choice.

He ended up going to the Kentucky Colonels.

I was the better basketball player. I knew about defense and how to pass. Kitch just knew how to get passed at. His stature made up for his shortcomings

I love Kitch as much as anything in this world. So it makes me very sad that for a long time, the biggest, mangiest, most miserable thing about my life has been the fact that my brother is thirteen inches taller than me.

But now, with my grey mare gutted and my finger cut off, a bigger, mangier, more miserable thing had arrived.

• • •

The cows were ready for their evening squeeze. Whether I was sad or not, whether my finger stump hurt, or whether my dead toes didn't feel anything, whether the bed stunk like piss or my head felt like hell, those girls needed to be milked.

I got up, went to the bathroom, and peed for about half an hour. Then I found the crutch and headed for the barn. I milked the cattle, then went to the chicken house to gather the eggs. I had too many damned chickens. My nine hens gave me a total of nine eggs a day when I only ever needed four. I tossed the five extras at the evergreens that grew to the west of the house. Let the coyotes eat.

• • •

The next day, I drove to Strattford for the livestock auction and won a mare for eighty-five dollars. She was a warm-blood roan with a star on her forehead. The auctioneer claimed she was ten years old. I put her at closer to fifteen. If I kept her away from blizzards, she'd make it another five.

I brought the horse home and introduced her to her new stall. I let her nuzzle with the dairy cows and I fed her handfuls of hay. Then I set her loose in the pasture. She ran along the fence, enjoying the opportunity to stretch out. She avoided the feeder cattle and they avoided her. She looked like a good one.

CHAPTER 6

The days came and went. I was tempted on several occasions to go to Dorsey for a bottle of whiskey, but I stayed home.

Afternoons, I bridled the horse and led her around the pasture until my foot would start to throb. The roan was of a friendly disposition. If I had to stop and catch my breath, she let me lean on her.

On Thursday, I drove to Strattford so the doctor could have another look at me. First, he examined my foot. He made me wiggle my toes. The two black ones didn't move. They were shriveled up now, and starting to curl inward. He made me walk around bare-footed. He showed me how to work my ankle so I could best keep my balance.

"How's the pain?"

"Negligible."

"Those toes are like dead twigs on a tree, just waiting to dry up and snap."

"Cut 'em off, then."

"Save yourself the money, Johnny. They'll likely fall off on their own."

"How about my finger?" I looked closely at the stitches on the stump.

"It's not going to grow back, if that's what you're asking."

Doctor Shepard must have seen some sadness on my face because he said, "By my last count, thirty-six people in Strattford County lack at least one finger. Combines, augers, blasting caps, you name it. And they're all managing to survive. You're not bad off, believe me. After spending the night in that blizzard, you're lucky your ears are still attached to your head."

"I'm a lucky one, I guess."

"Before you leave town, buy yourself a pair of wool mittens and some wool socks. And get a wool hat, too."

I nodded.

"And you might want to pick up a slide rule while you're at it."

"Why's that?"

"So you can count to twenty." He thought that was funny.

"I don't get it."

"People sometimes count on their fingers and toes. You're down to just seventeen digits."

"Oh."

He said, "You cattlemen spend too much time alone."

He took a snipper and a pair of needle nose pliers from a drawer and started working on the stitches on my finger nub.

He said, "How's the whiskey treating you?"

"Only when necessary."

"Good."

When I stood up to leave, Doctor Shepard said, "Happy Halloween."

"When's that?"

"Tomorrow. You got candy for the kiddies?"

"My place doesn't get kiddies."

"Stay away from the ghosts."

"I ain't had much luck with that lately."

I drove to Main Street and went to the outfit store. I bought wool socks, wool mittens, and a wool cap. They had a shelf of cowboy hats as well. I tried several and settled on an off-brand that fitted my head. The brim was wider than I like, but the red of the felt matched the color of my new horse. I like my hats to match my horses.

Back home, I checked the mailbox. There was a postcard from Kitch. Lovely Indianapolis.

Bus ride good. Meeting lots of people. Cheerleaders!!!!

Hangovers!!!! Talk to you soon. Don't forget to answer the phone.

I did my chores and went to bed.

CHAPTER 7

Halloween was a windy one. Corn husks blew into the yard and scratched against the windows. It's the time of year when everything gets sick and dies and comes unloosened from its moorings.

After dinner, I sat on the front step, smoked cigarettes, and watched tumbleweeds chase their shadows in the orange of the setting sun. The temperature, which had been tolerable, began to drop.

My thoughts drifted to unhappy subjects. Blizzards, fingers, horse guts, revenge. If it had been earlier in the day, and if I'd had a saddle and felt capable of sitting atop a horse, I might have ridden north and looked for arrowheads, loping, looking, calming myself. But that was not a possibility. My other option would be to turn on the TV and drink until I passed out in the recliner.

For that, I needed whiskey.

Dee's Liquor had been decorated for Halloween. A scarecrow leaned next to the front door. Construction paper bats were taped inside the windows.

When I walked in, Dee said, "Johnny Riles. How's your brother?"

I said, "He scored in his very first game."

"Is he keeping out of trouble?"

"You know Kitch."

I bought two bottles of whiskey and two bottles of cola. Before I pulled my pickup out of the parking lot, I rolled down the window and poured out half the pop from each cola bottle.

Then I filled them to the top again with whiskey. I hoped this would slow my drinking for the evening and thus prolong the enjoyable aspects of the process.

Instead of driving west, toward home, I headed east. I was out, I might as well stay out. I sipped my concoction, lit a cigarette, and drove Highway 36 the two miles to Dorton High School.

The parking lot was full and the lights were shining on the football field. I had no desire to pay fifty cents and sit in the stands and shiver next to my neighbors and cheer for our boys like a normal person would do. Instead, I made a U-turn and headed back west until I came to an intersection, where I went south and parked at the edge of the pasture that was adjacent to the football field. I felt safe here. A quarter mile away, my view was mostly blocked by the windbreak on the west side of the field, with only the end zones being visible. I left the engine running and the heat on and I rolled down the window. Across the fallow land, I could faintly hear Neal Koenig's amplified voice announcing the starting lineup.

I put the radio on the rock station and drank from one of the cola bottles. The DJ played Sister Golden Hair, which is my second favorite song by my favorite band. It settled me down. This was better than being at home feeling sorry for myself.

I was too far away to see the scoreboard. But whenever the action got to one end of the field or the other, I could see around the windbreak and watch the kids knock helmets and chase into the end zone. As best I could tell, the Dorton Rangers were behind by twenty-four at the end of the first half.

By the beginning of the second half, I had finished both of the cola bottles and was no longer calculating anything. I began drinking the whiskey straight. I tapped the dashboard to the rhythm of the radio and smoked cigarettes until the field lights went dark and headlights began creeping out of the parking lot to split off east or west down the highway.

When the last of the cars had passed from view, I put the truck in gear and headed home. I drove slow thru Dorton so I could look into the windows of the Airline Café and see who was eating their post-game burgers.

With my eyes away from the road, I didn't see the hay bales.

I'd completely forgotten about the hay bales. It's a Halloween tradition. Kids douse bales with gasoline, light them on fire, and kick them out of the back of a pickup truck to tumble onto Highway 36.

Sparks exploded over the hood of the truck. Before I could steer away, I drove into another bale. Another burst of sparks. I veered to the left to avoid a third hay bale, which brought me headlong into a fourth hay bale. It probably seemed comical to the people sipping their milkshakes in the café.

With my spastic driving, the truck wanted to fling itself any direction but straight. It skidded back and forth across the road twice before I righted things. By this time I had passed thru Dorsey and was heading into the darkness of the nighttime highway. I looked in the rearview mirror. Flames on the road, flames in the bed of the truck.

I drove straight for a mile and then pulled over. I got out and patted down the fires. There was hay all over the bed. Hay stuck under the wiper blades. The front grill was bent some. My right headlight was busted out.

I lit a cigarette. It was cold out there. I could hear the sounds of guns. Kids were probably shooting the hell out of road signs. Go to town, boys. It's Halloween.

I climbed back into the cab and took another drink of whiskey. I had only a couple inches left before I'd have to crack the seal on the second bottle.

I drove on toward my place, but when I got there I didn't park next to the house as I normally would. Instead, I drove past the barn and then headed north thru the prairie. I went north and a little east until I could see the starlit trees along the banks of Old Stinkum.

I stopped a good distance from the river bank and shut off the engine. I walked thru the cottonwoods and down to the riverbed, carrying the nearly empty whiskey bottle. With minimal trouble, I found the '48 Ford that had saved my life. It was round and squat and comforting. I opened the door. It still smelled like fire inside. I stepped away and slammed the door. I climbed up on the roof of the old truck and finished the rest of my whiskey. I spoke at the darkness, "I'll find you. I'll gut you just like you did my horse. I'll cut your fingers off. I'll cut your paws off. I'll cut you into pieces and stuff those pieces in your mouth."

A big open space like that, your voice doesn't echo, it just disappears into the wind.

There was a rustling sound. I don't believe in ghosts. But there was a rustling sound, like a big cat, like a saber-tooth tiger. I heard breathing. I threw the whiskey bottle as hard as I could in the direction of the noise. I heard the bottle skid along the ground. I heard a scampering sound, as if an animal had moved out of the way.

I was on a shell of a pickup on the banks of Old Stinkum in the cold of Halloween. I squatted and listened to the wind pushing the cottonwood branches. I could barely see the outline of my pickup, twenty yards away.

Inside the truck below me, my horse's blood was turning black and flakey.

I stood. I filled up with air and shouted to the wind, "Leave off! Leave me off!"

Something groaned. It was no lie. Something groaned and moved about. I suddenly didn't want to be where I was anymore.

I jumped straight from the roof of the truck to the ground. I sprinted, stumbling with my bad foot, catching myself with my bad hand, pressing upright and running properly now. I could cover twenty yards in three seconds, thirteen strides. I pumped my arms, lifted knees. All inside me was panic.

When I reached my pickup, I yanked the door open, started the engine, and backed out of there with the devil on my hitch. I pounded over the pasture, badger mound after badger mound, until I saw my yard light. It beckoned, pulled me home. I looked in my rearview mirror. No beasts were perched behind me.

I parked and walked in to the house. I wanted to be calm. I couldn't. The phone was ringing.

"Happy Halloween, big brother."

"Happy Halloween, Kitch."

"Boy, am I messed up, Johnny. I'm drunk and we're two-and-oh. I scored four points. It's wild here in the ABA. One guy on our team keeps a bottle of wine in his locker. Another guy keeps a gun in his locker. Another guy keeps a girl. You do anything wild lately?"

"Not lately, no."

"You should get out more."

"I went out tonight."

"Go out again. Do something wild. It's fun to go wild."

"When are you coming home?"

"Not for a while. But the Nuggets are heading to Kentucky to play us this next Monday. You'll be able to get it on the radio. Or is that too wild for you?"

I was unstable. The voice on the phone was unstable.

Kitch said, "I've been seeing a girl."

"Yeah?"

"The prettiest woman you'll ever see. She's got dark hair. With lots of curls. She's here. We're right now getting ready to go to a costume party."

Thirteen inches taller. I lived on a ranch surrounded by demons and Kitch was in the upper regions of heaven.

He said, "You still there?"

"Yep."

"Guess what I'm going as."

"Going where?"

"The costume party."

"I dunno. A vampire?"

"Vampires are for dopes. I'm gonna be Dr. J. My girlfriend is going to lend me her wig. I'll be a knock out. I gotta go. Have fun sharpening your knife."

I sat at the kitchen table with my legs spread wide so as to prevent myself from tipping out of my chair. I took my knife out of the holster and held it to my wrist. Then I put it back. Halloween was no time for that sort of thing.

I went outside, thru the wind, and into the barn, intending to say hello to my new horse. She was asleep. I crawled into the stall. I curled up in the straw around her legs and closed my eyes.

My dead horse was out there somewhere. That saber-tooth tiger skull was out there. The thing that killed my horse was out there.

I was unhappy.

CHAPTER 8

NOVEMBER

The next day, after lunch, I poured a whiskey and sat in the recliner. Taking sips out of the glass, I removed my shoes and played with my dead toes. The black skin had grown hard. The toenails were loose so I pried them off and dropped them to the floor. The toes, absent the nails, resembled the nub tails on newborn pups.

I couldn't stay here, playing with my toes. It was time to get on the new horse.

I bridled her and stood her next to the wooden fence of the corral. I climbed up the rails and got on her back. She accepted my weight without complaint. I tapped her sides with my boots, prodding her into a few steps. I hadn't rode bareback since before Kitch was born. I said, "Let's start easy, okay?" She walked. I heeled her up to a trot.

It's calming to be on a horse. I pointed her northward, toward the riverbed. The weather was fair. No clouds in the sky or elsewhere. Where the sun landed, it was warm, where it didn't, it was cool.

We crossed the prairie, ambling easy. When we came to Old Stinkum and the abandoned pickup, I stood the roan next to it and climbed onto the hood. I slid to the ground and wandered about, playing tracker. I located the whiskey bottle I'd thrown the night before but I couldn't find any footprints other than my own. Amongst the scrub and half-dead tree branches, I found some broken twigs. I didn't see any fur caught on the snapped ends. They had been broken by something, though, and, judging by the size of some of the broken twigs, that thing had been of substantial weight. The sounds that had frightened me that night had been real. No matter how drunk I'd been, I knew this to be a fact. Something had been lurking, watching me. I would find it, whatever it might be. In the bargain, I hoped to recover my saddle.

The sun had begun to sag and I did not wish to remain in that place after dark. I would have to continue my search later. I climbed back atop the pickup, got on the roan, and pointed her toward home. Bareback isn't an easy way to ride. Without stirrups, you can't brace yourself for bumps.

We arrived home before twilight. I put the roan to her stall. She seemed fond of me already. I was fond of her. I did my chores and then it got dark. Inside the house, it was silent. I swallowed a glass of whiskey.

We owned a pair of binoculars. Dad got them during his time in the army. I suspected he would not have brought them with him to Saint Francis, as there was very little to look at in Kansas.

I went to Mom and Dad's old room. I found the binoculars in the closet, next to a box of broken pocket watches. I pulled the binoculars down and looked out the front door. It was too dark to see anything but stars so I went to bed.

CHAPTER 9

I did my morning chores quickly, then I proceeded with my real work. I draped my saddlebags over the horse's haunch and set to filling them up. Binoculars, spare water canteen, and, in case it grew cold, coat, wool socks, hat, and mittens. I boiled three eggs for a snack.

I retrieved my twelve-gauge from under the sofa and strapped it across my back. I suspected the thing that killed my horse would not be out in the daylight, but I also knew that if it was, I could not stab it to death with Excal.

I climbed on the roan and kicked her flanks and we trotted north.

When we reached Old Stinkum, we paused at the abandoned pickup. I climbed off the horse, pried off one of the truck's two remaining hubcaps, and placed it in one of the saddlebags. I intended to keep it as a souvenir of the derelict that had saved my life.

I rode the roan for hours, searching for a place I'd been but couldn't remember. We trotted at random, weaving left and right, always heading north, finding nothing but grass, cactuses, and sand. Not even an arrowhead. The land entered into gentle rolls that disallowed me from seeing more than a quarter-mile in any direction. At regular intervals, I'd rein in the horse, hold the binoculars to my face, and watch the wind twitch the leaves of grass on that dry expanse.

I didn't have a clue as to where my grey was, where her bones were. Still, I knew I'd find those bones and I'd find my saddle. Then I'd find the creature that killed her. I'd shoot it in the face and gut it with my knife.

In the late afternoon, we crested the top of a short hill and came to a stop. I ate my hardboiled eggs astride the roan. We had been out for some time and we had found nothing. Neither horse bones, nor arrowheads, nor any idea how to sensibly go about this thing. The shotgun had been bouncing against my back all day long. By this point, the horse was thirsty for water and I was thirsty for whiskey. It was time to go home.

I turned her around and we trotted toward the ranch.

CHAPTER 10

The next morning, I took a moment to consider how to proceed. First, I decided to leave the shotgun at home. It was heavy and it irritated my shoulder where it hung. Instead, I packed my thirty-two caliber revolver in one of the saddlebags.

Second, I came up with a systematic approach to my search. The night of that blizzard, I'd been stumbling in the dark, with no sense of direction, no idea of anything. Judging by how long I'd wandered about, I estimated that the incident could have taken place anywhere within a six-mile radius of the site of the abandoned pickup. I knew that the incident had taken place to the north of Old Stinkum. I hadn't crossed the riverbed during my blizzard wanderings. There was a distinct edge to the banks of Old Stinkum and, had I stepped into the riverbed, I would have known it, even in that blindness.

Using the abandoned pickup as my starting point, I would ride the roan in expanding semicircles with Old Stinkum as the southern border.

In this manner, I was sure to find my saddle.

The first few passes were short. They expanded quickly. I'd keep the horse tracks from the previous pass ten feet to my left, until I came to the river, and then I'd expand my semicircle by ten feet and ride back around to the other side. I scanned every sagebrush, every weed, every clump of dirt. Every few minutes, I'd stop and lift up the binoculars. After some hours, I witnessed three coyotes arguing in the distance. I rode out to see what they were up to. They took off before I reached them. I kept my eyes on the spot where they'd been messing around and rode there directly. They'd been chewing on a deer carcass. I couldn't tell how it had died.

I returned to my semicircles. I'd covered quite a bit of dirt by the late afternoon. My spine began to ache from the bareback riding. I decided it was time to conclude the day's hunt. No horse. No saddle. Before we turned back for the ranch, I removed the hubcap from its place in the saddlebag and dropped it to the ground where I'd ended my search. Next time I came out, I'd start right back up at the same spot.

After my chores, I went into the house and took account of the cupboards. I was low on bread, beans, and carrots. It was nearly six o'clock. The Dorsey store would close soon. I drove fast and made it thru the door just as Charlie Morning was about to flip the sign from Open to Closed. She spoke on the phone with her boyfriend the whole time I was there. She winked at me as I paid and hustled out the door with my bags.

On the way out of Dorsey, I stopped by Dee's and I bought two bottles of whiskey. As she rang me up, Dee told me I sure must be excited.

"Why's that?"

"Your brother's on the radio tonight. The Colonels are playing the Nuggets."

"It's Monday already?"

"All day."

There was a noise from the back room. Dee turned around and shouted, "You mess around and bust something, I'll skin you alive."

She turned back to me. "My kid's a god damned idiot."

I got home and ate a hamburger. Then I washed the dishes, poured a glass of whiskey, turned on the radio, and stretched out in the recliner.

The game was midway thru the second quarter. Denver's announcer was excited. "Fletcher outlets to Petit who kicks it back out to a trailing Kitch Riles. He stops, pops, and swishes! Threeeeeeeeeeeee-pointer!"

The Louisville audience cheered for my brother.

"Bobby Flowers drives hard to the lane, fakes a dish, and stops for a jumper. Yowza! Kitch Riles just blocked that thing right into the stands."

More applause for Kitch.

"This is odd. After two impressive plays, Riles has sprinted off the court. Oh, man." I heard the crowd groan. "Ladies and Gentlemen, I don't know how to say this, so I'll just say it. Kitch Riles has just lost his lunch right in front of the scorer's table. His teammates are laughing it up. I pity the man who has to clean up that mess.

"And look now! Riles is right back on the court and he's waving at the crowd. You gotta love this guy."

Over the remainder of the first half, I drank another glass of whiskey and Kitch scored six more points. The Colonels led by two at the halftime break.

The phone rang. I answered. Heavy breathing.

"It's me. It's Kitch."

I said, "I'm listening to the game."

"Amazing, isn't it?"

"The radio guy said you threw up."

"He said that?"

"Correction. Lost your lunch."

"I have a hangover. That's what happens. Gotta go. Wish me luck."

The Colonels won, 106 to 103. Kitch scored fourteen points.

The broadcast ended with a reminder that Kitch and the Colonels would be in Denver on November fourteenth.

As I lay in bed that night, it occurred to me that I might want to get rid of the dairy cows. After all, I didn't use the milk. All those cows did was keep me from sleeping in.

CHAPTER 11

While I ate breakfast, I made a list of things to do:

1) Retrieve my saddle and the bones of the grey mare.
2) Avoid infection in my hand and foot.
3) Get rid of the dairy cows.
4) No more whiskey.

Item one would be easy. If I continued my semicircles, I'd find what I was looking for.

Item two was taking care of itself. Already, I barely even noticed my missing finger. The wound had shrunk to a little pink mouth on the stump. The toes were dried up nubs. No pus, no swelling.

Item three would require some effort, but nothing super-human. I'd haul the cows up to the auction barn in Strattford next Saturday and sell them.

Item four. I currently had less than two bottles of whiskey. Once I finished them, I wouldn't buy another. I pulled a bottle down from the cabinet and poured a glass. I drank, feeling much better having taken that step towards sobriety.

With my list solidified and my ambitions known to myself, I did the morning milking and feedings.

After chores, I fixed some hard-boiled eggs, filled my canteen, and climbed on the roan. In the full morning sun, things below the horizon were reflected backwards and upside down against the edge of the sky. Tiny, upside down trees, smudges of grey.

The roan marched across the prairie and across Old Stinkum, right up to where we'd stopped the day before, right where the previous day's tracks ended, right where I'd left the hubcap.

The hubcap was missing. The horse sniffed the ground. Knowing it'd be difficult for me to climb back on her, I slid off and squatted to poke around. The hubcap would have left a ring in the dirt where I'd dropped it, but instead the ground was smooth. It made sense. The roan, when she'd been sniffing and snorting, had blown the dirt around, erasing all traces of hubcap.

If the hubcap had blown away, it would have slid along the ground, leaving a trail. There wasn't any trail. All I saw was a spot that no longer contained a hubcap. If the wind had blown hard enough to relocate the hubcap, it would have also blown away our tracks from yesterday, but our tracks were still there. Which meant the wind hadn't moved the hubcap. This left one conclusion: some sort of creature had taken it. A hawk could easily pick up a hubcap. What better way to start a nest than with a shiny round hubcap from a 1948 Ford pickup? A hawk, then.

I touched the roan's nose. "I'm going to scare you, but not on purpose." I walked behind her a few steps. She turned her head to look at me. I ran directly at her, jumped as high as I could, put my hands on her rump, and propelled myself onto her back just like a cowboy in a movie. She didn't buck. I hugged her neck tight so she knew I still liked her.

I rode my semicircles, looked thru my binoculars, ate my eggs. No hubcaps, no saddles, no horse bones. When the sun slipped low, I rode home, did the chores, and went inside for dinner. Sitting on the kitchen table was my list of things to do. I crossed off item number two: ~~Avoid infection in my hand and foot.~~

Before bed, I polished off one of the bottles of whiskey, which meant it wouldn't be long before I could cross off item number four.

● ● ●

For three more days, I continued to not find the remains of my dead horse. I did not despair, even though the semicircle sweeps had expanded to more than two miles long. The riding kept me calm. The weather was cooperative, the horse had an easy lope, and I knew that there was plenty of land yet unexamined.

Eventually, I'd discover footprints or a jaw bone or some such thing. I was thorough and I'd find my answers.

That third evening, as I rode home with the southern sun warming my face, I went over my list of things to do.

> *1) Retrieve my saddle and the bones of my grey.*
> *2) Avoid infection in my hand and foot.*
> *3) Get rid of the dairy cows.*
> *4) No more whiskey.*

This coming Saturday, I would bring the dairy cows to the auction, which would leave me with just two simple tasks to complete.

The whiskey was coming along nicely. The final bottle was nearly empty. So, really, just one task.

That night, the younger of the two cows sat still as I squeezed four gallons of milk from her udders. But the old cow started fighting before I'd even set the stool next to her. She kicked and snorted and acted like a mean old biddy. And then, after all kinds of effort on my part, she gave me barely a gallon of milk.

I didn't particularly care how much milk that old cow put out, but if I took her to the auction, the person who bought her would. There's only one person who'll buy a mean old cow that doesn't produce milk. That's the fellow who comes down from the dog food factory in Denver. And for what he'd pay, it wouldn't be worth hauling her up to Strattford.

I wondered if there was some way that cow could help me find my dead horse.

After dinner, the phone rang.

"Hey brother."

"Hi, Kitch."

"The San Diego Sails are folding." He laughed.

"Oh?"

"We beat them tonight. I got twelve points. I was the first forward off the bench. Have you ever seen the rain?"

"No, but we got that blizzard a couple weeks ago."

"I'm at the airport in Cincinnati. Rain is streaking down the windows. I can see reflections. People with babies and jackets."

"That must be something."

"I took six shots and made four. I shot eighty percent from the line. One assist. Four rebounds. The rain."

"You sound sleepy."

"Sleep is death."

In the background, an announcement came over a loud-speaker.

Kitch said, "I have to go. The showers bring life."

CHAPTER 12

The next morning, I was particularly gentle as I milked the old cow. She gave me a half gallon of milk, then kicked the pail over. Normally, I'd have twisted her ear, but I just said, "That's okay, girl."

I put a leader line on her, climbed on the roan, and we rode north. The cow led well. She enjoyed being outside, exercising in the sunshine. The weather was good again. Mid-fifties, sunny. No wind.

When we reached the end of my tracks from the day before, I climbed off the roan, pounded an iron stake into the ground, and then tied the leader line around it. I dropped a couple of flakes of hay in front of the cow. "I'm going to leave you here for a minute or two. How's that sound?"

She mooed happily and bent down for a mouthful of hay.

I rode south, until I could barely see her, all alone out there, staked to the ground.

I got down from the roan and sat on my ass with the binoculars against my eyes. The cow's sand-colored hair made her hard to see against the bare land and dead grass. I smoked cigarettes, drank water from my canteen, and sipped from the whiskey bottle.

The cow stood there, nibbling on her straw. Sometimes, she'd flap her tail. Every few minutes she'd let out a faint moo.

I finished the last drops of whiskey. The day was uncommonly warm. I grew tired.

I awoke to a rough wet tongue scraping my cheek. The horse was licking my face. The sun had mostly gone down. My cowboy hat was on the ground. The temperature had dropped. I got a panic. Dummy. I shouldn't have drunk that whiskey.

I lifted the binoculars. I couldn't spot the cow. Likely, she had lain down and blended right into the twilit landscape. I listened careful. I didn't hear her mooing.

I gathered my belongings and jumped on the horse's back. It wasn't full dark yet, but it was headed that way. The world would soon change from full color to black and white, and from there to just black. I ran the horse out toward where I'd staked the cow. I found nothing but empty dirt and dead grass.

There wasn't any way in the world that I'd be spending the night in those parts. The cow would have to fend for herself.

Home, I did my chores, ate dinner, and considered driving to Dorsey. No point. It was almost seven o'clock, the liquor store would be closed. I sat in my bed and smoked the last of my cigarettes.

• • •

The next morning, as soon as it was light enough to see, I rode the roan north again. The cow was still gone, the stake was still gone. No hoof prints, no blood. Not a hint of her existence.

I rode home, fed the cattle, gathered eggs. Then I drove to Dorsey and parked in front of the liquor store. It was after ten in the morning but the place was closed and Dee's car wasn't even there. I sat in my truck, staring in at the shelves of bottles, waiting for Dee to show up and apologize for sleeping in. I heard a bell gong. The Baptist church was letting out. Of course the liquor store was closed. It was Sunday.

I drove home. On the way into the yard, I stopped at the mailbox. There was a letter from Kitch. I cut it open with my knife. Two tickets to the game this coming Friday. The Kentucky Colonels versus the Denver Nuggets at McNichols Arena in Denver, Colorado. There was a note, scrawled on hotel stationary. "Come to the locker room afterwards. Tell them you're my brother. They'll let you in. Don't dress like a hick. Be ready to party."

I did not want to go to that game.

I spent the rest of the day in bed, smoking the dry stubs of old cigarettes, wishing for whiskey, unable to sleep due to the simmering guilt I felt about letting my cow disappear.

• • •

On Monday morning, I drove to Dorsey and bought four bottles of whiskey and a carton of cigarettes. For the next few days, I did my chores, smoked, and drank as much liquor as necessary to keep from thinking. There was nothing to think about. The cow was dead, the horse was dead, the saddle was gone, and I would see Kitch play in Denver.

Kitch called on Wednesday.

"I'm going to be cut. I can feel it."

"Say again?" I was drunk.

"Now that the San Diego Sails are out of business. They're having a dispersal draft."

"Oh."

"Do you know what that means?"

"No."

"It means we're going to pick up at least one of their players and that means somebody from the Colonels is going to get cut."

"Should I still go to the game?"

"Of course."

CHAPTER 13

On the morning of Kitch's game, I lay in bed, hungry, unbathed, smelling of whiskey, and with my tongue coated with ash. Meanwhile, I imagined Kitch in a hotel, drinking orange juice, packing his duffel bag for his first ever basketball game in Denver. Secure, satisfied, and tall.

I climbed out of bed. From the kitchen window, I watched a cloud move from the western horizon all the way to the eastern horizon.

I placed the tickets in the sink and set them on fire. Kitch would have to play without me.

• • •

The next morning, as I was milking the young cow, she kept squinting at me like I was a bum. For skipping Kitch's game, for smelling like whiskey, and for leaving her all alone in the barn without her friend.

She stepped toward me sideways so I had to stand up or get knocked over. I slapped her hard on her flank and she settled back over the milk pail.

"You should be glad I didn't leave *you* out there."

She turned around and sent forth a flood of piss. I scooted away, but not before my britches were good and splattered. As the piss soaked into my jeans, I got awful damned angry. I couldn't tolerate one of my animals questioning my authority like that. I made a rope halter and got on the roan and led that judgmental little cow out north.

I brought her to the same place, roughly, where I'd staked the other one. I pounded another metal rod into the ground and tied the lead line around it. With the heel of my boot, I dragged a circle, about twenty feet in diameter around the cow. I made three or four passes until it was good and deep. The cow watched me with slitty eyes and chewed her cud.

I hopped on the horse and rode homeward. I glanced back one time. She'd lain down, the lazy thing.

The afternoon was warm so I sat on the front step and sipped whiskey. As I crept deeper into the bottle, I started imagining sounds, like a cow was shrieking from far away.

I had been foolish. You don't leave a cow to be murdered just because it peed on you.

The day was coming to an end, and so was the warmth. I put on my mittens and my wool hat and climbed back on the roan. By the time we trotted out north, the sun was touching the horizon. We rode quickly. Before we crested the last hill, I stopped the horse and pulled out the binoculars.

The sun was gone now, leaving the sky a blend of orange wiped into black. In the failed light, I spied out to where I'd staked the cow. I marched the roan toward the circle. The cow was right where I'd left her. I scanned around and didn't see anything lurking nearby. I trotted the horse forward.

The circle was entirely intact. The cow didn't look at me funny. I untied the rope and left the stake in the ground.

I put the horse into a trot and the cow matched us step-for-step. It was dark. All of us wanted to get home.

After we got back to the ranch, I led the cow into the barn. I scratched her back for a long time. "I shouldn't have done that."

I could tell she was tired. She probably hadn't got this much exercise her whole life. Before she lay down, I tugged her udders a couple of times, just to see if she'd give me anything. I only got a gallon out of her. No wonder. She hadn't drunk hardly any water all day long. I'd been cruel.

I did my chores and went to sleep without touching the whiskey.

• • •

The next morning, I said hello to the cow, squatted on the

stool, and squeezed her udders. This time, she didn't even give me half a gallon. She was still upset at me. I stood and patted her forehead. "Forgive me, girl. I get in a mood sometimes." I looked deep into her eyes. They were cloudy. They were the eyes of an old cow. This was an old cow.

Cows can be hard to tell apart when it's dark. Jerseys, especially. But in the light, it was obvious. The cows had been switched at the stake yesterday. The old cow that I figured for dead was standing right in front of me.

It took me several cigarettes before I was calm enough to consider the situation. I was dealing with something that had thumbs. You can't switch out a lead line with paws and claws. That ruled out coyotes, mountain lions, saber-tooth tigers, and hawks. It didn't confirm that I was dealing with a human, but it certainly seemed to lean in that direction.

On the bright side, I could start sleeping in if I wanted. The old cow didn't need to be milked but once a day.

That afternoon, I rode out north. The circle was still in the dirt, the metal stake was still hammered into the ground.

I placed a bottle of whiskey next to the stake and then rode home.

• • •

The next day, I put six eggs in a pillowcase and rode back to the circle. The whiskey bottle was gone. I left the pillowcase where the bottle had been and rode home knowing that I'd learned something about my opponent. Which is, he was thirsty.

• • •

The next day, the eggs were gone but the pillowcase was still there. I now had a use for my spare eggs.

I left a rotten tomato and a tooth brush.

• • •

The next day, the toothbrush was gone. The rotten tomato remained.

I put out a pillowcase filled with eggs, toothpaste, a pair of

Kitch's old socks, and a pocket-sized copy of the New Testament.

• • •

The next day, everything was gone except for the New Testament sitting atop the empty, folded-up pillowcase. No footprints. Never any footprints.

CHAPTER 14

Here's what I knew. The horse killer preferred young cows to old ones, and I suspected the young cow was still alive. The horse killer did not want a bible, which could mean that he didn't believe in God, or had already memorized the Bible, or plain couldn't read. The horse killer had cold feet and he had dirty teeth, which meant that he was poor but understood the importance of dental hygiene. The horse killer liked whiskey and eggs but did not care for rotten tomatoes, which meant we had some things in common.

Whiskey and eggs stay fresh for a long time. What if I were to put out some good food that would go bad quick? The horse killer would have to fetch it before it spoiled, before the coyotes got to it. I happened to have a pound of ground beef in the refrigerator.

I brought a screwdriver to my bedroom and unscrewed the bells from my alarm clock. I put the clock on my kitchen table along with the pound of beef, a half-empty bottle of whiskey, the binoculars, my thirty-two caliber pistol, and four hardboiled eggs. I placed the goods in a pillow case and brought it outside, pleased with myself.

The roan had been in the pasture, eating grass next to the cattle. She approached the gate, eager for a ride.

I pulled the pistol out of the pillowcase and wedged it between my belt and my jeans, then I slung the pillowcase over my shoulder and climbed upon the horse and kicked her sides.

The circle and the stake were still there. I hopped off the horse and took the meat out of the pillowcase. I peeled open the butcher paper and placed it on the dirt with the ground beef lying atop.

I cupped my hands around my mouth and hollered, "This here's quality ground beef from the Keaton Locker." I walked around in a circle as I spoke. "It's raw ground beef. I raised the steer myself. I'm going to leave it here now and ride on home. In about ten minutes, it'll be covered with ants. In twenty minutes, I figure the coyotes will come."

I jumped on the roan and we trotted south to my watching-spot over the edge of the hill. I climbed off her back and made a show of removing the eggs and whiskey from the pillowcase. The alarm clock, I left within. I shelled and ate the eggs and drank some swallows of whiskey. I expected that the horse killer knew right where I was. He was watching me and waiting. He knew how long it'd be before the ground beef went bad. He knew everything, almost.

I leaned on my elbows and put the binoculars to my eyes. I spent a few minutes like that, watching the stake. Clouds glided slowly across the sky, dragging shadows below.

The rhythm of the shadows and the sunshine made me tired. I didn't fight it. I wanted the killer to see me fall asleep. I wanted him to hear me snore and I wanted him to feel safe.

Just before my eyes closed, I took off my hat and stuffed the alarm clock inside it. I set the hat on the ground and used it as a pillow. The clock went tick-tick against my ear. I had it all timed out. In eight minutes the clapper, absent the bell, would go off, silently vibrating against my ear. Then I'd wake up and watch as the horse killer sneaked up to the stake. I didn't know what I'd do then. Maybe shoot him. Maybe just watch.

By the time I awoke, the sun was almost down. A hell of a lot more than eight minutes had passed. In the darkening day, I saw my hat lying in front of my face. In my sleep, I must have rolled away from it and slept right thru the alarm clapper. A waste of a plan and a waste of good ground beef.

I peeked over the crest of the hill. The light was too far gone to see anything.

I reached for the whiskey bottle. It was gone. He'd been here. He'd taken it.

I patted my hip. I still had my pistol.

I hurried to the roan and felt her flanks, her neck, her nose, just to make sure she was alive. She looked at me like I was over-reacting.

I galloped her north, toward the stake. We reached it just as the sun went below the horizon. I had left the block of meat on top of the flattened butcher paper. The meat was gone and the paper had been folded up in a neat square on the ground. A line of ants led away from it.

I climbed off the horse and squatted next to the paper. I couldn't see any footprints. I didn't expect to. I pulled my knife out of the holster and poked at the paper. I tried to act like I was curious, but I was plain scared.

I scooted the paper toward me and opened it up. Three Polaroid pictures of me curled up on the ground with a half-empty bottle of whiskey at my side. In all of them, there was a shadow draped over me. The horse killer was real enough to block the sun. I dropped the pictures and jumped on the horse. We ran straight home.

When the horse and I arrived at the barn, the stars were out and the yard light was on. Parked beneath the light was a shiny red Corvette.

Kitch had come home.

CHAPTER 15

He was in the living room, sitting on the recliner, watching TV with the volume up. Kitch always liked everything loud. The chair was fully reclined. A pair of crutches lay on the floor. One of his feet was in a cast.

The room smelled like cologne. I breathed thru my mouth.

Kitch didn't look at me as I walked in. He said, "Have you seen this new show?"

On the TV, a group of men were standing in an alley, arguing. One of them pointed a pistol at a building.

I still had my gun stuffed into the right side of my pants. I twisted myself so Kitch wouldn't see it.

I said, "I don't look at the TV very often."

Kitch turned around to face me. He had grown a moustache that spread thick from one corner of his mouth to the other. His shirt was decorated with bright flowers.

I said, "What happened to your foot?"

"You didn't hear? It's a story. I'll tell you after the show's over."

I said, "You eat dinner?"

"I got a burger in Last Chance. But if you're cooking."

He turned back to the TV.

The smell of the cologne wasn't as strong in the kitchen. I took the gun out of my pants and hid it in the cabinet, behind my whiskey bottles. I fried three eggs for me, scrambled six for Kitch. During a commercial break, I brought out Kitch's plate along with a bottle of Tabasco sauce, which he required on anything he ate. I asked if he wanted something to drink. He shook his head and held up a half-empty glass of milk.

When the show concluded, Kitch crutched to the TV, turned down the volume, and crutched back to his chair.

He said, "Good show, huh?"

"I liked the joke at the end."

"Whaddya think of that brunette? Gorgeous, ain't she?"

"Hard to tell. I've never met her."

"You always say that."

I shrugged.

Kitch said, "I happen to know a couple people who *have* met her. You meet a lot of important people in my business. Apparently, she's a wildcat." He winked.

I brought the empty plates to the kitchen. Then I opened the cabinet, took out one of the bottles of whiskey, and poured a gulp into my mouth.

I returned to the living room and sat down on the Davenport on the end closest to Kitch's recliner. The TV was still playing, with the sound off. I put the ash tray between us. It was a fancy one, with a narrow stand. There was a button you could push which would spread the metal halves open and drop the accumulation of ashes into the bottom of the bowl.

Kitch pulled a shiny blue packet from his shirt pocket. The writing on it looked French. He took a rolling paper out of the packet and sprinkled it with tobacco. He saw me staring and said, "You want one?"

"I got my own." I shook one of my reds out of my own pack and lit it with a strike-anywhere match. The smoke helped with the cologne. The whiskey was helping me relax.

Kitch rolled his cigarette small and tight. He lit it with a silver flip-top lighter and took a long drag.

He said, "You gotta love the French."

I nodded.

He said, "You're probably wondering what happened to my ankle."

I nodded.

Kitch tipped the milk glass to his mouth and drank it empty. He wiped the excess moisture from his moustache with the back of his thumb.

I stood up. "I'll get you some more milk."

"Water, please. I'm milked out."

"Okay."

"You're sure being an accommodating type."

I brought his glass to the kitchen and rinsed it and put it under the faucet. In the time it took for it to fill with water, I poured another slug of whiskey into my mouth. With all the smoke and the cologne, I figured Kitch wouldn't notice the booze on my breath.

Back in the living room, Kitch was rolling another cigarette. His first one was still smoldering in his mouth. I handed him the water, sat back down on the Davenport, and lit a smoke for myself. The room was getting hazy.

I said, "So you're still on the team."

Kitch leaned way back on the recliner. "Hell yes I am. I'm a rising star in the American Basketball Association. After our game in Denver, which you didn't come see me afterward, thank you very much, Coach started working me into the regular rotation. He kept me on even after we got Caldwell Jones in the dispersal draft because, as he said, I had a knack. Well, that Denver game, where you saw me score five points in the waning moments, that was the knack Coach was looking for.

"My job is to hustle, get rebounds, and make sure no one messes with our point guards. We played the Pacers last Tuesday and I was in for most of the third quarter. I scored five points, got five rebounds and picked up five fouls. We lost, but after the game, Clovis—he's our center— said, 'Gimme five for your three fives.'"

Kitch laughed hard. "That big spade hadn't spoken two words to me since I joined the team. But there he was, giving me five for my three fives."

I said, "What's a spade?"

"It means 'Negro.' Except they don't like to be called Negroes. They don't like to be called colored either anymore. Depending on who you're talking to, you can sometimes say Afro-American. That's the more, um, scholarly term. But it's easiest just to call them black. Spade is a word you use if you know the guy. If two spades are talking to each other, they'll call each other nigger, but *you* hadn't better call one of them nigger. As far as Caucasians go, there's only three of us on the team so the spades call us whatever they want. Mostly, they call me Riles. Sometimes they'll say honky, but only if we're all partying together."

Kitch paused a moment and then said, "What was I talking about?"

I said, "Your ankle."

"Yeah. A couple days ago, we played the Spurs down in Texas. Halfway thru the fourth quarter, their backup center took it to Rollie real hard on a fast break. Rollie is short and he's old. Nobody takes it to Rollie. So, on the next trip down the floor, I gave their boy an elbow to the ribs. A fight ensued. Technicals. Next thing you know, I'm sitting with Coach in the locker room, waiting for the game to finish. Both of us were ejected and dejected. We were up by six when the fight happened. We ended up losing by seven."

Kitch lit his second cigarette and began rolling another.

I said, "And that's how you hurt your ankle."

"It is not. After the game, we went out to a bar with the guys from the Spurs. We partied with them until curfew. They're a quality bunch of fellows, even their piece of shit backup center. I got good and drunk and started singing for everyone. You know how I can sing."

Kitch could sing like a lawnmower. Loud and sharp.

He took a drink of water and rubbed his forehead. "It's so dry out here. It's bad for you skin. You should get a humidifier."

"Your ankle."

"Yeah. As we were getting into the cab to go home, I stepped on the curb funny. Twisted the hell out of it. My ankle. When I woke up the next morning, it was so swollen I couldn't hardly walk."

I said, "So you broke your ankle by getting into a cab?"

"It's only a sprain. I'm on injured reserve, which means I can't play for fourteen days. Coach gave me permission to come home for a night since I won't be able to make it out here for Thanksgiving next week."

"That's nice of him."

"Did you see my car? I rented it at the airport. From Stapleton to here, it took me barely an hour. I must have averaged a hundred and twenty miles an hour."

"How'd you shift, with your bad ankle?"

"On the fly, like Dad showed us."

Our conversation paused for a moment. Talking about Dad meant thinking about Dad.

Kitch said, "Apparently, he's the only watch repairman in all of Saint Francis."

"That's fortunate."

Kitch said, "He says he's getting some feeling back in his leg. Said he's just about ready to come back out here and kick your ass." Kitch laughed. "You shoulda shot him twice."

Kitch's eyes were red. Presumably from all the cologne fumes.

I said, "More water?"

"Hydrate me."

I brought his glass to the kitchen, filled it, and then took a long, long slug of whiskey.

When I returned, Kitch was puffing on another of his cigarettes. Entering that smoked-up room was like looking thru a cataract.

Kitch said, "Why didn't you say hello afterwards?"

"After what?"

"After my game in Denver. The one I gave you tickets for."

"I couldn't get into the locker room. They wouldn't let me in." I'm not much of a liar. Fortunately, Kitch was never much of a skeptic.

"Did you tell them you knew me?"

"I didn't want to make a big deal of it. I couldn't have hardly stuck around anyway. I had to get home for the cattle."

Kitch looked at his glass. "You know how I was drinking milk when you came in? After I got here, I went to the barn to fill a glass and say hello to the girls. But Polly wasn't there. It was just Eleanor. What happened to Polly?"

Kitch named everything. Polly was what he called the young cow, the one I'd most recently given to the horse killer. Eleanor was the old cow, the one the horse killer had given back to me.

I said, "You know how cows are."

"Did you see me milk that cow at halftime of that game? I milked her good, didn't I?"

"It was a marvel to see."

"Who'd you bring with you?"

"Bring where?"

"To the game. Who'd you use that extra ticket on?"

"I ended up going alone."

"Really? That's a hot ticket, seeing Kitch Riles play in Denver. I figured everyone would want to go with you. You could have asked Charlie. You see her all the time at the store. She's plain-looking, but she's funny."

"She has a boyfriend."

"What about Mandy Churchouse? She's always willing."

"I didn't have time to ask every single person in Dorsey. I've been awful busy. It's a lot of work taking care of a ranch on your own."

I shook another cigarette out of my pack. I already wanted more whiskey. I cleared my throat a couple of times while I struck my match. I brought my cigarette to my face and coughed. I said, "I reckon I oughta get some water for myself."

Kitch said, "I know. It's so dry out here."

While I was slugging the whiskey, Kitch hollered, "You got anything stronger in there?"

I pretended I didn't hear him.

Kitch hollered again, "'Cause Mom used to always keep that bottle in the cabinet above the sink. We ought to have a sip."

I said, "Let me check." I made noises like I was looking around and then I said, "Why, here it is. Right where she left it. You want a glass or do you want to drink from the bottle?"

"Glass. On the rocks."

"That means ice, right?"

"Yes, dummy."

The bottle was three-quarters empty. I pushed my spare bottle to the back of the cabinet. If Kitch found out about that, we'd end up drinking every last drop of booze in the house and I'd have to make a run to the liquor store first thing in the morning.

I found Mom's old serving platter, a blue, flowery thing that Kitch and I had given to her for her birthday several years prior. I loaded it with two glasses of ice, a glass of water, and the whiskey bottle. I carried the tray out and set it on the empty side of the Davenport, between me and Kitch.

Kitch ran a finger along the side of the bottle. "She didn't leave much for us, did she?"

"She's good at that."

As I poured the whiskey, Kitch took another long drag of his cigarette, pinching it tight between his thumb and forefinger. He was down past the point where the tobacco could possibly taste any good. He looked carefully at the remaining bit of the cigarette and then popped it into his mouth and swallowed it.

I handed him his glass and I held up mine. We took a moment to admire the liquid inside. I'd been annoyed to see Kitch at the house, but I was starting to warm up, thanks to that liquid.

I said, "That's some mustache you've got."

"The ladies like it." Kitch snapped his fingers. "Don't let me forget. I've got something in the car for you."

I said, "What kind of something?"

"Not 'til later, brother."

Good ol' Kitch. He was all right. Mom was all right. I was all right. Dad was far enough away that it didn't matter.

Kitch said, "You know what?"

I said, "I know very little."

Kitch thought that was the funniest thing anyone had ever said. He laughed for about a minute. When he calmed down, he said, "What were we talking about?"

"How amazing you are."

"Yeah. I met a woman after a game the other day. In Denver, in a bar. She was a looker. I kept looking at her and she kept looking at me. She entered the place with some guy in a suit, but she left with Kitch Riles. She said I had the prettiest eyes she'd ever seen."

In addition to being bloodshot, Kitch's eyes were now half-crossed.

I said, "She's a damned liar."

Kitch thought that was the brand new funniest thing anyone had ever said. I put another inch of whiskey in his glass. The bottle was getting dangerously low.

Kitch said, "She works at the dog pound." He exhaled a string of smoke and looked around the room, at the Davenport, the TV, the cracked plaster walls, the carpet that hadn't been vacuumed in a couple of years.

I said, "Wanna play Horse?"

Kitch pointed to the cast on his foot. "I can't play. That's why I'm here."

"I'll put you on a chair. We'll sit on chairs and play Chair Horse."

The rim was bolted to a homemade plywood backboard, which was screwed to a telephone pole on the east side of the barn.

I set out two chairs in front of the hoop. I got Kitch situated in his chair, propping his bad foot atop a wooden pail. I went back to the house and brought out the whiskey, the ball, and, for laughs, the fancy ash tray.

Between the moon and the yard light, we could see well enough. Kitch and I sat side by side, just in front of where the free-throw line would be on a proper court. It was cool enough to see our breath.

Kitch looked up. "The stars really get after it out here."

I looked at the house and the barn, grey in the moonlight. The chickens were sleeping. The feeder cattle were ambling towards us across the pasture. Somewhere to the north, the man who killed my horse was eating ground beef.

Kitch raised the whiskey bottle. He said, "We'll play for the final sip."

He squeezed the ball, making sure it had enough air, and then tried a one-hand sitting jumper. The ball flew past the backboard and into the dark.

When I came back from retrieving the ball, Kitch was smoking another of his cigarettes. I lit one of my own, the last in my pack. With my cigarette dangling out of my mouth, I tried a sitting granny shot. It bumped the rim and came right back to me, knocking me in the face and busting my cigarette in half. Brand-new funniest thing in the world. I even laughed a little.

I said, "That was my last smoke."

Kitch said, "If I know you, there's a whole carton in the freezer."

"Yeah, but it's all the way inside."

Kitch handed me his cigarette. I took a drag and handed it back. I said, "The French make some good-tasting tobacco."

"They sure do."

We traded a dozen shots. Kitch was the first one with a make, a bank that plopped thru the net and bounced to a stop on the ground. He whooped. I fetched the ball and took my seat for a follow-up.

Kitch said, "You'll miss."

I concentrated hard, compensating for the fact that I was seated, and took a two-hand set shot, which didn't come close to entering the net. The ball scraped the bottom of the rim and rolled out toward the barn. Kitch erupted in laughter. He was a little kid and I was his big brother. I felt mighty drunk, mighty good. Kitch and I were having a time.

I followed the ball to where it had rolled, right up against the barn. As I bent down to pick it up, I heard something beyond where I could see, around the corner of the barn. I stood with the ball in my hands, peering at the dark border where the barn blocked the yard light and where the moon did not shine. I took steps toward the sound, into that darkness. I whispered, "I'll murder you. I'll murder you over and over."

I glanced once more into the darkness and then I turned and walked back toward Kitch. It was hard for me to step out of the shadow, like it was stuck to me.

Kitch said, "I finished the whiskey."

"You ain't won yet. Alls I have is 'h.'"

"I got the feel for this. Observe." He took the ball from me and shot left-handed. It swished thru the net. "You want to keep going?"

I said, "I do not. Since you drank the rest of the whiskey, perhaps you could roll me a cigarette, at least."

I sat in the chair next to him as he fiddled with the tobacco and the rolling papers.

Kitch said, "Don't feel bad. I practice a lot." He handed me the cigarette. I took it with my left hand.

Kitch yelped. "Holy fuck! What happened to you?"

"What?"

"Your finger."

"What finger?"

"The one that isn't there."

"You're drunk."

"I can still count, dummy. You're missing a finger."

"It's always been like that."

"Bull."

"It has."

He considered this.

I said, "I can't believe you never noticed."

He considered this some more. "No. You've flipped me off with that finger."

I had to remain cool. The horse killer was watching. I said, "It got bit off a few weeks ago."

"Bullshit."

"Nope. That cow. Eleanor."

"Polly."

"Yeah. Polly. I was milking her and she started choking on her cud or something. I pried her mouth open."

The story was happening in my head. I could feel her lips and the snot.

Kitch said, "You're not supposed to put your hand in a cow's mouth."

"It was an emergency. She couldn't breathe. I reached in, up past my elbow. I found a corncob stuck sideways in her throat. I grabbed on. Just as I was yanking it out, she coughed and then, snap! She clamped down."

"Polly bit your finger off?" Kitch was astonished.

"Not all the way. She just crunched the hell out of it."

"What'd you do?"

I pulled my knife out of the holster and showed it to him. "What do you think?"

Kitch nodded. "Excal. No way."

I put the knife away. "Yeah. No way. I hollered like hell is what happened. Then I jumped in the truck and drove to Strattford as fast as I could. Doctor Shepard cut it off. It's not a big deal. If it'd been the pinkie, that would have been serious."

Kitch stared at the stub where the finger used to be. He reached out and tried to touch it.

I brought my hand to my chest. I said, "Don't be a weirdo."

Kitch said, "And that's why Polly's not around. She bit off your finger and you got rid of her."

"Sold her the next day."

"Do you get any of those phantom pains, like the Civil War guys get when their arms are amputated?"

"Not much. I dream about it sometimes."

"Wow. Nine fingers."

"Seven, if you don't count my thumbs."

Kitch looked at my hand some more. I allowed him to touch the stump.

He said, "Shit."

I took a drag of the cigarette. I got dizzy.

CHAPTER 16

The sun shone thru the window and coated my closed eyelids with warmth. Judging by the scratchy fabric under my shirt and the way my legs were half-folded up, I concluded that I had spent the night on the Davenport.

The living room smelled like cigarettes, farts, and cologne. I let my eyes open just enough to let in the orange glow of morning. Then wider, so I could look thru the blurry streaks of my eyelashes. And then, full open to stare at the plaster ceiling.

Since I was on the couch, I concluded that Kitch was sleeping in my bed, stinking it up and dotting the sheets with cigarette burns.

A clattering sound erupted from the kitchen. The clatter grew louder and then a miniature poodle sprinted out of the kitchen doorway and onto the living room carpet and then, with a wild leap, it landed directly onto my lap.

The dog had, at one point, been shaved bare except for poof-balls around its ankles, chest, and head. The poofy bits had lost their poofiness and the shaved areas were growing back. The poodle was not pretty.

The little creature stood on one of my thighs, grey and ridiculous. Its feet kept slipping off my leg. It stared at me with its pink tongue hanging out, panting.

I put my hand under the dog's belly and placed it on the floor, then I went to the bathroom. The dog tried to follow. I pushed it away with my foot and quickly closed the door. Pieces of greenish flakes were floating in the toilet. Kitch must of had the shits. I pissed for about an hour and then went to the sink and splashed water on my face.

The dog followed me to the kitchen. Lying on the table was a record album, still sealed in shrink wrap. The record was *Tonight's the Night*, by Neil Young. I'd heard some of his songs on the radio. The cover was a black-and-white photo of Mr. Young standing in front of a microphone. He looked like he'd just woke up after spending a night drinking with Kitch.

Beneath the record was a letter.

J.R.,

Happy birthday. I did your chores. The milk's in a bucket in the barn. The eggs are in the basket on the stove.

The dog's name is Prance, but you can change it if you want. Just call her something, okay? Ha ha. I got her from my friend at the pound. I left a bag of food in the mud room.

We play in Denver the day before Thanksgiving. Mom and Dad are coming to the game. I expect you'll want to avoid that scene.

You're twenty-seven now. Don't die. Ha! Like Jim Morrison (The Doors) or Janis Joplin (Me and Bobby McGee) or Jimi Hendrix (Purple Haze) did.

From: Your Big Little Brother

I looked out the kitchen window. The corvette was gone. Kitch was speeding back to the airport with his arm hanging out the window and a cigarette in his teeth, leaving a trail of stink.

I opened the freezer and pulled out the carton of cigarettes. I took out a pack and took out a smoke and lit it.

The dog would be a problem. I like animals. I don't like it when they get killed. As a kid, I was in 4-H and every year when my steer got hauled off to the locker at the end of the county fair, it tore me up. You can't get attached to things if you're going to outlive them. And this dog here was coyote bait. Hawk bait. Horse killer bait.

I ashed my cigarette on the floor. The dog sniffed and then ran around the table, acting generally happy to be alive.

A miniature poodle wouldn't be safe outside. I wasn't about

to let the thing live in the house. Dogs are meant to run. Correction. Some dogs are meant to run. This one was meant to be stored in a duffle bag. I had to get rid of it immediately. I decided to put up a 'Free Dog' sign the next time I went to the grocery store.

The poodle looked at me with dumb eyes.

Kitch had left a ten-pound bag of cat food in the mud room. I opened it and took out a handful of kibbles. I brought them to the kitchen where I placed them in a bowl on the floor. The dog looked at the food and then walked to the area in front of the stove, where it started licking grease stains.

I cracked an egg and poured it on top of the cat food. The dog ran forward and slurped up the egg and chomped the kibbles, her tail wagging happily.

"Eat your breakfast. I'm going to ascertain what kind of damage Kitch has inflicted upon the livestock."

I pulled on a vest, pushed my hat on my head, and opened the front door. The dog shot between my feet and ran outside. She ran down the steps, making a dead line toward the chicken house. The chickens were pecking in the dirt in front of their coop, protected by a four-foot-tall fence. The dog, who had apparently never before seen fowl nor a fence, ran straight into the chicken wire, which slung her onto her back. She bounced right up and started barking at the chickens, who commenced to flapping and clucking and preparing for the end of the world.

The dog barked until the last of the chickens had run into the coop. She gave a few more yips and then sprinted away.

Hurdling cow turds, she ran around behind the barn, out of sight. I followed, walking fast. By the time I rounded the barn, she was in the pasture, galloping straight toward the cattle, who stood at attention a hundred yards away.

Most of the vegetation in the pasture had been chewed and stomped short but there was still some sickly sagebrush for her to dodge. She weaved and yipped and ran.

Quick, she spun around, leaving a burst of dust. She made a wild screech. I walked faster, watching carefully. The dog growled at the ground.

I crawled thru the fence and started toward her.

She lunged a few times and then took off after a ground squirrel, a pale beige critter with white spots on its back. It was nearly as long as she was.

The chase didn't last ten feet. The dog pounced. She and the squirrel rolled in the dirt. Then the dog stood up and the squirrel lay down. The poodle glanced at me and then plunged her face into the belly of the squirrel.

I didn't have to worry about this dog being outside.

I left her alone with her prey and went to the barn to check on the milk cow. The milk was in the bucket, the cow was still in her stall, the stool had been put away. Kitch hadn't screwed anything up.

I climbed into the hayloft and threw eight bales out to the ground. Then I climbed down and cut the twine off and dumped the flakes into the feed troughs.

The warm night had left the stock tank free of ice. A breeze picked up, spinning the windmill. Gulps of water slurped into the stock tank.

I leaned on a fencepost and watched the cattle cross the pasture for their hay.

I owned thirty-nine head of cattle. One bull, twenty mama cows, and eighteen feeder calves. You couldn't tell by looking, but every last one of those mama cows was pregnant. In the spring, they would give birth to a new batch of feeder calves. In April, when this year's calves were up to weight, I'd sell them to whoever was willing to pay, usually the stockyard in Greeley. My feeder calves had one job. Get fat and don't die.

I walked amongst the cattle as they ate their hay. Check for bloat. Look for streaks of shit on their backsides. Listen to their breathing. When weather changes, cattle can get pneumonia. Check for pink eye. Look at their coats for signs of ringworm.

Everybody was healthy.

My horse was pastured with the cattle. She allowed them to eat before she approached and finished any hay they had missed. I gave her an extra flake for her patience.

After lunch, I took a nap. I awoke in the late afternoon. I pushed the dog to the floor and sat up to get dressed. Before I pulled on my boots, I brought my legs up in the Indian fashion of sitting and held my bad foot as close to my face as possible. The frostbit toes were smaller and drier than before. I squeezed. I could feel the tiny bones grinding under the hard mummy skin.

In the evening, I drove to Dorsey with the dog on the seat beside me. She stood up on her back legs and put her paws on the dashboard so she could watch the fence posts pass by.

My first stop was the grocery. I left the dog in the truck. Inside the store, there wasn't anyone at the register. Charlie was probably in the back, counting cereal boxes.

All I needed was a loaf of bread and a few cans of vegetables. Charlie came out of the back as I approached the register. She had a smirk on her face.

"How's Johnny?"

I said, "Still upright. How's Charlie?"

"Can you believe this weather?"

"Seems pretty seasonable."

"The weather is a fascinating subject, don't you think?"

I said, "Not particularly."

"Failure to talk about it is grounds for dismissal here."

Charlie was two years older than me. She graduated in '66. She started working part time at the store when she was in eighth grade. Fourteen years later, she'd made it to full time, stocking, pricing, ringing, and making small talk. She was a smart ass and I liked her for that. She had a well-publicized boyfriend in Goodland, eighty-five miles east. I didn't particularly care for that.

I said, "You wouldn't have any use for a poodle, would you?"

"Is she cute?"

"She's in my pickup. My brother gave her to me yesterday night."

"Kitch is in town? Where's the parade?"

Charlie was the only person I knew who didn't worship my brother.

"He took off this morning. He gave me a miniature poodle for my birthday."

Charlie said, "Happy birthday, Mr. Riles."

She stepped from behind the register, took me by the arm,

and we walked outside. She put her face against the driver's side window of my truck. The dog was asleep on the seat.

Charlie said, "Can I hold her?"

I opened the door. The dog was instantly awake. She dove out onto the ground and began running figure-eights around and between my legs. Charlie scooped her up to her bosom.

With her nose scratching the back of the dog's head, she said, "Keep her, Johnny. You're lonely out there on the farm."

"It's a ranch."

"Whatever it is, you're all by yourself, which means you're lonely."

I said, "You sure know a lot."

"I do. For instance, I know that, just as soon as you're paid up here, you'll drive across the highway and head into Dee's Liquor. I watch people go into that store every day. They're either lonely or they aren't; I can tell by whether they're smiling or not when they come out. You never smile."

I smiled real big, so big my lips felt uncomfortable dragging over my gums.

"See?" said Charlie, "That's a phony smile. Keep the dog. Girls like dogs, I hear."

I said, "You still dating that fella from Goodland?" I stretched my smile wider.

"Yes. And if I wasn't, you think I'd date a younger man?"

I let my smile go flat. "I should probably get out of here."

Charlie handed me the dog. I started getting in the truck. Charlie said, "Don't forget your groceries."

Dark had settled. I turned on the headlight. I drove out of Dorsey without stopping at Dee's. The groceries were in the back of the truck. The temperature being around forty degrees, I wasn't in any rush to get to my refrigerator, so I drove all the way to Strattford for two bottles of whiskey. It was an eighty-mile round trip. Even with gas being fifty-six cents a gallon, it was worth it.

When I got home, I went to the barn and filled a glass with a few squirts of milk straight from the cow. I came back to the house and poured it into the dog's bowl. She lapped the milk until the bowl shone. That old cow was finally being useful.

The dog scratched on the front door, then turned to look at me. She tilted her head sideways.

I said, "I'm not letting you out. There's coyotes."

She scratched the door again.

"You have been warned."

I opened the door. The dog sprinted out. A couple days ago, she'd been stuck in a cage waiting for someone to put her to sleep. At least now she could die with dignity, as much as that's possible for a poodle.

I poured myself a glass of whiskey. I couldn't believe how normal I was feeling. I'd had a good night and a good day. Kitch had been thoughtful, in his own way. The dog was okay. Even Charlie had been nice.

I put the Neil Young record on the hi fi. He sang about a man who drove a van. I fell asleep on the Davenport.

I woke up in the middle of the night and remembered that I'd forgotten to let the dog in. I got up so fast I became dizzy. I ran sideways thru the kitchen and to the mud room and opened the front door.

The dog was sitting on the step, gnawing on a rabbit's foot. The temperature was close to freezing outside.

I said, "Sorry, pup."

I scooped her up, with the rabbit foot dangling in her mouth, and brought her inside. I brushed my teeth and then got ready for bed. The dog jumped on the mattress next to me. She chewed on the rabbit foot all night long.

CHAPTER 17

The next morning, I let the dog follow along as I trotted the horse north. It took me a long time to find the spot. And even then, I wasn't sure I'd found it. The stake was gone. Everything was gone. The circle I'd dragged into the dirt, the footprints, gone. No pillowcase.

I sighted the binoculars across the land and walked the roan in a circle. The season was such that the sun stayed south all day long. Even at noon the shadows were stretched. The horizon formed gentle waves.

I climbed off the horse and drank water from the canteen. I poured some in my hat and let the dog slurp it out. When the dog finished, I put the hat on my head and let the moisture cool my brain.

I closed my eyes to ponder. If Kitch still lived with me, I'd put him in a giant box and then leave him out in this spot. Then, when the killer approached, Kitch would spring out and shoot the fucker in the face. Or become best buddies with him.

I said to the horse, "What do you suggest I do now?" I put my ear to her mouth. She nudged her nose up and knocked my hat off.

I retrieved my hat, jumped on the horse, and rode home with the dog running along. Already, her grey fur was turning brown. She was turning into the landscape.

After lunch, I walked around the cattle pasture to check the fence. I tugged the wires at every post, making sure all the staples were tight. The ones that weren't, I pounded with fence pliers.

As I worked, the dog chased between the legs of the cattle. They didn't mind her at all.

On the western border of the pasture, I found a lizard hanging on one of the fence barbs. There's a bird that catches lizards and impales them on barbed-wire fences. This lizard was withered and small, about the length of the finger Doctor Shepard had cut off. I poked at the empty leather of my left glove.

A mist of clouds covered the sun. The light of the world went grey, shadows dissolved. Wind stirred small pieces of dead things and slid them across the ground. It was going to snow again. I pounded the last fence staple and went to the barn to put the pliers away.

By the time I stepped outside, the wind had grown. Tumble-weeds rocked back and forth, preparing for an evening roll.

I whistled for the dog. She hurtled out of the pasture and followed me inside.

After sunset, I stood at the kitchen window and watched snow-flakes whip past the yard light like swarms of insects. I poured a glass of whiskey, then returned to the window. The snow got thicker. The wind got stronger. Snow pinged against the walls of the house. I could barely see the yard light. The furnace came on and stayed on.

This could be another bad one. I swallowed my glass of whis-key.

I exchanged my cowboy hat for the wool hat. I put on my coveralls and wool socks and wool-lined gloves. Then I went out to check on the old cow in the barn. She seemed happy. Wind hummed thru the cracks in the walls. Gusts made the whole barn creak. The lights flickered.

I went up to the loft and tossed out six bales for the feeder cattle. The wind was blowing so bad the bales almost flew back in when I pitched them.

I climbed back down and went outside to put the hay in the feeder troughs. The cattle and the roan had all gathered up at the barn with their asses to the wind. Their backs were already white with snow. The water in the stock tank hadn't yet frozen over. The windmill was spinning like crazy. I pulled the lever and shut it off.

I whistled to the roan. I opened the west door of the barn and brought her in and led her to her stall.

The barn at night is always pleasant, even at the start of a blizzard. I wasn't afraid of anything in there. I used to sleep in the hay loft as a little kid, especially in the winter when the spiders moved slow and the mud wasps were still worms in their nests.

I said good night to the roan and the cow and then I walked back to the house, leaning sideways so the wind wouldn't send me flying away. The snow struck me like pieces of sand. It put my mind right back to wandering in the pitch dark with horse hair in my boots and horse blood frozen on my pants.

Quick steps and in a moment I was back in the house with the dog pawing snow off my leg. I took off my coveralls, rubbed my hands. I warmed a can of soup and sat in the kitchen with a blanket over my shoulders.

I gave the dog some more cat food with milk. When she finished, she scratched at the door to get out. I opened it up and she stood watching the snow swirl outside. She didn't want to go out there, but I knew she needed to pee. I carried her to the south side of the house where the wind was more settled. She pissed as fast as she could and then jumped into my arms.

Back inside, I brought a bottle of whiskey to bed and drank some sips, then some swallows, then some gulps. When I wasn't drinking, I'd stop up the bottle with my finger stump and hold it upside down, a little bit of whiskey oozing down my hand.

The wind rattled the windows and the snow ticked on the walls and I wondered what sort of weather the horse killer was listening to in his bed.

CHAPTER 18

At sunrise, the dog jumped onto my chest and told me to let her outside. I got up and opened the front door. The snow had stopped, the clouds had moved on. The landscape was drifts and curves. Icicles hung from the eaves, pushed at forty-five degree angles by the wind.

I stomped a flat spot into the snow on the front step and put the dog down. She made a little yellow stain and then ran back into the house.

It was a little after seven o'clock. Chores could wait another half-hour. I made eggs and sausage. I gave the dog a fried egg with her cat food.

I lit a cigarette, enjoying the way the smoke hovered in the room. Kitch called.

"Hey, big brother." He was talking loud.

I said, "Just getting up?"

"Naw." He paused. "Just going to bed. What's the time out there?"

"The sun's been up for about twenty minutes."

"Hell, the sun's been up a couple days here in Louisville. At least I have."

He was drunk.

He said, "How'd you like your birthday presents? That's some dog, ain't it?"

"She's all right."

"Suzanne said you'd like her."

"Who's Suzanne?"

"The gal who works at the dog pound. You like that Neil Young record?"

"It's good."

"Sorry I couldn't find the one with Horse with No Name."

I said, "Neil Young doesn't sing Horse with No Name."

"Sure, he does."

"It's by a band called America."

"America's not a band name. It's a country. No wonder nobody's heard of 'em. You want something good? Listen to the Ohio Players or the Brothers Johnson. The spades know all the good stuff. You ever sleep with a colored chick? Oh, man. You know what else they got here in Louisville? Some real good hillbilly girls. Little girls with straw in their ears. Probably never made it with anyone outside their family. Har har. After every game, there's a line of 'em outside the locker room. Man, once—"

I said, "How's your ankle?"

"Much improved. I'll be back to practice in a couple of days. We played Saint Louis last night. We beat those fuckers like a bad dog. They're supposed to go bankrupt any day now. This whole league's going broke. And the Spirits are going broke faster than the rest of us. Speaking of us, we smuggled a bottle of vodka on the plane. Coach Brown knew about it but he didn't care 'cause we won. The night before, Bird was so hungover he had to run off the floor during a time-out so he could puke in the locker room. I once puked on the floor. Did I ever tell you about that? At the start of the third quarter, Marvin Barnes hit Clovis right in the stomach. The refs didn't do anything. Shit like that wouldn't happen if I wasn't stuck sitting behind the bench with my damned ankle."

I said, "The poodle caught a ground squirrel. She ate it."

"We're playing in Denver on Wednesday. That's the day before Thanksgiving, in case you don't have a calendar handy. Mom and Dad are coming. They want you to come, too, so you can all sit together. I don't want to get in the middle, you know. But they said that."

"I've got a lot of work around here."

"I'll let 'em know."

"I appreciate that."

He said, "So how do you like the dog?"

"She's all right."

"What's her name again?"

"Toby."

"That's right. I better hit the sack. I need my sleep so my ankle can get better. They're always itching to cut somebody here. The ABA has all the talent, none of the money. Excepting Dr. J, of course. He has both. Time to go. Don't forget to milk the cow."

He tried to hang up the phone but I heard it miss the cradle and clunk to the floor. I hung up and let him fight it over with himself.

I went outside and chopped the ice in the stock tank. I tossed hay to the cattle. The day was cold. Twenty-five degrees and cloudy enough that the sun didn't melt anything. The air crinkled with the sound of settling snow.

When I went back in the house, the dog wanted to go outside. I dropped her onto a drift just outside the front door. She fell right thru the snow and started whining for help. I plucked her out and brought her back to the house where she alternately barked at the closed door or sat on my bed and whined. She needed exercise. I told her to hang on a minute.

I found an old sock and cut holes in it so I could poke the dog inside with her head and tail and four little legs sticking out. I left her in the house in her sweater while I went out and found an old car tire in the junk pile behind the barn and tied a rope around it. I dragged it from the barn to the house, leaving a nice, wide swath. I opened the front door and the dog tore out and ran along the drag-path all the way to the barn. I followed her and let her inside where she sniffed around the stalls and squirted piss in the corners.

I greeted the roan in her stall, then went to the tool bench and found another length of rope. I rigged up a figure-eight harness I could loop around my shoulders. I put the harness on, led the roan out of the barn, and tied the harness to the tire rope. I climbed atop the horse and heeled her gently. As she walked forward in the snow, the harness sank into my shoulders.

We dragged the tire behind with the dog following in the flattened path.

We meandered around the property. We walked under all the eaves on all the buildings and I punched at the icicles. The dog ran behind us, happy as hell in her sock sweater. I couldn't believe her feet didn't freeze off.

I allowed the horse to go where she pleased. She took to the north, with the dog running behind and with me leaning forward against the pull of the tire. The sky was hidden by an endless white cloud that merged seamless into the horizon. A white soup in every direction. I felt tiny out there. This is exactly how I'd imagine heaven to be. I was grateful the sun wasn't out. The world was plenty bright without it.

My mind meandered of its own accord.

High School basketball would start soon. It's always warm in the gym. The floors are always slick with dust, no matter how many times the janitor sweeps. Get your rebounds, points, and assists. Hustle for that ball.

And then you're a senior and it's spring and it's the last game in the last tournament. A loss, unless you win state, which you won't, unless you're Kitch. You put your clothes in your duffel bag, find an empty seat on the bus, and lean your head against the cold window and wonder if you'll ever, in your whole life, see a pair of naked titties.

Kitch won his final high school basketball game, he saw the titties.

And now he was playing in the ABA. I figured he'd play professional basketball for ten years and he'd win his last game. Then he'd become a senator and marry an actress and buy a mansion filled with statues. He'd live longer than anyone had ever lived, two hundred years, ten thousand years, a million years. But one day, after everyone else in the world died of old age, he'd be alone, dribbling a basketball in his driveway and the only applause he'd hear would be the flapping of the crows. Even Kitch would one day be irrelevant.

The gauzy sky peeled back to reveal the sun. Every bump on the snowy prairie became a pale blue shadow. I had moved out of heaven and onto Venus.

The tire was dragging a fine path but the rope harness had started my shoulders to aching. The dog was keeping up fine. With the sun out, the top of the snow had begun to crust over. The horse's hooves made crunch sounds as they broke thru. The dog jumped out of the tire path and was able to stand atop the drifts without sinking in. She ran along now in a straight line, just behind us and to the side. We'd come a couple miles already and the dog was still going full throttle, all warmed up in her sock sweater. I stopped the horse, shook out of the tire harness, and slid down. I punched a small bowl shape into the snow and poured some water for the dog to lap up.

I removed the rope from the tire and coiled it up and put it over my shoulder. Then I climbed back on the horse. The sun was brightening things up. I squinted and watched the world thru my eyelashes. I left the tire on the ground. I didn't want to haul that thing anymore.

The horse wanted to keep going north, so I let her. I figured if the dog got pooped, I'd stuff her inside my coveralls.

The wind, gentle as it was, kept a steady hiss of snow moving about.

The dog started yipping. Balanced on top of the snow, she sprinted from one place to the next. Sniff a moment and then sprint to the next. I whistled for her. She didn't listen. I slid off the horse and walked toward her, wishing she'd stop screwing around.

As I approached, she looked up at me and then resumed her bounding from spot to spot.

She was barking at footprints. Each one, an impression of a heel and the flat point of a cowboy boot.

The prints led northeast in a wobbly line. Me and the horse and the dog, we were out there in the sun on the white plain, visible for miles. I ran to the dog and scooped her up. She didn't like being held. I didn't care. I put my hand over her mouth until she stopped yipping.

I stared at the footprints. The horse killer had taken these steps. By the way his boots had punched thru the crust on top of the snow, I surmised that he'd been here recently, maybe within the last hour

I retrieved the binoculars and my pistol from the saddlebag. I put the pistol in the inside pocket of my coveralls, next to my cigarettes. I held the binoculars to my eyes and pointed them in the direction the tracks were heading. They disappeared into the horizon.

I had four options.

I could stay put and wring my hands until it got dark and cold and maybe freeze off a couple more fingers.

I could go home and drink whiskey until my eyes closed.

I could follow the tracks forward, hoping I could sneak up on the bastard.

I could follow the tracks backward and see where the bastard had come from.

I chose number four.

CHAPTER 19

I stuffed the dog in my coveralls and jumped on the roan's back. I kicked her into a gallop. We followed the footprints south and west. I bent down as low I could without squishing the dog and watched the tracks pass by. It was just like hunting arrowheads.

We continued over the gentle curves of land. The horse took tired breaths. I reined her into a trot. I let the dog poke her head out between the buttons of my coveralls. The sun was starting to drop.

The footprints veered to the right. I slowed the horse to a walk and we followed a few yards until we came to a place where the snow had been stomped down flat.

In the center of the stomped down snow was a solid brown turd.

I climbed down and let the dog out of my coveralls. She didn't seem interested in the turd. I squatted next to it. The thing was medium-sized, I'd say. Darkish in color. On either side of it, I could see where the killer had planted his boots.

There was some yellow stain on the snow around the turd. No toilet paper. However, there was a ball of snow with some brown on it. That's how he wiped.

He didn't cover his shit up, which meant he was in a hurry. Or he didn't care who found his turds.

Owl shit consists entirely of bones and fur. You can tell exactly what they eat from what comes out of their ass. Same with coyotes. In the summer, their crap is usually filled with beetle carcasses. You never see coyote turds in the winter.

This turd didn't tell me anything. It didn't even have a smell.

I took out Excal and poked at it, half expecting the thing to jump up and run away. But it just sat there as I pushed the blade into it. I pressed all the way thru and split the turd in two. The outside was frozen hard. Inside, it was still soft. With it opened up like that, I could smell it some. There was nothing about the aroma that set it apart from any other turd.

I wiped the knife blade in the snow several times and then put it back in the holster.

There was my clue, a lump of shit.

I put the dog in my coveralls, jumped back on the horse, and recommenced following the tracks south and west.

We came upon a hill, very gentle. When I crested it, I felt conspicuous and vulnerable. Dark was approaching. It was past time for me to head home. Clues or not I had no intention of spending another night wandering blind in this country.

Before we turned back, I climbed off the horse and put the dog on the ground. I walked a slow circle, trying to memorize the horizon. Then I took off my mittens, and peed. The dog peed. The horse peed. As I was zipping up, the horse perked her ears. Not in a worried way, but in an excited way. The dog got excited, too. I got curious. Maybe it wasn't yet time to go home.

I said to the horse, "What ought we do?"

She whinnied, acting like she wanted to keep after those tracks.

"If we don't find something soon, we're turning back."

Dog inside coveralls, leap, ride. The land was more shapely now. Broad, low hills, about a quarter mile wide, maybe twenty feet tall. Arroyos here and there, with snow flaking off their steep sides.

We climbed up and up. This hill was taller. We reached the top and went over, down the side, into the deepest valley I'd ever seen in this country. Not a valley, really. It was a bowl, a depression a good fifty feet lower than any other land around here and at least a half mile across.

At the bottom of the bowl was a tight stand of cottonwood trees. Cottonwoods always look dead. As a rule, half the bark has been blown off, exposing white wood underneath. The topmost branches have snapped and are hanging upside down from the bottommost branches. Every third tree has a black lightning smudge running down the trunk. I don't know how the god damned things survive. But wherever they are, you know there's water.

The horse knew what those trees meant. She pounded down the hill right into the bowl. I leaned back on the reins, but she went faster and faster, right toward the cottonwoods.

As we clattered to a stop in front of the trees, a flock of black-birds burst out and circled around in the sky. The horse walked right into the stand and right up to a puddle of water. She dipped her head and started drinking. I slid to the ground and set down the dog, who ran to the edge of the puddle.

The snow was stomped with all sorts of animal tracks. Coyote, rabbit, raccoon, deer, and various birds had been here. So had the horse killer. His boot prints were right on top. They led away from the puddle. Right next to them was another set of tracks that didn't belong there.

When I heard the sound of my cow mooing, I knew where they'd come from.

CHAPTER 20

She was hidden in a shelter of branches woven together with rusted barbed wire. The walls of the shelter were taller than me and the branches were so close together that even the poodle couldn't squeeze thru. I saw where coyotes had tried to burrow their way in. The branches' bottoms had been poked deep into the ground. It was a sturdy fortress.

I walked around, looking for the gate. I couldn't find it. Peeking thru the branches, I saw that the cow had a clean bed of grass. The stall was roomy enough for her to turn around. She approached the fence. I stuck my finger thru a gap and let her lick.

The horse grunted. I was fairly confident we hadn't been followed. But it was growing dark. Every time I blinked my eyes, a little more color left the world. It was time to go home.

I told the cow, "I'll remember this place. I'll come back and I will find the man who stole you and I will bring you home."

I did my chores in the dark, then I went inside the house. When I flipped on the light in the mudroom, I saw footprints.

I thought, This is why I drink. I've been chasing a ghost for over a month and when I finally find his trail, cut one of his turds in half, and locate my missing cow, he's squatting behind the shower curtain ready to beat me purple with a baseball bat.

I stood for a solid minute. I could run. I could enter the house. I could stay where I was.

I reached into my coveralls and pulled out the pistol and my pack of cigarettes. I lit a cigarette and smoked it down to the butt.

I entered the kitchen, gun in hand. There was a piece of paper on the table. Looking left and right I walked forward and picked it up.

Johnny,

> *Dad and I stopped by. We're going to Denver so we can watch Kitch's team play the Nuggets the day after tomorrow. We'll head back to Saint Francis the next day (Thanksgiving). This snow is something else. Hope you're well.*

Mom

I placed the note back on the table and poured a glass of whiskey, raising a toast to the horse killer. If it hadn't been for him, I wouldn't have been chasing footprints all afternoon, and if it hadn't been for that, I would have been home when my parents showed up.

Around ten o'clock, it started snowing again. It never snows three times before Thanksgiving. Not like this.

I had no complaints. The horse killer would have to return to the cow tomorrow to milk her. Without this storm, he'd have seen that I'd found the hiding spot. Instead, with the snow covering my tracks, I was invisible.

I had avoided Mom and Dad. Good. The dog was still alive. Good. I had found my cow. Good. My tracks were covered. Good. I had whiskey.

Good night.

CHAPTER 21

It was still snowing when I awoke the next morning. Thanksgiving was two days away. I thought about driving to Dorsey to buy a turkey, maybe seeing Charlie Morning in the store. But my truck was two-wheel drive and the snow was shin-deep.

Other than going out for chores, I stayed inside all day. I petted the dog now and again between sips of whiskey.

I took a bath that night. I soaked in the tub until the last bubble popped, then I got up and toweled off and put on my pajamas. It wasn't until I crawled into bed that I realized my frostbit toes were missing. Where they'd been before, there were now just two raw pinholes.

My missing finger was one thing. It had to go because it was infected. But my toes, they hadn't been hurting anyone. I wanted them back. I pulled my socks from where I'd left them on the floor and shook them out. No toes. I looked in my boots. No toes.

The bathtub. The warm water had probably loosened them. The tub was empty. I checked the floor, checked the rug in front of the toilet. No toes.

I leaned over the edge of the tub and stuck my finger in the drain hole. The cross-stop left plenty of room for two toes to flow downward.

I went to my bedroom, rolled back the rug, lifted the trapdoor, and looked down into the crawlspace. Dark, of course, and certainly full of black widows.

Still wearing my pajamas, I pulled on socks and boots and ran outside, thru the damned snowflakes, and into the barn, where I retrieved the trouble light and a pair of plumber's pliers. I ran back to the house, shaking and stamping to get the snow off. I poked the light into the crawlspace and descended.

The pilot light hissed in the furnace. I crawled until I reached the plumbing under the bathtub. I waved the trouble light back and forth, looking up and down and left and right the whole time. When I squatted to look at the u-trap, I saw a shiny black body retreat into a gap in the floor boards above.

I hung the light on a floor joist. I loosened the bathtub's drain pipe. Water seeped out and spilled over my hands. Carefully, I removed the trap then tipped it over sideways and poured the water out onto the dirt floor. Some hair, some sludge, no toes.

As I was reattaching the trap, I bumped the trouble light. It fell hard onto the dirt floor. There was a quick flash and a pop. Then it was dark. The spiders would return soon.

I finished tightening the drain by feel, then I crawled to the trap door and lay on my back and stared up at the light fixture on the ceiling of the room above me. Out there, that's where the trouble was.

The furnace came on with a gentle roar. I listened as the heat exchanger warmed up and the fan kicked in.

From here on, I only had eight toes. Eight toes and nine fingers. I could only count to seventeen. What was I doing in a crawlspace full of spiders, looking for two shriveled toes? Only a dummy would go into a crawlspace.

Underground.

The horse killer lived in a hole in the ground. That's why I couldn't find him. He lived near that shelter he made for the cow. Not right next to it, because a hole in the ground there would be filled with water. But in the bowl, somewhere on one of the sides of that bowl. He had water just a few steps away. A fine place for a lair.

Tomorrow, I would find that fucker.

CHAPTER 22

By morning, the snow had stopped. The sky was a mass of low-hanging clouds, the temperature just below freezing. I put on my coveralls and went out for my chores. The snow was almost up to my knees. The top ten inches or so was soft. Below that was the crunchy layer from the previous storm. I walked careful so I wouldn't twist an ankle in a hidden footprint. I left the dog in the house.

The cattle gathered to eat their hay, chomping and pissing and shitting into the clean snow.

One of the old mama cows looked like she might be getting a touch of the pink eye. She probably didn't have pink eye. That was a summer sickness, brought by flies. But there was some pus and her eye was kind of pink.

I went to the barn and found the box of antibiotic powder. I took off my right mitten and picked up a handful of the stuff. I sprinkled some in the cow's eyes.

I went back in the house and filled a vacuum thermos with a can of chicken noodle soup. I put the pistol in the inside pocket of my coveralls. The dog begged me to take her outside. I wasn't gonna drag a tire behind me this time. I told her, "If you come, you'll have to ride in my coveralls and you'll have to wear your sweater." She agreed to these terms.

Before we left, I drank a full glass of whiskey. I considered leaving the booze at home and then I reconsidered. Whiskey was invented for cold, sunless days. It came with me; the whole bottle, not the flask.

As the horse loped us north, I fought the desire to kick her into a gallop. I had to be slow. I had to be sensible. With the dog curled comfortable next to my belly, I rode in the general direction of the bowl, stopping every few hundred yards for a quick scan of the landscape with the binoculars.

We went past the same arroyos and over the same gentle hills, the horse and I breathing bursts of steam that stayed behind as we marched on.

When we crested the edge of the depression, the horse wanted to march directly down to the cottonwoods, to the water, to the cow. I tugged on the reins until she stopped. I made her sit still while I scanned for signs of humanity. The bowl was a half-mile across, a bellybutton in the pure white landscape. I didn't hear or see anything odd, only fresh snow, still air. I felt very tall and very visible.

I walked the horse around the rim of the depression. She wanted that water. I had to twist her ear to get her to stop fidgeting. We walked a few steps and then waited. Then we walked. Then we waited. The horse kept fidgeting. I climbed off and led her by the reins, stomping thru the snow. I undid a button on my coveralls so the dog could poke her head out.

We were two-thirds of the way around the edge of the bowl when I saw an indentation, like the way the dirt sinks on top of a coffin. It was fifty feet away, down the slope of the hill. I walked the horse forward. The sunlight on the snow made tricks. The indentation came and went as my eyes moved over it. I started walking fast, then I started running. I dropped the reins and let the horse follow as she pleased.

My feet felt light, like I was running on top of the snow. The indentation was bigger than it had looked from up the hill. You could have parked a car in it.

The excitement had me panting. I took my bottle of whiskey out of the saddlebag and drank a swallow. I took deep breaths.

The dog squirmed against my belly. I stamped a flat spot and set her down. She walked back and forth, poking her nose into the walls of snow around her.

I left the dog there and walked to the edge of the dent. I dug into the snow with my mittens. The bottom eight inches were the crusty stuff from the previous storm. I dug thru that until I came to solid dirt. I took off a mitten and pressed. It seemed like the ground might have been slightly warm.

I continued digging. As more ground grew exposed, I brought the dog over and set her next to me. She tried to help. The horse watched.

I went to my hands and knees, removed my mittens, and felt in the dirt for proof of humanity. I grunted and wheezed. I made no attempt to be quiet. If the horse killer was down there, he knew I was up here. I sat on my ass and kicked at the dirt with the heel of my boot. I scraped and scraped. There had to be a door, a lid, an opening.

The roan started toward the trees. If she wanted her water, let her have it. I kept kicking at the dirt. I took out Excal and began stabbing the earth. The dog yipped in my ear. I told her to shut up, but she kept on. The horse killer was down there. I shouted at the dog to shut up. She continued yipping.

Exhausted, I sat down with my legs spread wide and took deep breaths. I was digging a hole on the edge of a bowl in a snowed up country under a sky of lumpy grey clouds. I needed to think, but I couldn't. Not with that damnable dog and her racket.

I hollered at her to shut up. She barked louder.

I lifted her up and tossed her. She spun in a flip and landed ten feet away with a poof of snow. She stopped barking. I resumed digging. Kicking. Fighting. That fucker took my toes. That fucker took my finger. He took my cow. He took my picture. He killed my horse. I felt a sadness in my head, a Noah's Ark of sadness. Inside the ark was one of every stupid, bad, wrong, or foolish thing I'd ever done or thought. Half a Noah's Ark. My foolishness had no companions, no mates, no chance to start a new world. Just a braying, shitting, fighting mob of fur and teeth. I punched the ground. I spat upon it. I was digging for a monster that I'd never, ever find.

I pulled the gun out of my pocket. I didn't know where to point it. I pointed it at the sun. I pointed it at the ground. I pointed it at my temple. I pressed it against my forehead. I couldn't make my finger touch the trigger.

The dog resumed her barking, louder than before. Excited, bothersome yelps.

I lowered the gun and walked to where I'd tossed her. She'd burrowed out a spot for herself, big enough to spin in circles. I pointed the gun. I said, "Do you know what this thing does?"

She did not acknowledge me. She barked and spun in circles and pawed at the snow. Then she paused and looked at me, almost irritated. She scraped the snow with her little feet until she exposed a patch of dirt. She bent down and gnawed on something, trying to pick it up.

I put the gun in my pocket and kneeled next to her and scraped away snow and more snow until I came to a lip and an edge and a square, flat piece of wood with a chunk of rope attached to it.

We had found the hatch.

I tugged it open.

CHAPTER 23

On my belly on the snow, I poked my head into the hole. A tunnel led straight and dark into the earth. The sounds of the world became amplified. I heard the coo of a dove. I heard the clicking settle of the snow. I heard the cow sigh down by the cottonwoods. Mostly, I heard my heart beating. I had to relax. I slowed down.

I crawled into the hole. The dog remained perched at the edge.

The tunnel went down at a slight angle. It was large enough that I could crawl on my hands and knees. A basketball would have rolled down it, but not quickly. The walls and floor were hard-packed. My body blocked most of the sunlight behind me.

After ten feet or so, I came to a drop-off. I felt with my hands and found something like a step. I leaned forward and found another step. This was rock, crumbly like limestone. I turned around and looked back. The tunnel had curved just enough so I couldn't see the sky. Only a hint of light made its way inside. Just enough to see that I'd stirred up some dust.

I backed down the steps one by one. Five solid stairs and then a flat floor. I could stand up here. I was in a room. Beyond the outline of the tunnel I'd just crawled down, all else was as dark as the inside of a cow.

I moved my hand until I touched a wall. I rubbed my way along, feeling for some proof of humanity. Only smooth, hard walls.

I moved further along. My fingers rode over something knobby. There was something familiar about it, this thing sticking out of the wall. A bone, but very large. The biggest bone on a bovine would be the thigh. This thing was bigger than that. I couldn't get my hand around it. It was halfway exposed, the rest embedded in the wall. What I could feel was at least a yard long. The knob on the end felt bigger than a bowling ball.

When I was six years old, I got the chickenpox. I remember lying in bed at night, feeling the scabs on my scalp, certain they were the size of pennies. Huge scabs. But when I'd peel them off and examine them in the glow of the nightlight, they were small enough you could have sucked them thru a straw. Likewise, this piece of bone that I couldn't see probably wasn't even half as huge as I thought. Just an old cow thigh.

As my eyes adjusted, I started to get a sense of depth in this cavern. I still couldn't see anything, it just felt less infinite.

I shook out a cigarette, stuck it in my mouth, and lit a match. The sulfur flashed and stunk and settled into a flickering glow and then the room was partially revealed.

My cigarette remained, unlit, in my mouth.

The room was deep and broad and tall. In the dimness, I saw furnishings. A bed maybe. The walls appeared to be smudged with different colors of paint. There was a solid mass several feet in front of me.

With my free hand, I took several more matches out of the box and held them to the flame of the one that was burning. These matches alit brightly with an air-sucking hiss. The mass in front of me was revealed. It was a saddle, sitting astride a sawhorse. It was my saddle. I walked toward it.

At that moment, a wild howl flew down the tunnel and erupted into the room. I dropped the matches to the floor and crushed them under my boot, then I backed against the wall.

The howl happened again, just as wild, but familiar now. It was my mad little poodle. The cavern gave her voice a lower pitch, like she maybe was capable of scaring someone. Like there was someone out there who needed to be scared, and that prospect scared me. I drew the gun from my pocket.

My horse killer had come home. I would stay here and shoot him as he crawled down the tunnel. I'd never shot anyone on purpose.

Nothing happened. The dog kept howling. I kept breathing.

My tongue found the cigarette, dry-stuck to my lower lip. I licked it free and then struck another match. I brought it to the cigarette and took a deep breath. Before I exhaled, I held the match to the wall and looked at the bone I'd felt there. It was even bigger than I'd imagined. I'd never imagined a bone like that could exist.

I didn't want to be there anymore. Not with my poodle and my horse outside. I shook out the match and climbed into the entrance tunnel, gun in hand, cigarette in the corner of my mouth, smoke irritating my eyes.

Crawling fast, I was soon able to see a partial patch of grey sky. I crawled faster.

It's a wonderful thing to be at the very edge of a moment that will alter your life.

The circle of sky grew large and as bright as anything to my dark eyes. If I could burst out, I might be able to surprise him.

I reached the opening, put my hands on the edge, gun still gripped tightly, and heaved myself into the day. I fell into a crouch, ready to live or die, glad I wasn't dead already. Every moment was pure joy. The ark was empty, the sadness had retreated. The blizzard, the semicircles, the waiting, and my terror had gone with it.

The grey had been a good horse. My finger had been a good finger. My toes had been good toes. I would do them honor.

Still crouching, I spun around, looking for anything. It was dastardly bright. I blinked and puffed on my cigarette. An eternity of sun bounced off every crystal of ice on the plains on the bowl before me. The dog leapt onto my lap. She barked and pawed at my face.

I clamped her mouth with my left hand. I heard the sound of a horse's hooves walking thru the snow. My eyes began to see. I turned to face where the sound was coming from, down in the bowl. A shadow of a horse was approaching.

The dog squirmed out of my grip and stood next to me, emitting the occasional yip, no longer fully committed to her frenzy. She'd done her duty by getting me out of that hole. I was in charge now.

I remained squatted. As my eyes grew accustomed to the

light, the horse became a roan. The animal grew thicker, wider, and then split into two separate objects, horse and human, less than a hundred feet away.

I stood. I lifted the gun from my side and pointed it. I kept my elbow bent, the gun a little higher than my belt buckle, like I was ready to use it and didn't need to bother aiming.

My roan was being led up a slope of snow by a short man dressed like a tramp. His coat was of rotten leather. He had two rabbits tied by their feet and slung around his neck.

He was wearing a cowboy hat, the one I lost during the blizzard.

His face looked like it'd gone sour. Brown and wrinkled, with sun-pinched eyes.

He led the roan right up toward me. In case he hadn't seen it, I waved the pistol to the left and then to the right.

A few steps away, he stopped. He smiled, yellow teeth laying out distinct against his dried up lips.

I said, "You killed my horse."

He said, "I was hungry."

There was something wrong with his voice. It sounded high, like a woman.

PART II

MUSKRAT LOVE

CHAPTER 24

Under the shade of the cowboy hat, two pale eyes stared at me like drops of candle wax. She was old, at least fifty and maybe as much as sixty. Her face and hands, the only skin I could see, were brown. I couldn't tell if it was from the sun or if she was part Mexican. Or if it was because she hadn't taken a bath.

Her nose was up, like she wanted to sniff me. Like she wanted to take a bite out of me.

I said, "I ought to kill you."

She said, "Whua." It was the sound a teenager makes when you ask how was your day. Take it or leave it, I do not give a damn. If she'd had a creaking voice, like a witch, or a hoarse voice or some other kind of voice, I might have shot her right there. But the sound that came out of those withered lips was soft and it was altogether unconcerned with the lethality of the situation. It made me feel like I hadn't communicated my threat properly.

I spoke again, but with more growl. "I ought to kill you."

She said, "Noted."

I considered for a moment and then said, "Fuck yourself."

She tilted her head a bit and said, "I suppose I should thank you for the milk."

The dog stood watching us. The horse pulled back her lips and licked her teeth.

I said, "And I suppose I should thank you for this." I held up my left hand and showed her the nub of my missing middle finger. "I damn near froze. I slipped in my horse's guts. My toes fell off. I been riding bareback for weeks. All on account of you."

I pointed the gun right at her face. We were ten feet apart.

She tugged on her ear, looked at the weather. This was not going as I'd hoped.

I said, "I can't sleep. I'm all alone. I drink and I smoke. I haven't been happy for a long, long time. She was a good horse. I had her blood on my blue jeans. People don't kill horses. People don't eat horses. Look at you. You're a woman. You're a short tramp of a woman. God dammit, you should have been tall."

I pinched my eyes but the tears squeezed out and ran down my face. The woman took a step toward me. I shouted, "Stay put!"

She took another step. I pointed the gun at the ground between us and pulled the trigger. The bullet zinged into the snow without leaving a mark. I fired again and again until the chambers were empty.

The woman didn't move or say anything.

I stood there, trying not to weep. This wasn't what I'd expected. I'd wanted a monster. I wanted to dispatch a devil and walk home cured. Instead, I was shouting at a trampy old lady.

Suddenly, she ran straight at me and knocked me down. Before I could fight, she had me on my back, in the snow, with my arms spread out and pinned under her knees. Straddling me, she pulled the gun from my hand and wedged it in the front of her trampy pants. She felt around my waist, found my knife, and stuck it in her belt. She was strong.

We sat there like that, me breathing heavy, failed sobs, and her looking down at me. The cowboy hat had fallen off her head. Her blonde hair was short and cut ragged. She looked ready to do anything.

She removed my knife from her belt and put it up to my neck.

She said, "I could gut you right now and dry your meat and eat you all thru spring. I could tan your hide and wear you when it rains. I could put your testicles on a stick and eat them like marshmallows."

She let me ponder the meaning of that last statement while snow melted underneath me and climbed up the cuffs of my coveralls. Then she stood up, leaving me splayed, and said, "You found me, you little pissant. What's your plan? I'll tell you. You will keep your mouth shut. Don't think about me. Don't ever talk about me. This is my place and you needn't come here again. You should have left me be."

I sneezed and snot went out of my nose.

She shook her head as if she were disgusted, then she went straight into the hole. I could have run, but I stayed put, with the dog licking the tears that were dripping out of my left eye. I didn't particularly feel like going anywhere. And, anyway, if she were to come out with a rifle there wasn't anywhere for me to hide on that snowfield.

A few seconds later, my saddle squeezed out of the opening, followed by the woman. She deposited the saddle next to my head, then she walked to my horse and reached into the saddlebags and extracted the bottle of whiskey. She uncapped it and drank. "Coming up here with your liquor and your little gun. You thought I was a big, mean man. But I'm a withered old witch. I know where you live. I know what you eat. I'll kill you dead as a ghost if you come up here again."

She handed me the bottle. We looked at each other for a minute and then I handed it back to her. I said, "Keep it."

With the bottle held close to her chest, she backed into her hole until I could only see her head. She said, "I fixed your cinch." Then the door went down and I was left alone with my dog and my horse and my saddle.

I gathered my things and put the saddle on the horse and cinched it up. The woman had repaired it well. The dog sat quietly on my lap on the ride home.

Once there, I closed the curtains and sat at the kitchen table smoking one cigarette after another. I'd given away my last bottle of whiskey to the woman who'd killed my horse. God damn, if there was ever a time for whiskey.

I always get myself worked up about things and they never come out as I hope.

I slept poorly that night.

CHAPTER 25

The next morning was Thanksgiving, which meant that the liquor stores were closed. The prospect of a day without liquor did not sit well with me.

I went outside without eating breakfast. Water dripped from the eaves. Every few minutes, an icicle would break and fall to the snow.

I gave the cattle an extra bale of hay for the holiday. Two of the heifers had pus in their eyes. I slapped antibiotic powder on them. They stood blinking, dripping ooze. Pink eye doesn't like the cold. They'd be okay.

I walked around the barn and checked for new footprints in the snowmelt mud. I saw no signs.

I went back to the house and tried not to think about the way that trampy woman had done me. She'd surprised me by being a woman. If it wasn't for that, she'd be dead. Yessir. She told me to stay away. I wasn't going to stay away, not for long. I don't care if you're a woman who lives in a hole. You don't get to kill my horse.

Before I did anything, though, I needed a sip of something. I went thru the cabinets, hoping I'd overlooked a bottle. The only thing that seemed remotely promising was a bottle of vanilla extract, stuck to the bottom of the Lazy Susan. I unscrewed the cap and sniffed. There wasn't more than a shot's worth. I pinched my nose and drank it all. It tasted awful, and it also reminded me of homemade ice cream and summers with Kitch. I leaned back in my chair and let the liquor creep into my blood.

Instead of wringing her neck, I'd wept.

The phone rang. I answered it.

"Yo, Johnny. My man. What happenin'?"

I said, "Nothing is happening, Kitch."

He said, "Cool. Very, very cool."

"You're talking funny."

"Whatcha talkin' about, bro? I'm just moving my lips and squeezing my lungs, same as you."

"You're talking like a colored person."

"Black, Johnny. When *you're* born, you're pink. When you grow up, you're white. Stay in the sun too long and you turn red. When you're sick, you're green. When you die, you turn purple. But me, when *I'm* born, I'm black. When I grow up, I'm black. When I'm in the sun, I'm black. When I get sick, I'm black. When I die, I'm black. So tell me again, Mr. Rainbow, who's colored?"

"That's fascinating."

"Suzanne gave me that. She's the woman from the dog pound."

I said, "She's black?"

Kitch said, "Obviously. So, yo, tell me. You ready for the parents?"

"What do you mean?"

"They said they was gonna stop by."

"Stop by where?"

"There."

"They're coming here?"

"Precisely."

God damn the whole world.

I said, "When?"

"They came to my hotel room after the game last night and we rapped for a while. They said they was gonna pay you a visit on their way back to Saint Franny."

"When are they getting here, Kitch?"

"I don't know. Lunch, I assume. It's Thanksgiving."

"Jesus. Why didn't anyone warn me?"

"Chill, brother. I got some good news. First, happy Turkey Day. Second, my ankle's almost better. I'm gonna be off injured reserve in six days. Third, we busted Denver down last night. We fucked them up. That rookie of theirs, Bobby Flowers. He can dunk but he can't stop big, bad Clovis Fletcher. Fourth, I'm in love. Suzanne is the finest chicken I've ever licked."

I said, "I think I hear a car."

Mom and Dad walked into the kitchen just as I hung up the phone.

Mom was wearing a big floppy straw hat and white gloves and her eyelids were decorated with powdery blue makeup. Dad looked like his old self, in his loose clothes, limping on his bad leg. He was carrying two grocery bags.

Mom squatted down and petted the dog. "There you are, cutie. Kitch told me all about you!"

Dad said, "It smells like vanilla in here."

I said, "I didn't know you were coming."

He said, "How are things?"

I said, "Fine." I omitted the part about the lady in the hole in the ground.

Dad put the bags on the kitchen table and began pulling out white paper boxes.

"Thanksgiving dinner," said Mom. "I figured you wouldn't have anything decent to eat so we bought Chinese take-out from Denver. Those people don't celebrate Thanksgiving, apparently. You two watch football. I'll warm everything up."

Dad and I went to the living room and turned on the game.

I stared at the TV, saw nothing. My parents were in the house, they wouldn't be leaving until dinner was over, and the only liquor in my body was a swallow of vanilla extract. My guts were tight. The animals inside my head pawed at the floorboards of their ark, ready to tear each other to bits.

Dad pulled a fob watch out of his pocket and rubbed it with his thumb. "I can't believe they allow Dempsey to kick with that foot of his."

I said, "Huh?"

"Tom Dempsey. He just made that field goal. He doesn't have any toes on his right foot so he gets to wear that club of a shoe. It gives him an unfair advantage."

"I don't think I've heard of him."

At the start of the second quarter, Mom called us into the

dining room. I'd never had Chinese food before. Rice and noo-dles, chunks of vegetables and meat covered with shiny brown sauce. Mom had set the table with my best plates, which, at one point had been her worst plates.

Dad sat in his old chair at the head of the table, which meant I had to sit in my old chair at the side of the table. Mom hardly sat at all. She skipped to the kitchen and back, bringing salt and a pitcher of ice water and whatever other things that could possi-bly render our meal marginally better. Finally, she settled down.

Dad said a quick grace, with Mom adding, "And please look after Kitch's ankle!"

Dad said, "There's no silverware, honey."

Mom pointed to the two wooden sticks next to each of our plates. "None necessary. We're eating like the natives." She gave us a tour of our dishes. "That's chicken, that's pork, that's beef. And shrimp with snow peas. Those taco things are egg rolls. We have a Chinese restaurant in Saint Francis. You're going to love this food. Put some rice on your plate and then scoop one of the other dishes on top."

I filled my plate and started struggling with the wooden sticks. Dad tried to pick up a piece of chicken but it slipped from his sticks and landed on the floor. The dog raced over and gobbled it up. Dad said, "I'm getting a fork." He scooted his chair out.

I said, "Get me one while you're up."

Mom said, "Sit down. I'll do it. You two are no fun."

When she returned, she said, "You moved the glasses into the Corning Ware cabinet."

I accepted a fork from Mom. I said, "They're easier to reach now. And, anyway, you took the Corning Ware."

I scooped up a piece of meat and chewed it. God damn I wished for whiskey.

Dad said, "That's quite the group of individuals on Kitch's team."

Mom said, "That man, Mr. Fletcher, is one tall cookie. I never thought anyone could make Kitch seem short."

Dad said, "And very polite for a colored."

I said, "Kitch didn't give you his lecture, apparently."

Dad said, "He introduced us to the whole team."

I said, "Was he talking funny?"

Mom said, "He told a couple jokes." She turned to Dad. "What was the one he said about the bear and the rabbit?"

Dad said, "You know I'm no good at jokes."

I said, "Is the punch line, 'And then the bear wiped his ass with the rabbit?'"

Dad said, "No, it was something funny."

Mom said, "The place looks nice. No one would mistake it for anything but a bachelor pad, but even so."

Dad said, "How's the livestock?"

"I expect I'll be able to sell them for a profit."

Dad said, "If prices had been this good a few years ago, I never would have left."

Mom said, "But Saint Francis has been wonderful."

Dad nodded.

Mom said, "He's the only watch repairman in town. He's got a waiting list a month long."

Dad's hand went to his pocket and he pulled out his watch.

Mom said, "There are six restaurants in town. Your father and I go out to eat once a week. We can walk to church. We hardly drive anywhere anymore. With gas being so high."

She scooped a pile of rice onto my plate.

She said, "It rains more in Saint Francis. We don't have to water the grass as much. Did you get hit by that blizzard in October? I heard it was something. Guess what? Your father is considering a run for the school board."

Dad said, "I'm not considering it. A couple people asked me, is all."

Mom said, "The mayor and the pastor are not just 'a couple of people.'"

"There's plenty of people—qualified people—who actually want the job."

Mom said, "They need someone with a logical mind."

"I don't have the temperament."

Mom said, "Yes, you do." She looked directly at me. "He does, Johnny. It's been a long time."

Dad blushed.

I moved some rice from the left side of my plate to the right.

After a moment where nobody spoke, Mom said, "Maybe we should have some wine. Yes, absolutely. Vernon, go to the car, please, and get that bottle of white."

I would have hugged the woman, except I was aggravated that she hadn't mentioned it earlier.

While Dad was fetching the wine, Mom said, "He doesn't hold it against you. Nobody does." She removed some sauce from the corner of her mouth. She looked younger than I remembered. Her skin was smoother. Her hairdo looked modern, straight to her shoulders with an outward curl at the bottom. She'd become a city person.

I said, "I'd be fine if we didn't talk about that." My urge to hug her was fading.

Mom looked like she'd expected me to say exactly what I'd said. "As we were driving out here, your father told me he wants you to know that he's made a lot of progress. He just doesn't know how to communicate with you. He's been so good to me. He brings me flowers at least once a week. He goes to church. You'd be proud."

I said, "Vernon Riles bringing his wife flowers? That's something."

"Everything's different now. Yes, we wouldn't have moved if there hadn't been the accident. And I know he misses this place. But that accident—and it was an accident—was a blessing. We're doing well in Saint Francis. I actually have friends, Johnny."

I said, "I'm very happy for you."

She looked at me suspiciously and then, deciding that I wasn't kidding, her eyes got watery.

She said, "It's been two years now. It's okay to let it go."

"Like you did to me and Kitch?"

She sighed a motherly sigh. "We're here now, Johnny. And we just came back from visiting Kitch. And we invited you to join us all in Denver."

"I have a ranch to take care of."

"You're saying you don't need us."

"I'm saying there are obligations and I'm the only person around to fulfill them."

Mom took a deep breath. Before either one of us could say

anything else, Dad arrived with the wine. She and I both I stared at the bottle as he placed it on the table.

Then Mom stood up. "I'll get some clean glasses."

Dad picked up the plates and followed Mom into the kitchen. It occurred to me that my father was getting old. His hair was mostly grey, his back stooped. His shoulders didn't fill out his shirt like they used to. Plus, he still had that limp.

As I sat there, waiting for Mom to come out with the glasses, I realized that she wouldn't be able to find the corkscrew, seeing as I had relocated it from the silverware drawer to the junk drawer. I went to the kitchen to help her find it and thereby hasten the opening of the wine.

Dad and Mom were kissing right in front of the sink. When they saw me, they stepped apart. Dad looked embarrassed.

Mom started poking around, opening cabinets. She said, "I didn't leave you any wine glasses?"

I said, "We can use coffee cups."

She said, "That's not very sophisticated."

Dad said, "Chinese food, coffee cups. I don't think we need to worry about sophistication today."

I pulled the corkscrew out of the junk drawer. "At least we have one of these."

We seated ourselves around the dining room table and Mom poured the wine. She held up her cup. "Happiness and thankfulness."

We clunked. I drank half of my glass and then set it on the table, trying not to appear greedy. I wanted to upend the bottle and pour every drop into my gullet.

Mom said, "This wine was a gift from your brother. It's from France."

We took turns trying to decipher the label. We all agreed it was good wine. Half a glass and my mood was improving.

Mom said, "Kitch told us about your finger."

Dad said, "Let's see it."

I let them fondle my hand. No, it didn't hurt. Yes, sometimes it felt like I still had a finger. They agreed that, although it was a shame to get rid of such a productive cow, I'd done the right thing by selling Polly. Or Eleanor.

Mom said, "I wish you'd told us when it happened."

I said, "Who wants to tell people they got their finger bit off by a cow?"

Mom said, "It must have been hard, taking care of the farm while your hand healed."

I shrugged.

Dad said, "Kitch gets to be a star and run around the country and you're all alone, milking cows. You must be dying of boredom."

Mom nodded. It was like they'd rehearsed this.

I said, "I like it here."

Dad said, "The place looks good."

I finished my wine. Dad refilled my cup. Mom finished hers and Dad refilled her cup. He'd barely tasted his own.

Mom said, "Your brother claims the two of you whooped it up when he came out here. He said he was seeing cross-eyed by the time you were finished."

I said, "It's hard to keep up with him."

Mom said, "He's really something, isn't he? That game we went to last night. It was a hoot. We've never been in such a big building. If Kitch played for the Nuggets, we'd drive to Denver for every single home game."

Dad said, "His coach, Mr. Brown. He keeps a handle on things. With a bunch of young men like that out on the road, things could get rowdy."

Mom said, "It's a shame about your brother getting his ankle stepped on. And the player who did it never even got punished."

We all nodded at the injustice of it all. I swallowed more wine.

Mom said, "Would you ever consider coming to visit us?" She swallowed more of her wine.

"Maybe after I sell the calves."

The poodle started licking Mom's ankle. She scooped the dog up and gave her a hug. "At least you have this cutie to keep you company."

I said, "Kitch sure does know how to surprise a fellow on his birthday."

Mom said, "I tried to call, you know. I forgot to send a card. But I tried to call but there wasn't any answer." She raised her cup. "Here's to Johnny Riles."

We clunked our cups. I finished my wine. Mom finished hers. Dad sipped his. The bottle was nearly empty. Dad split the remaining drops equally between me and Mom.

He said, "Twenty seven, right?"

"Yep."

Mom said, "I should start on the dishes."

I said, "I'll take care of it. You've got a long drive. And I'll need something to do after you guys take off."

She protested—not very loudly—and downed the rest of her wine.

They shook my hands and walked down the front steps with Dad holding Mom's elbow, both of them lit orange by the setting sun. I wasn't sure about how I felt about the two of them. A little bitter, a little worried, a little jealous. I'd like to be able to hold someone's elbow someday.

After their car was gone, I finished my wine, and then I finished the half-cup Dad had left behind.

Then I decided that I ought to go for a drive.

Charlie Morning lived in an old buckled-down house in Keaton, just across the street from the meat locker. Keaton, with its two roads and its four-way stop. Even though we shared a school, the people in Keaton always acted superior to the people of Dorsey. They had a barber and a beautician and three churches. I didn't hold it against Charlie that she lived in Keaton. She was nice, always had been. And I hoped she had some liquor.

It was dark when I pulled up to her driveway. Staked in the front yard was a four-foot-tall piece of plywood, jigsawed and hand-painted to look like a turkey.

The bay window of her living room was decorated with Christmas lights. Watching thru that window, I could see Charlie, her parents, a couple of grandparents, and a blond-haired man about my age, the fellow from Goodland, I suspected. They were all dressed in sweaters, waving around glasses filled with red wine. Wondrous red wine.

The blond fellow grabbed Charlie by the waist and they started dancing. Pretty soon everyone was dancing. Laughing and dancing around an aluminum Christmas tree.

I had no business here, lurking about. I started the truck and backed out of the drive way. I took the dirt roads home. You see fewer cars on the dirt roads and I didn't feel like seeing anyone right now.

Well, there was one person.

CHAPTER 26

The sky was clear and the moon was halfway full. Sitting astride the loping horse in the silent bath of stars, I couldn't help but imagine the woman from the hole in the ground squatting nearby in the dark, bent low, ready to plunge a knife into my horse's neck and then drag me away by my ankles, throttle me, castrate me, whatever seemed her fancy. I kept on, though, because she might have some whiskey left in that bottle.

My parents had figured out how to be happy. Why couldn't I? Probably because, unlike them, I couldn't move away from me. It wouldn't have been altogether inaccurate to describe myself as suicidal at this juncture. Partially suicidal would be more accurate. I wasn't ready to take my own life, but I felt prepared to let it be taken.

I'd left the dog in the house and now I wished I'd brought her along. The critters in my head were moving about. The dog might have helped calm me. I ought to have turned the horse around and fetched her, but the promise of whiskey pulled me north, into the dark.

When we reached the edge of the depression, I dismounted. It was awfully nice to have stirrups again, to be able to climb off my horse without leaping.

Leading the horse by the reins, I walked in the direction of the hatch. I couldn't be sure exactly where it was so I went slowly.

I paused a moment. Down below, at the bottom of the depression, the cottonwood trees made creaking noises in the soft wind.

The ground next to me opened up. The woman held the door over her head and leaned her torso out of the hole. She was dressed in a white garment.

"I told you to stay away."

"It's Thanksgiving."

"Therefore?"

"I brought food."

"What sort of food?"

"My folks brought it from Denver. We couldn't finish it."

"Thanksgiving food?"

"Chinese food. It's tasty. I brought chopsticks, even."

She climbed out of her hole. "Show me your hands and step away from the horse."

I saw now that she was pointing a bow and arrow at my chest. The arrowhead was black. Her garment looked to be cotton, like a night shirt.

I did as she asked. She hooked the bow over her shoulder and put the arrow under her armpit. Then she pulled the saddlebags off the horse.

She poked her nose in one of the bags and sniffed. "You got any egg rolls?"

I said, "Yes. And there's shrimps, too."

Her white eyes became narrow. She said, "Leave the food and go home."

I said, "We'll eat it together."

Her stomach growled.

I said, "Is that obsidian?"

She looked at me funny.

I said, "Your arrowhead. Is it obsidian?"

She pulled the arrow out from where it was pinned beneath her arm.

I said, "Can I see it, please?"

She held it up for me.

I said, "That's a good point. You make it yourself?"

"I found it. There's lots of them out here."

"Not like there used to be. I used to be able to find a pocket full of them in an afternoon. Never found one as good as that."

"You need to know where to look."

"I usually hit that flat spot, just south of here."

She said, "Is that where you found your cat skull?"

"The big one? You have it?"

Behind her, a star sent a streak across the sky. I didn't worry about it. I don't take things as omens.

The woman said, "Come inside."

I followed her down the tunnel and into the cavern. The room was lit by an oil lantern sitting on a sawed-off section of cottonwood trunk, right in the middle of the floor. The shadows moved with the wiggling flame, producing a restless effect.

The room was roughly the size and length of the inside of a school bus. In one corner was a skinny bed that she must have dismantled and brought down piece by piece and then re-assembled. Next to the bed was a small potbellied stove whose chimney disappeared into the dark of the ceiling. The room smelled of dust and straw and wood and smoke and salt.

The walls and ceiling and floor were smooth, like they'd been covered over with plaster. It was hard to see in the lantern light, but the plaster looked to be decorated with paintings. What I could make out were childish renditions of animals, stretched out at a full gallop. There were things that looked like buffalos and things that maybe looked like deer and things that maybe looked like elephants.

This cave was old.

In addition to the bed and the stove, there was a narrow table, a small wooden chair, and two clay jugs on a shelf. Clothes and blankets hung from ropes that stretched across the ceiling.

Wherever I turned, there was something else to look at. A cream separator, a butter churn, a collection of tools.

I didn't see the whiskey bottle anywhere.

The woman hung the bow and arrow on a wooden peg that stuck out of the wall. I slid the saddlebags off my shoulder and handed them to her. She reached inside and removed the boxes of Chinese food. She placed them upon her table. The table was not big and the boxes took up most of the space.

She said, "I only have one chair. You'll have to sit on the floor. And I only have one fork."

I said, "I'll use the chopsticks."

She reached into her pocket and pulled out a fork. She

opened one of the boxes. "This smells better than the last time I had chink food."

I said, "Eat as much as you want. I reckon you're hungry."

"I will slit your throat if you pity me."

She plunged her fork into a chunk of chicken.

The woman chewed quietly. She didn't eat like a dog. She ate like a hungry person, reaching across the table for this or that, occasionally looking at me with a face caught between gratitude and suspicion. She handed me one of the boxes, saying, "This one's all yours. I don't care for peanut sauce."

Using the chopsticks, I pinched out what I could.

We ate in silence. I watched the color of the lantern shift on her brown skin.

I said, "You wouldn't have any whiskey, would you?"

"I might."

"I bet it'd taste good right about now."

She scooted back from the table and reached under her bed to retrieve the bottle. It looked to be a quarter full. I reached for it but she hugged it to her chest. She said, "It's better if you mix it with milk."

She removed one of the clay jugs from the shelf. She unscrewed the lid and smelled the contents. Then she found a blue glass and poured it halfway with milk from the jug and then filled it the rest of the way with whiskey. She took a drink.

She said, "You've never had whiskey with milk, I gather."

"I'll take whatever you're offering."

"I only have the one glass." She took another drink, not in any hurry to share it with me, and said, "So today is Thanksgiving, then."

"Yes, ma'am." The whiskey bottle was sitting right there on her little wooden table.

"Don't call me ma'am. Liquor store's closed on Thanksgiving, is it?"

"That is the case." I nodded toward the whiskey bottle. "I'm awful thirsty."

"Well, then." She handed me the glass. I drank it down at once. The liquor began to work even before the last drop had made it to my gut.

I told her that whiskey and milk was a good combination. She nodded.

I said, "Might I have some more?"

She filled the glass again with her concoction and I drank it down again. Then she said, "You may leave now."

I didn't object. I said, "Good evening," and then climbed the steps, passed thru the exit tunnel, and entered into the world, feeling much better than I had when I left it. The night had grown darker. Clouds obscured the stars and the moon was below the horizon. My horse's silhouette snorted at me. Before I lowered the door, I considered shouting something cheery down into the hole. Maybe Happy Thanksgiving or Good night.

It occurred to me that I could very easily put something heavy on that door and trap the woman in her hole.

I neither shouted cheery goodbyes nor weighted down the door. Instead, I climbed onto the roan and let her bring me home, completely free of fear.

CHAPTER 27

I awoke at sunrise and proceeded to pace around the house with the dog clambering behind. The liquor store would open at ten o'clock, assuming Dee could be bothered to come to work the day after Thanksgiving. Three short hours.

I went out for my chores. I shouldn't have even looked at the cattle. The pink eye had spread. Twenty bovines, oozing pus. I administered the powder as they ate their hay. I couldn't have my cattle going blind on me.

At nine-thirty, I left for Dorsey. Normally, it's a seven-minute drive, but I went slow, like an old-timer. Thirty-five miles an hour, watch the landscape, gauge the weather by the slips of cloud in the rearview mirror.

When I arrived, the liquor store was still closed. There were three other pickups idling in the parking lot. I wasn't the only thirsty person in town. I parked around back and found two more pickups. None of us waved to one another. We looked straight ahead, waiting for our pharmacy to open.

By the time Dee arrived at ten-thirty, there were eight pick-ups in the lot. No one complained about her lateness as we exited our trucks and entered the store. Dee had a very important job and we were grateful to her in our time of need. She served us one by one, repeating the same conversation eight times.

"How was your Thanksgiving?"

"Good. Yours?"

"Better than a pair of tight shoes. Will it be the usual?"

"Yes, please."

I bought three bottles of whiskey. By the time I got home, I was down to two and a half.

The phone rang in the middle of my afternoon nap. I crawled out of the recliner and answered. I expected it to be Kitch and it was.

He said, "What's the dumbest thing you've ever done?"

"The dumbest thing I ever did was sticking my hand in Eleanor's mouth."

"Polly, you mean."

"In a single act, I lost a finger and a fine cow."

"You'd say that was dumber than the time you shot Dad?"

"Dad was an accident."

"So was your finger."

"I suppose. But I felt bad after I shot Dad. I felt stupid after I let that cow bite my finger."

"Yes," said Kitch, "that does seem like a damned stupid thing to do."

CHAPTER 28

On Saturday, I ran errands. First stop, Dorsey Grocery.

Charlie was leaning over the counter, sharing a laugh with Sherry Williams. Sherry was a pretty gal, a couple of years older than me. I had a crush on her when I was a freshman.

They paused their conversation to say hello. I asked how their Thanksgivings had gone and they both patted their bellies.

Charlie said to me, "It must be lonely all by yourself."

"Not lonely enough. Mom and Dad made a surprise visit."

Both Charlie and Sherry gave me a concerned look. After my parents had moved, I suspect the whole town had concocted tales of misery and abuse.

I said, "It was a mighty pleasant day, all told."

A little boy came tearing out of the reefer aisle with a box of frozen peas in his hand. Sherry told Charlie, "He's a terror." She dragged him to the shopping cart and they disappeared down the aisle.

I found my bread and brought it to the register. By then, a couple of housewives had come in and started talking to Charlie about the weather. I paid and left.

I drove to Keaton, a few miles east, and visited the bank to withdraw a hundred dollars for spending money. The teller, Marvadene Veitenheimer, was nice and pretty. Twenty-two, stuck with a strange name, and married.

I went to the Co-op and bought eye powder for the cattle. The cashier was Candace Burman. She was nice, but married and a mother of four.

Relationship-wise, my options appeared to be limited.

CHAPTER 29

The next day was a warm one. Mid-fifties, no clouds, just enough of a breeze to spin the windmill. The snow was melting quick.

Most of the cattle had now caught the pink eye. All but a few were crying pus. Flies, too dumb to go south for the winter, crept out of their hiding places and licked up the green drippings. I patted powder on every one of the cattle's eyes. When I was done, I dolloped a little on my face for prevention.

In the afternoon, I cooked up a casserole of ground beef, scalloped potatoes, and cream of mushroom soup. After it came out of the oven, I wrapped the dish in aluminum foil and then bundled the whole mess in a towel. I loaded up the saddlebags and whistled for the dog. She ran out from under the front step. Her cheeks had dark feathers stuck to them. I hoped she wasn't killing robins.

I climbed on the horse, put the casserole on my lap, and we headed toward the depression. The sun was out and the snow was nearly gone. The dog followed on the wet dirt.

When we reached the opening, I climbed down and stomped the ground. A moment later, the door swung open and the woman leaned out. The dog sprinted to her and started licking at her face.

I said, "I brought you a casserole."

"What's the holiday this time?"

"No holiday. Just food."

We sat in her cave with a lamp burning. She spooned casserole into her mouth. The dog sat near her shoes, waiting for her to drop something.

I said, "You'd save lamp oil if you ate in the sunshine."

"And you'd save food if you didn't bring it to me."

I said, "You got a name?"

"Yep." She dropped a piece of potato for the dog.

"My name is Johnny Riles."

"Congratulations."

I said, "Are you part Indian?"

"No."

"Part Mexican?"

"Are you part idiot?"

"I told you my name. What's yours?"

"I do not share that information."

"I brought you food. Twice."

She held up a spoon loaded with dripping casserole. "Next time, you might want to use some salt."

I said, "Why are you hiding down here?"

"I'm not hiding."

"Did you kill someone?"

"Shut up."

The dog whined for more scraps. It was amazing how fast the woman could eat. She'd finished half the casserole.

I said, "You figure this place was made by Indians?"

She said, "Maybe it was made by a man. Just one man. You think about that."

I gestured toward the enormous bone embedded in the wall. "What about that thing? Where'd it come from?"

"Olden times."

I said, "You know that saber-tooth tiger skull?"

"The one that was tied to your saddle?"

"Where is it?"

"If I'm not looking at a thing, I can't say that I know where it is. Except my backside."

She lifted a leg and let out a fart.

"You have it, though."

"The skull? Maybe."

"If it wasn't for that skull, my horse wouldn't of gotten spooked and run up this way and I wouldn't of been caught in that blizzard. I'd like to think that, for all the discomfort it caused, I could at least see the thing."

The woman wiped her mouth on her shirt sleeve.

I said, "Would you like some whiskey?"

She said, "You think I'll start blabbing to you if you get me liquored up?"

"No. I just thought you might enjoy some whiskey."

"I would enjoy some whiskey."

"The bottle's outside. I'll be back."

I crawled out the tunnel and said to my horse, "I do not know what I hope to accomplish here." The horse didn't reply. I removed the bottle from the saddlebag and crawled back into the hole.

The woman had moved her chair away from the table. Sitting on her lap was my cat skull. It was bigger and meaner than I remembered.

She had already filled up her glass halfway with milk. I poured it the rest of the way with whiskey. She took a drink. I sipped straight from the bottle.

She breathed a few times, looking into the lamp. Her hair was a short, tangled mess. The shadows of the light made her sunken cheeks and thin arms appear more shrunken and thin.

She said, "I did not intend to kill your horse."

She drank from the glass without taking her eyes from the lamp. Milk stuck to her upper lip.

She said, "I was laid up with bowel problems. I hadn't eaten in a long time. A couple of weeks, at least. I knew that if I didn't get something in me, I'd rot in this hole. Food means rabbits usually. But you can't catch a rabbit when you haven't eaten in a couple of weeks. So I was lying on my bed, waiting for myself to die. And then I heard the footsteps outside. I climbed up the tunnel with my knife in my hand."

She reached behind and took a knife down from the shelf. She displayed it in the lamp light. It was considerably bigger than Excal. She said "Rezin Pleasant Bowie. That's a good name, isn't it?"

I said, "Sounds like a nice fellow."

"Rezin Pleasant Bowie invented this knife."

"Jim Bowie, you mean."

"Jim was his brother. Rezin invented the Bowie knife. Jim was the first person to employ one in the murder of another man. Consequently, everybody thinks he invented it. That is the nature of genius." She put the knife back on the shelf. "When I opened the door and poked my head out, it was colder than I anticipated. Blind dark, with snow flinging every which way."

I said, "I recall this."

"I heard something." She whinnied like a horse. "A sound like that. I looked up and there she was, stumbling blind and looking lost. I put the knife into her neck and then I pulled the knife out and pushed it into her chest two times. I figured her for a wild mustang."

"There aren't any mustangs. Not here."

"I was delirious from a bowel syndrome. I can be excused." She finished her drink. She dipped her cup into the milk bucket and then held it out for me to top with whiskey. I complied.

She said, "When the horse went down, she was still breathing so I felt my way to her throat and sawed in and that finished her. But then I discovered the bridle. And then I discovered the saddle and I knew that I'd killed someone's animal. I conjectured that anyone who lost a horse in this blizzard was dead. You don't climb off your horse in that kind of weather."

I said, "The storm came on quick. And the saber-tooth skull complicated my relationship with my horse."

She said, "I felt poorly, but it was done and I needed meat. So I cut thru the cinch and pulled the saddle off." She patted the skull in her lap. "That's when I found this thing. I cut it away from the saddle and then I gutted the horse. I was so weak I had to use both hands to hold the knife. And it was blowing. I couldn't see. I accidentally punctured the bowel. The stink of it."

I said, "I remember that. It made me throw up."

"Me, too. Except when I threw up, nothing came out." She made a rubbing motion on her face. "Then I heard a slick sound. And a grunt."

"That was me."

"I stayed still. There was stomping and cussing."

"You could of helped me." The memory of the moment drifted back.

"People don't accept charity when their horse is killed. And I wasn't in the mood to offer it. I waited until you went away, then I crawled back in here and waited for my hands to warm up. Then I went back out in the blizzard. I pulled the bowels away from the horse so they wouldn't spoil the meat. I took off a piece of the flank. I cooked it and ate it. It helped me to live. The next morning, I butchered what I could. I spent time smoking the meat and drying it. It kept me busy for a few days. The coyotes took what I couldn't use."

The woman looked straight at me with her pale eyes.

I said, "I have to go now."

She tapped the skull in her lap. "You want this thing? It's yours."

"Keep it."

"Will you leave the whiskey?"

"No."

She said, "When you come back, bring me whiskey and some properly salted food and I'll tell you my name."

I said, "I'm not particularly caught up in names."

The dog followed as the horse carried me south across the darkening wide. I stooped in the saddle, took sips from the bottle, and revisited the night of the blizzard. I imagined a world where I'd never dug up that black skull. A world where I was still riding atop my old grey horse, both of us with our guts intact.

How would life be different.

CHAPTER 30

DECEMBER

The next morning, I awoke early but stayed in bed and listened as the songbirds whistled up the sun.

The phone started ringing. I let it ring twenty times before I made the trip to the kitchen. I lifted the receiver just as the top of the sun showed its first light.

Kitch said, "I'm in a predicament." He was no longer talking like a black person.

I sat at the kitchen table and lit a cigarette. I said, "Proceed."

"I owe money."

"Who to?"

"A guy. It's not important why or how, so don't ask. What is important is that I can't pay him right now, at this juncture."

I said, "Perhaps he'll let you pay at another juncture."

The dog climbed out of her spot on the Davenport and stretched out.

Kitch said, "I want you to know how much I appreciate everything you've done to keep the farm going. And it's important that you understand that no matter what you say about this, you're my brother and you always will be."

"I feel the same about you."

"So can you help me out?"

"I'll need more details than you've thus far provided."

"It's a simple question. Yes or no?"

"What's the question again?"

"Can you be at Last Chance at noon? With four hundred dollars."

"Today?"

"Yes, today."

"Did you get any sleep last night?"

"How is that relevant to this conversation?"

I said, "You seem a little punchy."

"Who wouldn't?"

"Who do you owe four hundred dollars to?"

"A guy. Do you need me to drip blood on the phone so you'll believe me when I say this is serious?"

"It seems like four hundred dollars wouldn't be a big deal to a professional basketball player with a professional contract."

"I only get paid every other week. Come on, Johnny."

I laid the phone on the table and poured out a handful of cat food for the poodle. I could hear Kitch's voice coming out of the phone.

When I returned, he was saying, ". . . is a long-distance call. I know you're there. Stop being an asshole or—"

I interrupted him, "What are you into?"

"It's nothing. Gambling. I'll pay you back. I get paid in eleven days. My teammates and me were playing cards on the airplane. I've never gambled before, Johnny. It's for fun, you know. I won a few games at first and then I got ambitious. I went all in on a pair of somethings. But I lost and the code of honor says you have to pay up. I paid most of it already. All I need is four hundred dollars."

"They're your teammates. They'll understand. They know how much money you make."

"It's not my teammates. It's a guy. I told you this. He traveled with us for a few days. Everybody liked him, like a mascot. Turns out he's an asshole. Wants everything right now. You don't have to worry about this happening again. He's not allowed to travel with us anymore and Coach said if anybody else gets caught gambling, they're off the team. My ankle's almost better. I'll be back playing in a few days and I want to not have to worry about this shit. All you need to do is drive to Last Chance at noon today and give some guys four hundred dollars."

"I thought you said it was *a* guy."

"He can't be there in person. He's in Missouri or something so he's sending some associates."

"How will I know it's them?"

"They'll be the ones who look like they want money."

"You'll pay me back?"

"We're playing in Denver on December thirty-first. That's New Year's Eve. Come to the game, I'll get you the money. Guaranteed."

"What if I say no?"

"It's important that you don't. Anyway, I already told the guy you'd do it."

"You have a lot of faith in me."

"He's sending his boys to Last Chance. That was his compromise. He wanted you to drive all the way to Denver but I told him you didn't know how to get around the city."

"I know how to drive in the city."

"I'm saving you gas money. Will you do it?"

I paused long enough to make him worry. Then I said, "Whatever trouble you're in, I doubt this will get you out of it."

Kitch said, "Don't overcomplicate things."

"I've got to go, Kitch."

"Come on, Johnny." He voice was pitched up in desperation.

I said, "I've got to feed the animals and then go to the bank and withdraw four hundred dollars. And then I have to drive to Last Chance. And then I've got to hope that you don't do anything else stupid between now and the end of the month."

"I'll pay you back, Johnny."

I said goodbye.

The pink eye had spread to the milk cow. I patted powder on her and the feeder cattle, then I put the horse in her stall in the barn, separate from the milk cow, and powdered her as well. I couldn't have my animals getting sick.

I left the dog in the house and set out for Keaton, where I picked up four hundred dollars at the bank. When she was counting out the money, Marvadene said, "You been coming here a lot, lately."

I shrugged. "It's the holidays."

She said, "Say hi to Kitch."

"Will do."

Last Chance is fifty-six miles west of Keaton on Highway 36, just over a third of the way to Denver. The town consists of a handful of buildings all bunched together at the bottom of a dip in the road. There's a gas station, of course, and a few crusty old houses. No stoplights and no movie theatre. But they do have a Dairy King. It's not really a Dairy King. It's a yellow building with a hand-painted sign out front that says, "Dairy King." They sell hamburgers and soft-serve ice cream. Out front, right next to the highway, is a picnic table for tired travelers who want to enjoy their vittles along with the sensation of a semi-truck flying by at seventy miles an hour.

I parked in the dirt lot, next to a station wagon and climbed out. I had arrived forty minutes early.

Sitting at the picnic table were two men. They were white guys. This surprised me a little. They were dressed in bell-bottoms and paisley shirts. Their hair came down over their ears. One of them had sideburns. The other didn't. They were licking ice-cream cones.

The men watched me walk toward them. When we were still separated by fifteen feet, I stopped and said, "Are you the boys after Kitch's money?"

The men didn't reply. I figured they were nervous. City people always act uncomfortable around country people.

I repeated myself, "Are you the boys after Kitch's money?"

This time, Sideburns nodded. I approached. I said, "I hope I'm not too early."

Sideburns said, "We were enjoying some ice cream."

I said, "You wouldn't happen to know what Kitch did to earn us this trip would you?"

The man without sideburns said, "That's something you'd best take up with your brother." He took a nibble out of his ice cream cone.

I said, "How do you want to do this?"

Sideburns said, "Take the money out of your pocket and give it to us."

I reached into my shirt pocket and pulled out four hundred-dollar bills. I handed them to Sideburns. He handed his ice cream cone to his friend and then, one by one, he held the bills up to the sun.

I said, "I got them from the bank this morning."

Sideburns turned to his buddy. "Let's go."

They got in the station wagon and drove away, toward Denver. They left their ice cream melting on the table.

I went into the Dairy King and ordered a hamburger. The counter lady said, "Those fellas your friends?"

"Friends of my brother."

"When they came in here, they said they were looking for Johnny Riles. That you?"

"Until I'm told otherwise."

"Your brother wouldn't be Kitch Riles."

I nodded.

She said, "Tell him we're all rooting for him."

"Will do."

When I tried to pay, she said, "Don't worry about it. We're big fans."

I expected that the dollar fifty I saved on that hamburger was the closest Kitch would ever come to paying me back the four hundred dollars I'd given those characters.

On the way home, I stopped in at the grocery in Dorsey. I bought nine cans of soup. Three each of chicken noodle, split pea, and chili beef.

As she was ringing me up, Charlie said, "How's Kitch?"

"His ankle's almost better. He'll be back playing in a couple of days."

"I only ask because I know you don't like talking about him."

"I appreciate that."

Charlie leaned toward me.

"Did you hear? A couple of guys from Sterling are going to open up a miniature golf course on the east end of town."

I said, "What's miniature golf?"

"Maybe you use marbles instead of golf balls."

"You and Mr. Goodland can go there for a date."

"If we're still together. We got into it on Thanksgiving."

"I'm sorry to hear that."

She shrugged. "How's that dog of yours?"

I said, "She's a fine little bird-catcher."

"You name her yet?"

"You know me."

She said, "How do you call her without a name?"

"She reads my mind."

A station wagon pulled in, all covered with mud. Wynema Herndon climbed out and walked into the store. She was old, with big glasses and a hairdo that got washed once a week at the salon in Keaton. Wynema sold local Avon products, loved to talk, rarely listened.

Charlie said good morning.

Wynema said, "These roads are muddier than you-know-what. It's a miracle I haven't slid into a ditch." She gave me a looking over. "How's your brother?"

Charlie answered for me, "He'll be back on the team in a couple of days."

Wynema said, "How's Virginia treating him?"

I said, "Kentucky, actually. Louisville. He loves it."

"Does he get along with the negroes?"

"They prefer to be called black nowadays, apparently."

Wynema said, "Call 'em what you want. Those boys sure can jump."

After I got home, Kitch called. He said, "Thanks, brother."

I said, "Stay on the team."

He said he would.

CHAPTER 31

The next morning, I trotted the horse out to the depression with the dog skipping along behind.

When we arrived at the hatch, I climbed down and stomped. There was no response. I stood with the reins in my hand and peered into the cluster of trees at the bottom of the depression. I could not see any activity. I hollered, "Hey-o! Hey-o!"

Soon, I heard a reply. "Hey-ah! Hey-ah!" I walked down to the trees.

The woman was inside the homemade corral. Thru the opened gate, I could see her squatting on an overturned log, milking the cow.

She said, "This girl could use some hay. I chop grass but it's hard to keep up."

I leaned on a tree. "I've got plenty of hay. I don't know how I'd haul it out here, though."

"You own a pickup."

"I've never tried to take it across Old Stinkum."

"It's a dry riverbed. Just drive over it." She patted the cow. "I call her Janet."

I said, "That's a fine name."

The woman handed me the milk bucket. Together we walked up the slope. I carried the bucket, she led the horse. The dog ran around, sniffing.

The woman sat on the ground next to her doorway, looked to the sky. She said, "The morning is my favorite."

I opened up the saddlebags and handed her six cans of soup. She laid them on the grass.

She said, "My name is Jabez."

I said, "That, too, is a fine name."

"It's a man's name."

I said, "Seems like it could go either way. Jabez."

"Well, that's what I'm called."

I shook her hand. I said, "It's good to make your acquaintance, Jabez."

She said, "And yours, as well, Johnny Riles."

In the distance, the dog chased a ground squirrel into its hole and stood, splayfooted and barking at the entrance.

Jabez said, "How old do you think I am, Johnny?"

"It's easy to give a wrong answer to a question like that."

She said, "Let me try, then. I think you're twenty-six years old."

"I turned twenty-seven a few weeks ago."

"Okay. Now tell me, how old am I?"

I aimed low. "Fifty?"

"I'm forty-six."

I said, "That's why I didn't want to guess."

"It's this barbarian lifestyle."

"You're pretty strong, yet."

Jabez said, "The barbarian lifestyle doesn't allow for weaklings." She pointed at the ground. "You been wondering about my place, haven't you?"

"I suppose, yes."

"What do you mean, 'I suppose'? You saw that bone in the wall, and the paintings. There's something marvelous in those tunnels and all you can say is 'I suppose'?"

"Tunnels? There's more than just that one room?"

"Oh, yes. Aren't you curious?"

"Of course, I'm curious."

"You don't act like it."

I said, "I'm not very excitable, I guess."

She said, "How many chickens do you own?"

"Eight or nine. Why?"

"Bring one next time. I want to eat a chicken."

"I only have laying hens."

"I can slaughter a laying hen. Bring me a chicken and I'll show you the rest of the tunnels." She scooped a handful of milk out of the bucket and slurped it. "You can go home now."

Home, I went.

The pink eye had not retreated in the face of my powder applications. The horse was still fine but every last one of the cattle was crying pus. Some of their eyes were turning milky white. When I hollered, the herd followed my voice, turning their heads every which way, bumping into each other.

I applied the powder once again. If I didn't get this under control, I'd have to use the syringe.

After dinner, I loaded eight bales of hay into the pickup and headed north. Driving a truck on the prairie is different from riding a horse on the prairie, especially in the dark. A horse can dodge badger mounds. The pickup bounces over every one. I wondered if anyone had ever driven on this dirt before.

When I arrived at the riverbed, I turned west and drove parallel until I found a spot where the banks were low. My two-wheel-drive pickup was able to climb down the bank, over the river, and up the other side, no problem. Jabez had been right.

From the riverbed, it was a straight shot to the depression. I followed my headlight over the hill and down to the cottonwood patch. By the time I'd shut off the engine, Jabez was up and out of her hole. I watched her silhouette hustle down the incline.

The dog rushed up to her. Jabez bent and petted her and then came down to the truck. She had on a pair of cowboy boots and she was wearing her white night shirt. Little breezes pushed the fabric against her body.

She said, "Why are you driving all up here?"

"You asked me to."

"Not in the middle of the night. Your damn truck could cause a cave-in. And all that racket. Someone could follow you. And one of your headlights is busted. You ought to fix that."

"I brought you hay."

She poked a bale and then smelled her finger. "How old is this?"

"I don't know. It was probably cut six or eight weeks ago. It's hay."

She was shivering so I said, "I've got a coat behind the seat if you want to borrow it."

She opened up the tailgate. "Help me unload."

We stacked the bales just outside the pen. Jabez gave the cow a couple of flakes.

I said, "I'll back out the way I came."

She said, "Leave the truck where it is. Stay for supper."

We situated ourselves in the cave and ate split pea soup. Jabez sat at the table with her bowl and the spoon, I sat on the floor and slurped my portion straight from the can. We didn't talk. The dog slept in the corner.

I heard the flutter of the lamp and the hiss of the dog's breath. I heard the clack of Jabez's spoon in her wooden bowl. I closed my eyes and listened. There was another sound. I felt it on the hairs of my arms. I lifted my hand and felt it on my fingertips. The air was moving from one end of the cave to the other. It was barely audible. Two sounds, in harmony, lower than the lowest note on a pipe organ.

Jabez said, "You hear it."

I opened my eyes. She was wiping her index finger around the inside of her empty soup bowl.

She said, "It puts me to sleep." She licked her finger clean.

"I've never heard anything like it."

"You won't hear anything like it anywhere else."

"It sounds like ghosts."

Jabez stood up. She rubbed a hand against the bone that protruded from the wall. The dog raised an ear.

I squatted, trying to hear the harmony again. After a few minutes, I said, "It's gone."

"It never goes away."

"Where's it come from?"

She pointed to the far end of the cavern. "Farther in."

I said, "Can you show me?"

The look in her eyes suggested that she was about to say something mean. She stood there, flickering in the lamp light like a thing that was only half real.

She said, "You didn't bring me a chicken."

"I brought hay."

She lifted the lamp from the table and said, "Come on, then."

CHAPTER 32

The end of the room was farther away than I realized. What I'd taken for thirty feet was easily twice that. As we walked, the walls and ceiling became crowded with paintings. Deer with spotted backs, woolly mammoths, bears, lions. Details appeared that I hadn't noticed in the earlier paintings. These animals had eyes. They leapt and charged, always moving in the same direction, toward the tunnel's exit. I wanted to linger, but the lamp went with Jabez so I followed the lamp.

As we continued along, the room didn't end so much as get smaller. The walls and the ceiling pinched together until we had to squat and then crawl on our hands and knees. Jabez would look back occasionally and pause for me to catch up. The dog skirted in between our legs and arms, her toenails clattering on the smooth floor. No animal paintings here. Instead, the walls had red stripes running up and down. It was like crawling inside a barbershop pole.

After twenty feet, the tube expanded into a room that was just large enough to allow both Jabez and me to stand upright. Here, she stopped. I stood behind her. I could have reached out and touched the walls on either side. Directly ahead I could see that the room disappeared into another crawling shaft.

Jabez said, "Look up."

The ceiling was painted with smoky clouds. The clouds were dotted with hand prints and stars and a new moon. The center of the ceiling pinched off into a funnel that went up beyond the light of the lamp.

Jabez said, "Listen now."

I did. The harmony came to me almost at once. It was louder than my heart. Even the dog tilted her head.

Jabez said, "It comes from up there."

"How far underground are we?"

"A long ways. We're into the side of the hill. That funnel goes up and up. I think it's a vent. I've never found where it comes out. That's where the smoke from the stove goes. You can feel the air move."

I nodded.

She said, "Keep going?"

"Yes."

She led me thru the next crawling shaft. Like the one before, it was painted with broad red stripes. And, like the one before, after twenty feet, it expanded into another room. This room was different from the last one. It felt like the whole world had expanded. Jabez strode across the floor, lamp held high. The light barely reached the ceiling. The walls all around were distant and dark. My entire house would have fit in that room.

The dog did not follow us, choosing instead to remain in the crawling shaft.

The air here was a substantial thing. Something that willfully moved to make way for my body.

Jabez struck a match. On the floor was a lamp, which she lit. There were two other lamps on the far side of the room and she lit those as well. As their wicks settled in I saw that the size of the room was the least of it.

In the lantern light, the walls were revealed to be covered with red paintings similar to those in the first room, except these paintings were life-sized, looming versions of elk, antelope, wolves, bears, saber-tooth tigers, mammoths, and other creatures I couldn't decipher. They all crouched and slept and fought and ran, each one of them pointing its nose to the way out.

The animals had bones. That is, there were bones protruding from the walls. These bones were wonders, every one of them black and dull. A painting of a woolly mammoth had a skull. One half of the skull was buried in the stone, but the other half projected out of the wall. The skull itself was enormous. A grown cat could have slept in the eye socket. But the tusk, it was more than enormous. The thing came out and hung in the air, curved, ready.

Next to the mammoth was a painting of an elk-thing. It wasn't an elk, because elk don't grow that big. The head was, again, a skull. It came straight out of the wall, nose first. The empty jaws were exposed, the teeth still in the sockets. The antlers poured out of the wall, moose-like, flat, and so god damned big I wasn't sure I was seeing properly. Just one of those antlers would be too big to fit thru the front door of my house.

Bears and bear-things, cats and lion-things. Every painting had bones. Legs, ribs, skulls, antlers, strings of vertebras. I couldn't stare in one direction for long because there was always something else to see.

Jabez said, "You're not breathing."

I filled my lungs.

She said, "It's the bigness at first. But pretty soon you'll start wondering about other things."

I said, "How'd all this get down here?"

She smiled. "That's one of the things you'll wonder about. Walk around some. There's lots to see." She sat down against a wall.

I walked the edge of the room, the cavern, the cathedral. A painting of a tiger sank its fossil teeth into the leg of a painted horse with a half-exposed backbone. A bear on its hind legs stood as tall as a windmill. Its ribs poked out from the wall. Draped over them were several strips of dried meat.

I turned to Jabez and said, "Can I touch?"

She nodded.

I poked with my index finger. I expected the meat to be hard, bark-like. Instead, it was soft. Globs of fat glistened in the lamp light.

Jabez said, "Are you hungry?"

"You can still eat this?"

"Yes, but you wouldn't like it."

I said, "I reckon it's hard to chew, being as it's so old."

Jabez said, "It's fresh. From your horse."

I looked at her, not sure how to behave.

She said, "She gave me good meat."

My grey was just another dead animal in a room full of dead animals. I tore off a small piece of the jerky and I bit it in half. I put one portion in my mouth. The other portion, I handed to Jabez. She put it in her mouth.

I said, "It's good."

By that means, I made peace with the woman who killed my horse.

I walked around the room, touching the bones, smelling the walls. The quiet here was different from the other parts of the tunnels. When I breathed or walked there was a sound, but the walls didn't echo. Noise left me and didn't come back, just as if I were standing on the grasslands above.

After wandering and staring until my neck hurt, I sat on the ground next to Jabez. She said, "You can smoke here."

I lit a cigarette. When I exhaled, the smoke climbed and turned into grey nothing before it dissolved into the void.

Jabez said, "A gentleman would offer a lady a cigarette."

I shook one halfway out of the pack.

She said, "A lady doesn't smoke."

We sat quietly. When I finished the cigarette, I crushed the butt on my boot heel and put it in my shirt pocket.

For a long time, we continued not to speak. I smoked another cigarette. The unlikelihood of the situation became no less powerful. I was smoking cigarettes forty, fifty feet underground in a room full of dead, giant animals.

I said, "What are we inside of?"

"It doesn't matter."

"It mattered to the people who put it here."

"What do *you* think it is?"

"Well. All the animals seem to be moving in the same direction."

"Yes."

"So they're going somewhere. Which is out, right?"

"That's a good guess."

"And they seem to be running, fighting."

"Why do you suppose that is?"

"Because some animals want to eat and others don't want to be eaten."

"Naturally."

We were quiet for another spell. I lit a cigarette. After I finished it, I said, "Sometimes I imagine a whole ark of animals in my head. It's like Noah's Ark except there's only one of each animal. So they'll never get to breed. When one dies, that's the end of the line."

Jabez said, "Those animals in your head."

"Yes."

"Maybe this is where they come from."

"What's that mean?"

She laughed. "I'm just talking. It's been a while since I talked to a person. Sometimes I say odd things."

"The animals might have been killed by a volcano. Maybe this is an ancient lava pit or something."

"Could be."

"And then some old Indians found this place and painted the walls."

"Or maybe animals came from this hole and went to the world. But some of them liked it here and stayed. And maybe nobody painted the walls. Maybe that's just how they are."

"That doesn't make a lick of sense. And if it did, it doesn't explain anything."

"You're awful smart."

"I'm not trying to be smart."

She patted her knee. "Come on. You're about to be even less smart. There's another room yet." She stood up, pressing heavily on her knees. "It's a long crawl."

I followed her to the far end of the room where the walls pinched once more into to a crawling shaft. Jabez bent down and picked up a rag that had been lying on the floor. Inside it were two candles, which she slid into her pocket. She said, "This shaft is long and dark and narrow. There's no room for the lamp. The candles are for when we get to the room."

I whistled for the dog to follow us. She declined.

CHAPTER 33

In addition to being long and dark and narrow, this final crawling shaft was also full of twists and turns. The walls and floor were so smooth they almost felt slick. The size of the shaft varied. Sometimes we could crawl comfortably, other times we had to shimmy on our elbows and knees. The shaft wandered left and right and expanded and contracted. Always, we moved downward.

As I felt along in the darkness, the air grew tight. The center of the earth could not be far away.

I bumped into Jabez's ass. This made her laugh.

I said, "Why'd you stop?"

She didn't answer. Instead, she continued to laugh. This went on for some time. When it finally appeared as though she had gotten control of herself, she let forth with the most vile fart I've ever had the misfortune to take at point blank range in my entire life. The sound was like the earth tearing itself apart. And the smell. It was like being punched in the face by a fist of shit. My nose and mouth and eyes became filled with foulness. I scurried backward, but it meant nothing. The fart went on and on. And Jabez laughed and laughed while I cried tears of real pain.

I remembered that I had matches. I wedged a hand into my pants pocket and worked one out. Then I twisted onto my back. Jabez continued with her laughing. I struck the match against the top of the shaft above my face.

The match ignited and burned bright and then went to a dim yellow. I let the flame creep down to my fingertips before shaking it out. Jabez continued tee hee heeing. The smell had eased considerably. I blinked the tears out of my eyes and lit a second match. It burned less brightly than the last one, but with my eyes clear I was able to see around me some.

The shaft was covered with handprints. As far as I could see— and it wasn't very far—but as far as I could see there were handprints and more handprints layered on top of each other all over the shaft, the top and bottom and sides.

The handprints were all tiny, like they belonged to children, babies even.

I said, "Jabez. Can you see this?"

She must have heard the seriousness in my voice. She sobered up some. "Can I see what?"

I said, "Gimme your hand."

She reached back and I passed her a couple matches. She struck one and remained silent until the flame went out. Then she said, "Those are not meant to be seen. Let's get along. We're almost there."

I kept account of our progress. Each time I lifted my right knee, I counted another step. Fifty-six more steps and the shaft leveled out. Another nine steps and it got so small that I couldn't count steps any more. We shifted forward like worms.

Then Jabez said, "Ahhh."

I heard her scuttle forward quickly and then I felt the walls recede. We were out of the crawling shaft and we were into a room.

Jabez said, "Sit down. I'll turn on the lights." I heard her fooling around and then she struck a match and held it to each of the candles. The flames burned straight up.

The room was small and almost perfectly round. The size and shape reminded me of those giant iron balls scientists used to ride to the bottom of the sea. A bathyscope, they call them. The walls were shiny, glossy white. The room was ringed with a narrow ledge about waist high. Perched on the ledge were dolls. Little horses and people made out of sticks tied together with something that could have been yucca leaves. The dolls were simple. Stick figures made out of sticks, no more than six inches tall. But that wasn't anything. In the center of the room, the floor raised into a table, like an underground giant had pushed an indentation up with his thumb. On that table was a baby mammoth.

It was about the size of a two-month-old calf. It lay on its side, the snout dangling over the edge of the table. Although its skin had a shriveled, dried-up look to it, the long hair was soft and inviting.

I reached my hand toward the mammoth, but Jabez grabbed my wrist. She said, "We can't stay here long. There's not enough air."

I leaned forward, sniffing.

Jabez said, "Don't wake it up."

"It's dead."

"Whisper, please."

I whispered, "What is this place?"

"I suspect we're in an asshole."

"It's not an asshole."

She said, "Did you smell that fart I let?"

"Stop being wise."

"What do you want? You act like I should know everything. Look around, enjoy the scenery, and shut up. But do it quick, because we need to leave."

I tried to memorize the room. The height of the table, the number of figures, the gloss of the walls. The baby mammoth. One of its eyelids was half open. Between the lashes, I could see a glistening orb. The animal's sides seemed to move.

I nodded at the mammoth. "You're right. It looks like it's sleeping."

"Thus, we whisper."

"I could stare at it for days."

"I tried that before. There are no days in this room. There's no time at all."

She blew out the candles. "We leave."

CHAPTER 34

After we crawled back to the big room, Jabez lit a lamp and I lit a cigarette. The giant paintings and the bones in the walls felt comfortable, familiar. They seemed like things that humans would do. Not like where we'd just left, with the tunnels of hand-prints and the sticks and the baby mammoth.

After my cigarette, we passed into the vent room and then back into the living area.

Jabez and I situated ourselves, she in her wooden chair, sipping whiskey and milk from her glass, and me sitting on the floor, drinking the same concoction out of the empty soup can.

She said, "You didn't bring my chicken."

"And you showed me the tunnels anyway."

"You'll bring me one, yes?"

"Yes," I said, "I will."

"Don't cross a crazy person. You know I'm crazy."

I considered my words carefully. "Lady, I'm not sure what you are."

Jabez tapped the side of her nose.

I said, "What if you invited someone smart to come down here? To get answers?"

Her voice got growly. "I took you here because your horse died. And because you give me food and whiskey and hay. This is my place. You will not speak about it to anyone. I don't know if you pray, but if you do, don't even mention it to God."

"They say God can see thru dirt."

"He can't see this place. It's older than he is and twice as real."

Jabez finished her drink and poured another.

I said, "What's it for, then? All those stick dolls? And the hand-prints? What's that little baby mammoth doing down there? Does it—"

She took the soup can away from me, topped if off, and handed it back.

She said, "This smart person of yours, if he ever found these tunnels, he would haul everything out and put it in a museum. Then he'd rub his chin and say, 'This here deal was a temple to some sort of primitive god.' And *National Geographic* would take pictures. And then guess what, Johnny Riles?"

I fished a cigarette out of my pocket.

She said, "Don't light that until I'm finished."

I placed it, unlit, in my mouth.

She said, "There'd be no more sound in the caverns is what would happen. And your smart person would make up balo-ney about how the persons who made this place used babies for slaves. Or maybe they'd say that the persons came from the stars. But whatever they might say, it'd be smoke out of their asses. This place is whatever I think it is. It's whatever you think it is. If your smart people find it, then they'll get to tell us what it is. What's down here belongs down here. Even you and me. We belong down here. So keep your mouth shut. I swear, if you tell anyone anything, I'll gut you like I did your horse. Light that cigarette. You're making me nervous."

I did as told.

She said, "Don't you dare tell that brother of yours."

"What do you know about my brother?"

"I've seen him. When you were playing basketball. You re-member."

"I do."

"Your brother is not trustworthy."

I said, "You don't know that."

She said, "Have you ever smoked marihuana?"

"That's a crazy question."

"The cigarette he gave you that night. It made you feel funny, didn't it?"

I said, "We were drunk, that's all. You shouldn't have been watching us."

"It was marihuana. I could smell it. Your brother is a liar. I've known boys like him."

"You don't need to say things like that about my brother until you meet him, which will never happen. And I wouldn't tell him about this place anyway so this whole conversation is piss in the wind."

She raised her glass. "Good. We're all piss in the wind."

I said, "How do you know what marihuana smells like?"

She closed her eyes and moved her lips like she was talking to herself. Then she opened her eyes and set her cup on the table. "I got to know it in Korea. Remember that war? I was an army nurse. An unwise decision on my part, but I was young and I wanted adventure. My job was, I put my hands into the bellies of soldiers to keep their slippery parts from falling out.

"Some of the other girls tried me on it, the marihuana. They said it would help me sleep. A room without a bunch of snoring, farting women, that's what would have helped me sleep. The weed just makes you think about the things that keep you awake."

She took a drink straight out of the whiskey bottle and said, "If you think it was upsetting to find your dead horse, imagine what it's like to watch a boy with zits all over his forehead, to watch him bleed out from a hole in his leg."

"I imagine that'd be hard to see."

"Contrary to what your Sunday school teacher told you, beauty is not on the inside. Inside is nothing but meat soup, and outside is worse. And after I came home—"

"Where's home?"

"After I came home from the war, everybody either pitied me or thought me weak because I didn't laugh as much as an army nurse should. What kind of person laughs after a war? Korea taught me what people can do, and most of the things they do, I don't care for. When I came home, I just wanted to be left alone. But that wouldn't happen as long as I stayed where I was. Neighbors brought me chocolates, the preacher asked after me, drunken buffoons called me at night. No one would leave me alone.

"One day, I decided I was finished with the whole damn

business. I opened the front door and just started walking. It felt so good, I walked and walked, not looking left or right. I went up and down ditches, I crossed pastures and plains and fields, I climbed a hundred barbed-wire fences. I went on for days, until I couldn't hear any cars or see any buildings or smell any people. And there I stopped, at the bottom of a prairie bowl, where there was water and cottonwood trees and cottontail rabbits. A horned owl came out of a tree and slid thru the air. It climbed to top of the sky without even flapping its wings. I made my bed on the ground and slept there, right amongst the trees.

"Then, in the midst that night, thunder woke me. Before I could blink my eyes, it started raining like all the clouds in the world had piled atop one another. The bottom of the bowl filled up. I became so wet you could have squeezed me and filled up a bathtub. I climbed up the slope and there I found a hole in the ground. It looked like a coyote den. I'm not afraid of dogs. In I went and down I went. I was soaked and I'd been walking for days, trying to be alone. And here I was. Here I remain. The end."

I tapped the leg of her table. "Where'd you get your furniture?"

"Here and there. Nobody misses it."

"Was it you that put the door in?" I nodded toward the entry tunnel.

"It was."

I lit a cigarette. "Do you ever get lonesome?"

She said, "I thought I'd made it clear that I do not care for people."

"That's why you're down here."

"I'm down here because I like it down here."

"You're not running away from something."

She showed her teeth. "I've been in the same place for thirteen years. That's hardly running."

"Do you miss your family?"

"I don't have a family."

I said, "I don't either, hardly. My parents live in Saint Francis. My brother went off to Kentucky last year and now I'm alone. I notice every day that he's gone. I can't say that I miss him, though."

"He drives a fancy car, that brother of yours."

"He's a basketball star."

"He ought to be, as tall as he is."

"Well, he's not really a star. But he's a professional."

"The Celtics?"

"Kentucky Colonels."

"Like corn?"

"Not *kernels*. *Colonels*. Like Colonel Sanders. The Colonels are part of the ABA, which is in competition with the NBA. They're a real—"

"I don't particularly care about the details."

"My brother is a jerk."

"They all are."

Another moment of silence. I lit a cigarette.

Jabez pointed to the dark end of the room. "Don't think too hard about what you saw down there. You want to imagine that the place is full of magic. There's no magic here. It just feels that way. It's like a sunset. When the sun goes down, it looks like it's moving and it feels like the twilight exists just for you. But it isn't and it doesn't. It's the earth that's doing the moving and it's doing so because it can't do otherwise. Same with this place. It looks like it's full of magic. But it's just a place that some people found and decorated."

I said, "They did a hell of a job."

We took turns on the whiskey until it was gone. I yawned. Jabez yawned. The hum of the tunnels lulled me. The dog cuzzled up in my arm and an easy sleep descended.

CHAPTER 35

I awoke in the dark, alone. I spoke Jabez's name, whistled for the dog, and received no reply. A faint light shown down the cavern's entrance. I followed it up and out of the cave. The sun was past noon, a gentle wind tickled the grasses. My pickup was still parked down by the cottonwoods, unsightly in this place where there were no machines. I turned away from the wind and pissed my belly empty.

I heard a faint holler from down by the trees. Jabez waved, small in the distance. As I walked down to meet her, she began coming my way, carrying a bucket of milk. The dog followed her.

When we met, Jabez said, "Thirsty?"

I scooped some milk to my mouth. Unseparated, creamy, and warm, it went into my stomach and spread into my blood. I shook my hands dry. I had slept late, in a cave, and now I was outside in a place with no consideration for time.

I said, "I see why you live here."

Jabez smiled, the skin of her face crumpling in an old kindness. Then she squinted and her eyebrows came together, no longer kind, but worried.

She said, "What's wrong with your eye?"

"I'm hungover, I expect."

"That's not a hangover."

I touched my eye and brought my hand right back down to wipe it on my jeans.

I said, "Oh, hell."

Jabez leaned away from me. "What you've got there, it's contagious."

I said, "I'd best leave you to it, then."

I walked to the stand of cottonwoods and climbed in the pick-up with the dog. The engine wheezed and puffed but wouldn't start. I could see my breath in the cab. I waited a minute. You have to give it a minute in the cold weather. I tried again. She started up. I drove home over the river and thru the sagebrush.

There was a muddy station wagon parked in front of the house. Wynema Herndon, with her tall, grey hairdo and thick glasses stood at the top of the steps, Avon product bag at her side. She hadn't had a sale at my place since Mom and Dad had moved.

She waved as I pulled in. I followed the dog out of the cab and walked to meet her at the front step. The dog jumped for the Avon bag. Wynema pulled it out of reach.

She said, "Who's this little cutie?"

"A gift from Kitch."

She said, "We're all so proud of him."

I said, "How about this weather?"

She looked at the sky. "Winter's coming."

"Once a year."

Wynema said, "I've got some new toiletry supplies that you might enjoy."

I considered the lump of soap on the edge of my bathtub and the watered-down bottle of shampoo on the shower rack.

"I'm all set, thanks."

She poked around in her bag and pulled out a small red bottle shaped like a fire hydrant. "Maybe your brother could use some aftershave."

"He's well-equipped in that department."

"Christmas is right around the bend. A gift for your mother?"

"She has my dad. I can't improve on that."

"It's a matter of letting her know you love her."

"We're pretty clear where that stands."

Wynema said, "Something for a special lady, perhaps?"

"I need to save my pennies. With gas being so high."

"Gas is cheaper than liquor."

I turned my crusty eye to look directly at Wynema. She peered at me close, her eyes made big from her glasses.

Wynema said, "I believe you have the pink eye."

I said, "You don't say."

She put the fire hydrant back in her bag, hurried to her car, and drove away.

My eye was red and there was some crust around the lid. The itching was minimal. I made sure not to touch it with anything but a wet rag.

I ate breakfast and then went out to check the beasts. What I saw was not encouraging. The cattle still had pink eye and now so did the horse. The animals were getting worse rather than better. White, cloudy eyes, crust stuck to their eyelashes. I needed something stronger than the powder.

I picked up pink eye juice at the Keaton Co-op and then spent the afternoon injecting the livestock. The cattle went okay. Get them in the holder pen, peel back an eyelid and jam the needle into the red part of the flesh. The horse was smarter. She avoided me. But I lured her with half a loaf of bread and got her with two quick jabs.

Afterwards, I lay down on the Davenport with a pinch of powder stinging in my infected eye and turned on the radio for the cattle report. Prices were going up. I was tempted to pack the livestock into the gooseneck right then and haul them to Strattford, sell every last one of those critters. But they weren't yet up to weight, and who knew how high prices would climb. Anyway, it didn't matter. You can't sell cattle when they have pink eye.

CHAPTER 36

Three days after my night in the tunnels, I remained in a good mood, in spite of the sorry state of my eye. My improved demeanor was, I supposed, due to a combination of things. The shadow of the horse killer had been replaced by the strangeness of old Jabez, the injections appeared to have cured the livestock, and the weather had turned warm. Most of all, the climb into the tunnels and the things I'd seen there lingered in my head like a pleasant dream.

In the meantime, I waited for my eye to clear up. I spent my afternoons on the recliner, TV on, sound turned down, a glass of whiskey in my hand. I thought about the tunnels and the hands that had made those paintings and built the stick dolls and laid the baby mammoth in that tiny room. These things had been done by people who had lived on this very land, and although they were dead and their footsteps had blown away and their bones had been chewed up by worms, a person like Jabez could go on living in nature just like they had, more or less. It made the world seem consistent, I suppose.

I allowed that Jabez's actions toward my horse had been sensible given the circumstances of that blizzardy night and the nature of her existence. All this was to say, the world was still as mean as ever, but the meanness had begun to make sense.

Eventually, Kitch called.

"Howdy, pardner. Kitch Riles on the horn."

I said, "You're talking like a hick."

"I'm talking like I talk. I hail from rural America. I speak my native tongue."

"A month ago you were black. A week ago you were nothing. And now you're Gomer Pyle."

"I am simply a well-bred white boy from the sticks."

"Where are you calling from?"

"Louisville, from my lovely home. And I'm feeling mighty fine. Last night was my first game back. It was a doozy. Just before halftime, our man, Caldwell Jones, slapped their man, Fatty Taylor, in the back of the head. Thus commenced a wrasslin' match which concluded with half a gallon of blood on the floor and Caldwell getting his self kicked out of the gym. I was the first man off the bench in the third quarter. Immediately upon entering the game, I blocked a shot and chased the ball down for a one-man fast break that concluded with the prettiest finger roll you ever did see. Then I stole the inbounds pass and dished it to our point guard, Rollie, who swished a three. In less than a minute, I had a block, a basket, a steal, and assist. Coach left me in for the rest of the game. All told, I accumulated ten points, four rebounds, two blocks, and an assist. And a steal. I have returned, by golly."

I said, "Who won?"

"We beat 'em by nine points, thanks to me. And secondly. The second reason I'm feeling good is that I've just learned that I'll never get cut from this team, irrespective of my amazing play."

"How's that?"

"It's because I'm white. You heard that right."

"You're starting to talk like a negro again."

"Not negro, black. Of which I am neither. With all the trades lately—I've told you about the trades, right?—me and Rollie are now the only whites left on the team. While I was injured, Rollie was the *only* white guy. The people of Kentucky made it clear that they could not root for a team with only one white guy. There were demonstrations. Now that I'm back and playing like the second coming of Moses, everybody in Kentucky is happy."

"Everybody?"

"The whites, mostly."

"You feel good about that?"

"More comfortable than good."

"What about your teammates?"

"I keep them entertained. New line of thought. Tell me Johnny Riles, how come nobody ever calls you J.R.?"

"You mean like 'junior'?"

"Yeah. J.R. Junior."

"Because I'm not a junior. My name is Johnny and our dad's name is Vernon."

"But your initials are J.R."

"I prefer Johnny."

Kitch said, "You should reconsider. New line of thought. Are you still coming to see me play on New Year's"

"Will you have four hundred dollars to pay me back?"

"Of course."

"I'll be there."

He said, "You'll get your tickets in the mail, just like last time. Wish me luck."

"I already did."

CHAPTER 37

I continued to dab my eye with a moist hankie whenever it got stuck shut. I began to wonder about blindness. After several days of waiting for it to get better on its own, I dipped the cattle needle in boiling water, filled it with pink eye juice, drank a glass of whiskey, and gave myself a shot in the cheek. The needle was as thick as pencil lead and the injection felt like a squirt of molten metal, but it did the job. Within a few hours, the crust started to shed from my eye.

As for the cattle, they made it clear of the pink, with one exception. The bull developed an ulcer on his left eye. As the ulcer ran its course, the eye bubbled up and then collapsed, leaving an empty socket. No infection, though, so it wasn't something I'd call serious. A bull needs a nose, nuts, and a pecker, but it doesn't need two eyes. A horse does, though, and I was glad to see that the roan's had cleared up completely.

Of course, the moment me and the horse and the cattle got healthy, the dog picked it up. The crust got so thick, I had to pry her eyes open every time she woke up from a nap. One morning, I held her down with my knee and injected the last drops of the juice into her snout. When I let her loose, she ran into my bedroom and hid under the bed and refused to come out, even for a bowl of bacon fat.

It had been more than a week since I'd visited Jabez. She was probably hungry and I was healthy and ready to go back to the tunnels. I would not go empty handed. I left the dog under my bed and went to Dorsey for groceries.

Clyde Winstrom was working the register. He managed the store and generally avoided the public, preferring to stay in back, where he opened boxes and paid invoices. I asked him what Charlie was up to.

"She's under the weather."

I said, "I hear the pink eye's been going around."

"It's not that."

"Good."

"Not so good. Pink eye, you can cure. What she has is worse."

"How so?"

"Relationship problems. Something happened between her and that fellow from Goodland. She'll get over it, but until then I'd just as soon she kept away from the customers. She's been awful cranky."

I bought beans and various canned fruits and told Clyde to have a good one, then I crossed the highway and bought three bottles of whiskey.

When I got in my truck, I thought about Charlie, sitting in her house feeling bad. I liked Charlie. She was a good gal and she had no business feeling bad on account of relationship problems. I didn't consider myself any kind of expert on such things, but I figured it wouldn't hurt to say hello.

I drove to Keaton and parked in her driveway. The shades were drawn. The turkey decoration had been replaced by a plywood sleigh and reindeer. I got out and knocked on the front door.

An unhappy voice said, "Come in."

I came in. Charlie was at her couch, under a blanket. The Christmas tree looked like it wanted to sneak out the door.

I said, "I heard you was sick."

"Who told you that?"

"Clyde, at the store."

"That blabbermouth. He's worse than some women I know."

"Does your sickness have to do with that fellow from Goodland?"

She said, "That's none of your business, Johnny."

"If he did something—"

"You'll whup his ass?"

"No. Well, maybe. I never liked that fellow."

"You never met him."

"And I'm glad of it." I took off my hat, scratched the back of my neck. "I just wanted to see if you were okay. Hell, I feel stupid coming over here like this. I'll leave you be."

She sat up. "Stay."

"Stay?"

"You're here. I'm in a mood. You want a drink?"

I said, "I have whiskey in my truck."

Charlie shook her head. "I can't keep up with whiskey. There's beers in the fridge. Get us a couple."

We sat and drank beers and she told me about Mr. Goodland. The gist of it was that he had found another gal, closer to home, and he preferred her to Charlie. Adding asshole to injury, Mr. Goodland hadn't the courage to tell her in person, but instead conveyed the news via a drunken phone call.

Charlie concluded with a shrug. "He wasn't worth my time."

"I could of told you that."

"From a guy who never met him."

"Still, I was right."

Charlie shook the last drops of her beer into her mouth. I'd finished mine twenty minutes ago but I'd been pretending to drink out of it so I wouldn't look like a slob.

I said, "You want another?"

Charlie nodded. I fetched two more beers and we sat next to each other and stared at the Christmas tree and sipped from the cans. I'm pretty good at drinking in silence.

It was getting towards sundown. The clock on the wall ticked and tocked for seventeen minutes before Charlie spoke again. "Wanna do something?"

My mind trembled at the possibilities. I said, "Such as?"

"Such as, let's go to Strattford and see a movie."

Less than I'd hoped for but more than I'd expected. I said, "I need to do my chores first."

"Bring me along. I'll help you."

Charlie got in my truck and we drove to my place. When I opened the front door, the dog plunged out of the house and sprinted for the windbreak.

We went to the barn and Charlie watched as I tossed hay to the cattle. It's always a pleasure to work in the presence of a woman. You become aware of your muscles.

I wondered if Jabez was watching. I wondered what she'd think of me tossing hay bales for Charlie.

I drove us to Strattford with my window cracked. Charlie drank two more beers. I kept the bottle of whiskey laying sideways on the dashboard and sipped from it as necessary. I drove sixty-seven miles an hour. That seemed fast enough without being a show off. I smoked three cigarettes on the thirty-five minute ride.

When I pulled up to the theater, Charlie looked at the marquee and said, "*Apple Dumpling Gang*. Jesus. Why can't they get real movies out here?"

I said, "I'll pay for the popcorn. Does that make you feel better?"

After the movie, which we neither one cared for, we joined the string of cars and trucks driving up and down Main Street for the cruising hour. Swing around at the train tracks. Head toward the convenience store. Repeat. Car radios. Kids waving and hollering. Girls sitting up on the back seat of a Mustang convertible, dressed in coats and scarves for the December weather.

Charlie said, "Remember when we used to do this?"

"We never did this."

"Not in the same car. But we did it. I saw you go by a time or two."

"I was always a passenger, and unwilling. I never understood the point."

"It's to meet people. Find out where the parties are. Have fun. See those kids over there?" She pointed at a Thunderbird that was turning down a side street. "They're going to park out by the Baptist Church and feel each other up. Or they'll smoke cigarettes or drink some peppermint schnapps. Or maybe they'll get in a fight. Did you like fighting?"

"I've always stayed out of things. I mean, I fought with Kitch, sure. But that was just wrestling. We never hurt each other."

She made a sound that resembled a snort. "You're full of bull.

I saw you come to school with a black eye lots of times. You must have been a bust-up."

I said, "I wasn't no bust-up."

"Where'd you get those black eyes, then?" She was taunting.

"They weren't from fights."

Charlie rolled down her window and pitched her empty beer can into the bed of the truck. "So you got 'em from the door-knob, did you?"

"Yep."

She pried open another beer. "Was the doorknob married to your mother?"

I didn't reply.

She flipped down the visor and looked in the mirror and then flipped it back up. She said, "Well, then. You've got a reason for anything dumb you do from here on out."

I jerked the wheel back and forth so we swerved in our lane. The car behind us honked in encouragement. I said, "Any-thing?"

"And nobody'd blame you."

I said, "How about you? Did you ever get into fights?"

"Once. I was a senior. You were a sophomore; you must have seen it. It was lunch break and we were jacking around in the gym. Ralphie Dabner tried to pinch my tits. I boxed his ears just as hard as I could and he went down like a sack of shit. Got me two days of in-house."

"I bet it was worth it."

"Every time I see Ralphie, he reminds me he still can't hear right."

"What?"

"He still can't hear right."

"What?"

"Funny."

She turned the radio to Strattford's all-country station. Fred-dy Fender sang about teardrops. I thought the song was hokey and was about to mention this when I saw that Charlie had turned her back to me and her shoulders were trembling. Un-derstandable, seeing how she'd just lost her boyfriend. I raised the volume so as to cover the sound of her sobs.

Sensing that our evening was winding down, I headed south on Highway 59 out of Strattford. Charlie continued to sit with her back to me. I offered her my hankie. She accepted it without looking at me.

A few miles out of town, Charlie stopped crying and began staring, swollen-cheeked, out the front window. I noticed she was hugging her arms so I turned the heat up.

A George Jones and Tammy Wynette duet came on. Charlie started sniffling again.

I said, "Mind if I change the station?"

Charlie swallowed and said, "Don't you like country?"

"I live in the country. I don't need to listen to it."

As I centered the dial on the rock station, the indecisive strum of a guitar came out of the speakers. Here it was. A tight-throated voice began reciting the tale of a nameless horse and the fool who rode it along a stretch of desert. Then the band came in and the best song ever written made me feel like I was a drop of blood in the heart of a lion.

I sang along, tapping the steering wheel. I lit a cigarette, taking the longest drag I could. It was me and Charlie and America driving down Highway 59 on a Sunday night, right in the darkest place in the world and to hell with that son of a bitch from Goodland.

I sang all the words, all thru the end of the song, all the way to the *la-la-la* part. When the song ended, something amazing happened. It started right up again.

Then something else amazing happened. Charlie turned the radio up full blast, so loud it made the speakers buzz. She reached over and pulled the bottle of whiskey off the dashboard. She swallowed the last inch of booze and rolled down her window and threw the bottle into the night.

Together, we whooped and sang. At the end, Charlie sang the *la-la-las* with all her lungs. I hollered along.

After the fade-out, the DJ said, "Sorry, man. I think I played the same song twice in a row. Shoot. Why not? From here on out, it's double-duty Saturday. I'll play everything twice. Here's a new one from. . . ."

I turned the volume down to a reasonable place.

Charlie said, "You really like that song."

"I like the way it sounds."

"You know all the words. They must mean something to you."

I tried to sound intelligent. "It's about our dreams. We live in our heads. And our skin is like sand. Under the sand, that's where real life is. Under the sand, but above the dirt."

"You think?"

"And I like the parts about the horse with no name. I don't name my horses or dogs or stuff like that, so I relate. And, in the end, the singer sets the horse free. I really like that part."

"What if you had a baby? Would you give it a name?"

"I doubt I'll ever have a baby."

Charlie became morose. "Me, either. Gimme a cigarette."

"They're bad for you."

"Please."

"No."

She said, "I'm sleepy." Then she curled up. I'd known her for twenty years but I'd never noticed how small she was. She curled up tiny on the seat with her hair touching my leg and she went to sleep. I put my cowboy hat on her head, just for something to do.

As we approached her house, she sat up and stared out the window like a little kid. My cowboy hat was hanging off the side of her head. I left the engine running as I parked in her driveway. I said, "Would you be interested in another—"

She said, "Don't ask me anything, Johnny. I'm half asleep."

"Of course not."

She removed my hat from her head and placed it on the seat between us.

I said, "Maybe we could visit again sometime."

"Sure."

She climbed out of the truck and walked into her house.

As I lay in bed that night, my thoughts revolved around the way Charlie had said, "Sure." She was an honest person and, as such, she would have told me if she didn't want to spend more time with me. Of course, being as she was honest, if she really wanted to spend more time with me, she would have said, "Absolutely," and invited me inside for a beer. Then again, she had recently been mistreated by a man she cared deeply about and she probably harbored hopes, desperate though they may be, that their relationship could be shored up. At the very least, she would have felt some guilt for going to a movie with me so soon after Mr. Goodland had revealed to her that he was an asshole. Finally, she had been drinking. There was a strong likelihood that she would have preferred to say something other than "Sure," but that she was afraid to say it for fear that it would sound insincere due to her inebriated state.

I concluded, therefore, that it would be best to not assert myself too strongly. Instead, I would allow Charlie to grieve her lost relationship whilst also pondering how much she'd enjoyed our evening and then come to the natural conclusion that she should invite me on a formal date sometime in the near future.

Next, I turned my thoughts to Jabez and her hole in the ground. Those thoughts were considerably simpler. Jabez was a likeable, horse-murdering, pungent oddball. She was a mystery solved and a mystery still. I didn't trust her, but I didn't fear her. None of that mattered, though, because she lived in a damned fascinating hole in the ground, which rendered irrelevant any number of screwy personality traits.

I would visit her again soon, but as with Charlie, I didn't want to appear too eager. Jabez struck me as a person who would become annoyed if I showed up at her doorstep too frequently.

I would wait two days before riding north again and I would wait until Charlie called me before I attempted to visit with her again.

This settled, I went to sleep.

CHAPTER 38

Cloudless December mornings have a certain way about them. The air becomes watery. Not shimmery like in the summer, but like you've been crying.

Two days had passed, and I was good and ready to visit Jabez.

The cattle breathed steam when I told them good morning. The dog shivered in her sock sweater. The land was dead and brown. In the windbreak, crows lit from tree to tree. The snakes and toads and salamanders were curled up, sleeping underground.

Charlie hadn't called.

The ice in the stock tank was thin enough that I could punch thru it with my fist. I struck hard and fast and pulled my hand away before my glove got wet.

The cattle remained healthy, including the bull, who seemed to be adjusting to being half-blind. The horse was fine, I was fine, and the dog was fine. Not a fleck of crust, not a drop of pus. I had conquered the pink eye.

I needed to go to the grocery for some things I thought Jabez might find useful. I could have gone to the store in Keaton, but it was four miles further away than Dorsey. And there wasn't a liquor store in Keaton. And, anyway, there was no reason for me to avoid my grocery just because one of their employees had once said, "Sure," to me.

Charlie gave me a nod as I entered the store. I was the only customer. I nodded back, trying to be both friendly and cool, and then I immediately headed to the farthest aisle and began shopping. After what seemed like an appropriate amount of time, I brought some cans of soup and beans and some hamburger buns to the counter.

I said, "How's Charlie?" Just as normal as could be.

She started typing prices into the cash register. "You don't need to feel sorry for me."

I didn't expect her to say that. It put me on my heels. I said, "Hell, I don't feel sorry for you. I'm happy for you."

"You're happy I got dumped?"

"Not at all. Not a teeny bit. I'm sad that you got dumped. But I'm looking on the bright side."

"What's the bright side, again?"

"At least you didn't marry him."

"I never married Nixon, neither. I guess that means I should be the happiest gal in the whole world."

"Exactly. It's the little things you need to be thankful for. You're done with Mr. Goodland, you aren't married to Richard Nixon, and you know me." This last bit was a gamble, but Charlie's cheeks had gone just a shade pink. I suspected that she was enjoying this conversation. I certainly was.

"You're so right. I know Johnny Riles. Can you get me your brother's autograph?" The way she said that, all full of sarcasm, and, in a way, sympathy, it made me want to rub my lips all over her face.

I said, "I had fun the other night."

"We ought to do it again."

I said, "Sure."

She said, "You been to any basketball games yet?"

"I could have, but I skipped out."

"I've been to a couple and both of them were horrible. The boys are as bad as they've ever been. And the girls are worse."

She was talking about high school basketball.

Charlie looked out the window. A car pulled into the parking lot. It was Alice Churchouse, the local singing sensation. For forty years now, it didn't matter what denomination you were, you couldn't get hitched or buried without Alice leaning her head back and howling praises to the glory of God.

Charlie spoke quick, so as to get the conversation over before

Alice came in. "I have an idea. Let's go to a game somewhere else. Skip Dorton altogether. Maybe we could go to Calida. Sit in the stands and cheer for another team in another town for once. That way you won't have to hear a bunch of comments about Kitch and I won't have to hear a bunch of questions about my ex."

Alice was now walking toward the store.

Charlie pushed the grocery bag toward me. I handed her a ten-dollar bill.

Alice came in. She said hello, I said hello, Charlie said hello. Alice rolled a cart into the frozen food aisle.

As Charlie gave me my change, I whispered, "Let's do it."

She said, "Friday. Meet me here after work."

Before I picked up my bag, Charlie reached behind the counter and pulled out a box of powdered doughnuts and placed them inside. She put her finger to her lips. I winked at her and then left, feeling so good about myself that I forgot to visit the liquor store on my way out of town.

As soon as I got home, I saddled the horse and headed north, followed by the dog.

Jabez did not come out when I stomped on her door so I walked with the horse down to the cottonwood patch. There, I found her. She had her back to me, squatted down and scrubbing clothes in the seep hole. She had on a pair of baggy drawers and nothing else. No shirt or bra or anything.

It's a shock to see another person naked, especially on a cold day like this, especially a person like Jabez. Her bottom, even thru her underdrawers, looked like an upside-down, creamy white Valentine's Day heart. Her skin was tight against her ribs. Her shoulders had strength to them that lent an indelicate appearance to her back. Her hand-sawn hair made her look like a tramp. The overall impression was unsettling.

The dog started to barking and ran straight toward Jabez.

Without turning around Jabez hollered, "Is that you, Johnny Riles?"

I said, "That's me."

"Are your eyes clean?"

"They were until a moment ago."

"Turn around, go on in the hole, and wait. If you try to look at me, I'll stab you in the belly."

I whistled to the poodle and led the horse up to the hatch. I brought the saddlebags into the cavern, lit the lantern, and sat on the floor petting the dog.

Ten minutes later, Jabez climbed in, fully clothed and carrying a green army bag. She strung a length of rope across the room and then pulled out her wet clothes from the bag. I helped her hang them up.

She said, "I like to let my things dry in here. It makes the place more humid. I can't stand dry skin." She lifted the dog and looked into her eyes.

I said, "She picked it up, the pink. I had to give her a shot. She's better now, as am I."

Jabez said to the dog, "You took your medicine real good, didn't you?"

Jabez put the dog back on the floor and set out some milk for her. Then she said to me, "You've seen me in my panties. Are you happy?"

"Disturbed would be a more accurate description."

She said, "To think an ass as pretty as mine could fart so loud."

I laughed some.

Jabez said, "You bring me any whiskey?"

"I forgot. But there's some good soup for you."

"I like my whiskey."

"I'll bring some tomorrow."

"And bring me that chicken you promised."

"I will."

"You staying for dinner?"

"I can't."

"You got a date?"

"No."

"Then have dinner with me."

We ate chili beef soup, she from her bowl, me straight out of the soup can. We didn't conversate. Jabez slurped off her wooden spoon, I stared into the darkness at the end of the room.

As she wiped her finger along the inside of her bowl, she said, "You're acting funny."

I said, "How do you act normal, knowing about all the bones and tunnels and baby mammoths down there?"

She said, "I'm flattered that you would describe me as normal."

"Acknowledged. Still, spending all your time in this boring room, after seeing what's down there, it's like eating the cork and ignoring the wine."

"You want to get back in there."

"Very much."

"Bring me whiskey and a chicken."

"None of my birds are going to give you any meat. I told you, they're laying hens."

"And I told you I don't care. Just bring me a chicken."

"I will next time, I promise. Whiskey, too."

She nodded toward the end of the room. "This isn't a fun house. You can't live back there." She took the empty can from me. "Go home and sleep."

• • •

The next day, I rode north with a bottle of whiskey and two frozen chicken breasts from my deep freeze. I didn't want to give any of my birds to Jabez. The thought of her slaughtering another of my animals made me queasy. The frozen breasts seemed like a sensible compromise.

Jabez opened the door as I rode up. "You bring what I asked for?"

I showed her what I'd brought.

She took the whiskey, uncapped it, and drank. When she finished her snort, I reached for the bottle but she shook her head. "You said you'd bring me a chicken."

"I did."

"You brought me *parts* of a chicken. I want a whole bird. I like to take the feathers off."

"Fine." I started to put the chicken breasts back into the saddlebag.

Jabez said, "You might as well leave them, since you went to all the trouble."

I tossed the package to her and said, "You're welcome."

She said, "I'm serious. Don't come back here without a chicken. A live one."

I climbed on my horse and rode south. Jabez could be difficult sometimes. I didn't care. I had a date with Charlie in just two days.

As soon as I walked thru the front door, the phone rang. For once, it wasn't Kitch. It was a man with a high-pitched voice. He said, "Johnny Riles?"

"Yes."

"Tell your brother to keep his promises."

Click.

God damn it, Kitch.

CHAPTER 39

The next day, as I was gathering eggs, I tried to decide which of the chickens I ought to bring to Jabez. I had more birds than I needed, that was a fact. But as they strutted about, all white feathers and yellow legs, I couldn't think that any particular one of them ought to be boiled, plucked, and gutted.

That evening, I checked the mailbox as I headed in for dinner. Amongst the junk was a letter from Kitch. I opened the envelope before I went to the house. Inside, there was a pair of tickets to the Kentucky Colonels versus the Denver Nuggets at McNichols Arena on December 31, 1975. In addition to the tickets, there was a postcard with a photo of an old covered bridge. On the back, Kitch had scrawled, "We did it in the bridge. We're all in it to win the victory." Below that, a woman's handwriting declared, "We're all hot dogs! Johnny! Hot dogs!" The card was stained with something brown. I lit it on fire and watched it burn in the snow.

The tickets, I brought inside and put on my nightstand.

• • •

The next morning, after doing my chores, I noticed that the windmill was squeaking. I fetched the grease gun from the barn and climbed to the top of the tower. I smeared grease on all the bushings and bearings. I remained perched up there for a moment, enjoying the view. The cattle wandering about the pasture, Old Stinkum winding away in the distance. Further north, the empty prairie. Beyond that, Jabez was in her tunnels, waiting for me to bring her a chicken. To the south and east, Highway

36 drew a line toward Dorsey, where Charlie was presumably leaning against the counter in the grocery, talking about the weather with someone and, hopefully, getting excited about our date that night.

Kitch called after lunch.

"I scored thirty-six points last night. You should see the way those big guys shit their pants when I leap over them. They can't believe how fast I am. I could snatch a penny out of a bulldog's mouth. Bullfrog. You've never seen a bullfrog. They look like someone dumped green soup on the ground and decorated it with eyeballs. Next year, I'm going to put in to be traded to Denver. Can you imagine what that team could do with Eiffel, Flowers, and me? I won't be home for Christmas. But I'll see you on New Year's, right? I sent the tickets last week. We traded Caldwell Jones yesterday. He just wasn't fitting in. These Kentucky girls are something else. It's just like that Beach Boys song, 'Southern girls with the way they talk they keep their boyfriends up at night.' You ain't never lived until a southern girl's cooked you breakfast. The races are very similar in a lot of ways. White and black, yellow, red, and brown. We're all people. Color is just hue, man. Some of the guys I play with. They're crazy. They sneak drinks at halftime. They say one of the guys on the Pacers rubs chili powder on his nuts before every game. I ain't tried that yet. Don't need to. Ain't nobody can keep up with Kitch Riles. Look at the time. I gotta split."

He hung up.

I said to the dead receiver, "I hope you're keeping your promises."

I showered, shaved, and sat at the kitchen table, sipping as little whiskey as possible, watching the clock. Two hours later, the little hand finally pointed to six and it was time for my date with Charlie.

I drove to Dorsey and parked behind the grocery store.

Charlie came out the back entrance wearing a scarf and a cap and pair of red mittens. I reached across the seat and opened the passenger door for her. I smelled perfume. I tried not to look at her directly, but I sensed that she may have put make-up on her cheeks.

I said, "I been waiting for this moment all day long."

She didn't get in the truck.

I said, "You're letting the heat out."

She said, "I'm sorry, Johnny."

"It's just a little heat."

"I can't go with you."

I looked at Charlie, waiting for her to tell me she was joshing.

She said, "Bradley called today. He's on his way to my place."

I said, "Who's Bradley?"

"Mr. Goodland. He apologized. He wants to talk to me in person. I owe him this."

"You don't owe that peckerhead a damned thing."

"He owes it to me, then."

"Shit, Charlie."

"I'm sorry. We'll do it some other time."

She pushed the door closed and walked back into the store.

I drove across 36 and went to Dee's for a bottle of whiskey. As I walked out of the store, a truck pulled into the parking lot and Boyd Osthoff climbed out. Boyd was from Calida, same age as me. When I was a junior, in the 'sixty-six district finals, he made a miracle last-second half-court shot that took the game away from us. Calida went on to win state that year.

He shook the bejeezus out of my hand. "I heard your brother hurt his ankle." He made a concerned face but I suspected he was gloating. He was one of those true-to-your-school types, and jealous of Kitch's success.

Here was something strange. Somebody who was happy to see Kitch get hurt. Even stranger, it made me mad.

I said, "He's all better now. He scored fifty-seven points last night. Single-handedly won the game."

"You must be awful proud."

"He's the finest human being to ever set foot on the earth."

Boyd said, "Shit. If I had a beer I'd say a toast."

I said, "Here's to the tallest, dumbest, turd of a man you could ever hope to meet."

Boyd hesitated a moment, then said, "Amen."

We clinked imaginary glasses. Boyd went into the liquor store. I drove toward home wishing I'd socked him in the nose. He wouldn't have deserved it, but it might have made me feel better.

The dog was happy to see me. I sat with her on the front step. She barked at shadows. I drank whiskey and watched the windmill spin.

Late that night, after the bottle was finished and I was face down in bed, the phone began to ring and ring. I didn't want to talk to Kitch, I didn't want to hear any mysterious voices telling me that Kitch needed to keep his promises, and I didn't want Charlie to tell me that she'd fallen back in love with her bastard of a boyfriend.

It rang and rang and rang.

Or maybe Charlie was calling to tell me she'd sent Mr. Goodland home with a boot print in his ass and she wanted to apologize for ditching me. I draped a blanket around myself and went to the kitchen to pick up the receiver.

My optimism proved to be misplaced.

"Johnny Riles?" It was the man with the high-pitched voice.

"Who are you?"

"I apologize for the lateness of the hour. Your brother is making some poor decisions."

"Then call him."

"Just tell him to keep his promises."

"Is this about that four hundred dollars?"

"It's more than that."

"Such as?"

"You just tell him to keep his promises."

I said, "The hell with you," and hung up the phone.

It took me a long time to get back to sleep.

CHAPTER 40

A few days later, when I checked the mail, there was a magazine wrapped in brown paper. It was addressed to "J.R. Riles." I brought it inside and tore the paper off. It was a *Playboy*, with lots of naked ladies on the cover. I tossed it on the dining room table.

The phone rang.

"Twenty-six, twice. That's what I got in the last two games. I even hit a three-pointer. Mo Lucas calls me The Great White Soap. It's 'cause I shower after every meal. You gotta be tough to make it in this business. I drink more coffee than you can imagine. That's why I'm always so hyped-up. You getting your magazines yet? It would do you a world of good to get some sex into your life. That's not a dirty word, you know. Unless you get the clap. But they have pills for that. Ha. Ha. I can't wait to see you. New Year's Eve. I've told everyone all about you. Don't forget to wear your cowboy hat. These guys think I'm a hick, wait'll they see you. Mom and Dad are coming out for Christmas. All the way to Louisville. Their very first plane ride. I could be partying but instead—"

I interrupted him. "Kitch. I'm getting phone calls."

He didn't reply. It was strange for him to be silent.

I said, "A man called, twice. He says you need to keep your promises."

Silence.

"Do you know what he's talking about?"

"Sounds like a prank call to me. Or, maybe. Yes. I know what it is. It's a hillbilly who's worried that I'm corrupting his daughter. I'll talk to him. When I'm thru, he'll never call you again."

"Are you still gambling?"

"That's over with. You bailed me out and I'll pay you back. Contrary to what that hillbilly asshole is saying, I do keep my promises."

I didn't know what to do with that damned magazine. I read it. I looked at it.

CHAPTER 41

It was three days before Christmas. Since I'd be spending the holiday alone, unhappy, and drunk, I decided that I should at least cook a proper meal for myself. First thing I needed was to buy turkey, celery, potatoes, and various other whatnots. I drove the extra four miles to the store in Keaton in order to avoid seeing Charlie.

There was a whole line of folks and they all said hello as I came in. It's a nice feeling, sometimes, to be welcomed. Brenda Walters mentioned that she'd seen a segment on Kitch on the news. Apparently, his play the last couple of weeks had earned him consideration as a selection for the All-Star game. This set off a store-wide conversation.

"Kitch Riles in the All-Star game!"

"He might win a championship with that team of his."

"He's in the wrong league. Kitch Riles belongs in the NBA."

"The NBA is old-fashioned. ABA players are the true athletes."

"I just like the way they look in those shorts."

"Those black boys sure can get after it."

"And to think that our Kitch is right in there with 'em."

And on.

As I pushed a cart down the aisles, I ran into various so-and-so's and always thanked them for their appreciation of Kitch's miraculous talent.

Karen Winstrom was working the register, looking just as bright as a polished spoon. When she rang me up she said, "Your parents coming out for Christmas?"

"Nope. It'll just be me and the dog."

"So they're staying in Saint Francis?"

"Oh, no. They're going all the way to Louisville to spend some time with Kitch."

Karen said, "Why don't you join them?"

The people behind me in line were listening.

I said, "I need to stay home and watch the ranch."

In addition to being true, I figured my dedication to the family business would meet approval from my fellow shoppers. I heard at least two people offer up a kindly "hmmm."

As she pushed my bags toward me, Karen said, "Do you even know how to cook?"

I said, "More or less. I have low standards. And the dog's are even lower."

That earned some chuckles.

At nine-thirty that night, the phone rang. I closed the *Playboy* and lifted the receiver, hoping it would be Charlie.

It was Kitch. "Hey Johnny!"

Laughter in the background.

"Yes?"

"You wanna get laid?"

"What?"

"Do you want to get laid?"

"What do you mean?"

"Just say yes. Do you wanna get laid?"

"Yes."

"Crawl up a chicken's ass and wait."

There was an eruption of guffaws. I hung up.

• • •

The next day, when I gathered the eggs, I discovered that one of the chickens had died overnight. Hard to say what killed her. The dog wasn't interested in the corpse.

I tossed the dead bird in the trash barrel and set it on fire. It smelled sweet, the fat mingling with the bones.

The mail brought another magazine in a brown wrapper, something called *Hustler*. It was nasty, the things people were doing in that one. God damn Kitch.

I slid the magazine under my mattress, next to the *Playboy*.

That night, I got all-fired drunk and ended up walking around in the cold outside in my underwear, singing and hollering into the wind. At some point, I entered the chicken house and yelled at the birds, "Which of you wants to die next?"

I went to bed sometime after midnight.

CHAPTER 42

The morning of Christmas Eve, I did my chores and then started right to cooking. My family always used to eat our big meal on Christmas Eve. That way, Mom could relax with her shot glass on Christmas Day. I chose to follow that tradition.

I put on the radio, smoked cigarettes, wore my apron. Peel, chop, stir. Turn on the heat and listen to the lids rattle. Let that turkey bake.

By early afternoon, I had a proper meal. Sweet pickles, stuffing, taters, and turkey. I tuned the radio to Christmas music. Then I put on a nice shirt and clean jeans. I raised the thermostat to seventy-two degrees. The house smelled and felt like a proper Christmas. I put the food in white serving dishes and set them out at the table and sat in front of my empty plate. I put my hands together and thanked God for this grub.

And then I said the hell with eating alone.

I loaded all the food into pie pans, which I covered with tin foil and stacked into a pillowcase. Then I got dressed for cold and went out to the chicken house. I filled my pockets with eggs. I caught a hen, wrapped her in a towel, and hauled her and the pillowcase of food to the barn where I saddled up the horse and headed north. I left the dog in the house, seeing as she might not get along with the chicken.

I made the hatch just before dark. I stomped twice with the heel of my book and Jabez popped out, looking like she'd been waiting for me. She had on her blue jeans and a denim shirt. Her face was clean. Her hair was mostly clean. She looked as normal as can be for a person who'd popped out of a hole.

I said, "Merry Christmas."

She said, "You bring me a chicken?"

I shook the bird out of the towel. It flapped its wings and took off on a sprint in the general direction of the top edge of the depression. Jabez hooted and hollered and chased the thing in a scribble of a race. After much comical falling and laughing, Jabez snatched the bird by the ankles and held it upside down. She skipped back up to the hatch, waving her prize all the while.

We climbed in the hole and ate ourselves silly. The chicken clucked happily, marching from one side of the room to the next, pecking at the scraps we tossed her. Lantern, cigarettes, whiskey, milk. God, it was cozy down there.

After we'd sopped up the last of the food, Jabez said, "Care for some eggnog?"

I said okay. I'd never had eggnog before.

She cracked four eggs and whipped them in an enamel bowl. Then she poured in a dose of milk. Then she set the bowl on her little cow-shit stove and handed me a spoon.

"Stir."

I stood next to the stove and stirred.

Jabez nodded. "Just like that. I'll be right back."

She passed into the dark at the end of the room.

Ten minutes later, she returned, smiling and proud, with her left hand hidden behind her back. "You stirring that proper?"

"Yes, ma'am."

Still with one hand behind her back, she took the spoon from me and held it to her mouth for a sip. "Good. Now put about two inches of whiskey in there."

As I poured the whiskey, Jabez stepped up behind me. I didn't turn to look since I figured she was up to something silly and I didn't want to ruin it.

She said, "Close your eyes."

"Should I set this bottle down first?"

"Just close your eyes."

I did as she asked. I felt her approach from behind. I smelled her breath, which was not as rough as I expected. Sort of grassy smelling. She pressed up close. I felt her bosoms against my back. Then her arms went over my head. Something brushed against my hair. I kept my eyes closed. She made a huffing sound. It occurred to me that she might be laughing or she might be moaning.

She brought her hands down and placed something heavy against my sternum. I felt a cord press against the back of my neck.

I opened my eyes and spun around. In doing so, my ass knocked the bowl of milk off the shit-stove. The noise startled the chicken, who leapt up and flew one frantic lap around the room and then instantly forgot what the commotion had been about and resumed her clucking and pecking.

Jabez stood frozen, glaring at me like I was the worst person in the world. Her smile straightened itself into a mouth of teeth. She snatched the whiskey bottle out of my hand.

I felt for the thing that was dangling from my neck and held it up so I could see it. It was a rock, maybe a piece of coral, roughly the size of a brick and just as heavy. It was tied on either end with a heavily knotted string of leather.

Jabez said, "Haven't you ever seen a necklace before?"

Aware of her teeth, I said, "By God, it's a necklace. And a good one."

The chicken dipped her beak into the spilled eggnog.

Jabez leaned toward me. "You know what it is?"

"A necklace, like you said."

"But what *is* it?"

I held it up so the lantern shone on it. Wavy horizontal lines ran across the width of the thing. I said, "It's a fossil."

Jabez leaned back, which relieved me, and then swung her fist into my temple, which sent me directly into her shit-stove. I avoided knocking it over by grabbing it with both hands and shifting myself directly into the wall.

When the tumbling concluded, the stove was upright, I was on my back, Jabez was glaring at me, and the room smelled like burned skin. The chicken continued pecking at the eggnog.

I didn't move. The weight of the necklace made it hard to

breathe. My hands hurt from where I'd grabbed the stove and my head hurt from where Jabez had socked me.

Jabez walked away and pressed her forehead against the far wall. She let the whiskey bottle slip from her left hand and drop to the floor. It landed on its side without breaking. Whiskey spilled out the neck. Jabez made a whimpering sound.

With her forehead still against the wall, she said, "It's a mammoth tooth. Any dummy could see that."

I touched my temple with the heel of my palm and held my hand in front of my face. There was blood, all right, a big red comma of it. My fingertips had white spots on them from the stove burn. I looked at my other hand and it had burn spots, too. I could see my fingerprints thru the burns.

Jabez turned to face me. She was breathing shallow now, her eyes moist. "I didn't intend to do that. It's how I am sometimes. I just let loose. I'm better now."

I nodded to indicate that I'd heard her.

She squatted in front of me. She said, "You're afraid of me."

I shook my head. I could feel the blood coming out of my left eyebrow.

Jabez said, "I'll fix you up. I'm a nurse."

Whatever mood had gotten ahold of her, it was gone. She reached to her breast and tore the pocket off her denim shirt. "Hold this against your head. I'll be right back."

I pressed the shirt pocket against my eyebrow. Jabez picked up one of the empty pie pans and disappeared into the darkness at the end of the main room. A few minutes later, she returned with the pan filled with dirt. She poured some water into the dirt, then she sat on her chair and made me put my head in her lap. She worked a small portion of the mud into a patty, peeled the shirt pocket away from my eyebrow, and slapped the mud directly on the cut. A speck of the mud got in my eye.

Here's mud in my eye. I laughed. It was a laugh you get when the brakes have gone out, your steering wheel's frozen, and your truck's rolling downhill toward a box of sleeping kittens.

Jabez shushed me and pressed the shirt pocket on top of the mud patty. Then she reached up, pulled a sock from her drying line, and tied it round my head.

"Stand up. Let's have a look at your hands."

I stood. She smeared mud on my palms then she slipped on my mittens for me.

I had a mammoth tooth dangling from my neck, a sock around my head, and mittens on my muddy, burned hands.

Jabez said, "Johnny Riles?"

"Yes."

"I regret what happened."

"I appreciate that."

"But you're okay now."

"It's okay."

"And I'm okay."

"Yes, you're okay."

Jabez smiled. I allowed that the rules of behavior were different in the tunnels. It's perfectly normal for someone to tie a mammoth tooth around your neck, mistake your ignorance for an insult, sock you in the temple, and then smear mud on your injuries. We'd get by. After all, there was still some whiskey in that tipped-over bottle.

I sat on the floor and let the chicken peck strands of wool from my mittens while Jabez mixed up a new batch of eggnog.

I said, "You wouldn't give me something from this cave if you didn't feel like I deserved it."

I could tell she was listening. Her stirring got slower.

I said, "It's an honor to wear this necklace. I didn't show you proper gratitude. Please accept my apology."

Jabez pulled the ladle off its hook and scooped eggnog into her cup and into my soup can. She said, "I accept your apology. And I wish to let you know that I'm grateful for you. I'd be dead without you." She pointed to the floor, where the chicken had roosted into a towel. "And I'm very glad you finally brought me that bird."

Jabez handed me the soup can. I held it with both hands so it wouldn't slip out of my mittens.

I said, "You're a tough one, Jabez."

"You're a good fellow, Johnny."

She raised her glass. We clunked and sipped. Eggnog wasn't like anything I'd had before, or would ever want again. I said, "It's good."

Jabez nodded. "I wish I had some cinnamon."

I took another drink. "Lots of vitamins in here, I bet. A person could skip lunch if he had a couple glasses of this stuff."

We got drunk and visited. We discussed our favorite Christmas Carols. Halfway thru my attempt at Silver Bells, Jabez said, "You're a horrible singer, Johnny Riles."

I said, "And this eggnog tastes like a cat's afterbirth."

Hardeeharhars. I finished my soup can and beckoned for more drink. She filled me up. I lit a cigarette. We watched the lantern.

I said, "Jabez, there's only two people in this whole world I care to spend time with, and you're one of them."

"Who's the other? That worthless brother of yours?"

"Worthless is right." I thought about the phone calls I'd been getting.

Jabez said, "Is it your mom?"

"Nope. My mom's far away. Always has been. I prefer it to stay that way. Same with my dad."

"Your girlfriend?"

"I ain't got a girlfriend."

"Somebody you're sweet on?"

"Nope."

"You mean you live all alone on that ranch of yours and you don't lie in bed with your hand under the covers and think of someone?"

"There ain't nobody, Jabez. Not like that, anyway. The other person, she is a girl, though. We're friendly. We even went on a date. But she's got a boyfriend and she doesn't want anything to do with me anymore. So I guess I misspoke. You're the *only* person I'd like to spend time with."

"What's her name?"

"Charlie. She works at the Dorton grocery."

"Charlie's a funny name for a girl."

I said, "So's Jabez."

"Don't you worry about me."

"I'm not worrying about you. I'm just saying your name is—"

"Relax, kid. It's Christmas Eve. Be jolly. Tell me all about Charlie."

Even with mud on my temple and mittens on my hands, drinking whiskey and eggs out of a soup can, I don't know. I liked Jabez. She was the kind of person who could sock you upside the head and then tell you to be jolly and you'd comply. The eggnog helped.

We drank and I talked. I told her how Charlie was nice and pretty. I told her how I'd peeked in Charlie's window on Thanksgiving. I told her how Charlie had given me free doughnuts, how we'd gone to a lousy movie the day her boyfriend broke up with her. I explained that Charlie doesn't mind about my drinking. How much fun I had singing with her in my truck. And how we'd planned to go on a date but Mr. Goodland had fouled things up by coming back. And then, I don't know how it happened, but I told Jabez that I sometimes wondered what Charlie's nipples looked like.

I caught myself. I said, "Eggs make a person say strange things."

Jabez was holding the chicken on her lap, stroking the bird's head. "It ain't the eggs. It's this place. I've said plenty of strange things in my time here. There's not usually someone around to hear me."

"Do you think there's a spirit in these tunnels?"

"This is just a hole in the ground, Johnny. It's filled with dead animals that have been decorated by dead people."

"But those handprints and that baby mammoth. And the artwork. It has to mean something. And you just said the place makes a person say strange things."

"It's just a cave. And I'm just a crazy lady who lives here."

I said, "I don't think you're even a little bit crazy. I can see why you'd say you were crazy. You socked me on the head and you killed my horse and you live in a hole and never talk to people. But as far as I'm concerned, you've done real well for yourself, surviving under these circumstances. And I'm not upset about my head or the horse."

Her hand kept stroking the chicken's head. "You know who *is* crazy? That brother of yours. I don't know hardly anything about him; that's just my honest opinion."

"If you knew him better, your opinion wouldn't change. Any

kind of trouble, he'll find it. He digs a hole and jumps in, and the only thing that saves him is that he's big enough to pull himself out. Or loud enough to convince someone to lend him a hand. If he were the short one and I were the tall one, things would be different."

Jabez finished her eggnog. She examined the bottle of whiskey. It still had a some swallows inside. She drank a gulp.

She said, "That girl, Charlie. If you love her, you're going to tell her about me."

"I never said I love her."

"Once you see her nipples, you will."

"I won't tell anybody about you. I'll never tell. You're safe, Jabez."

I stood up and crossed my heart. Jabez stood up, too, and took a hold of my hand. She squeezed hard, so the mud squished between my fingers in the mitten.

We finished the whiskey, sitting on the floor with our backs against the wall. At some point, Jabez got up and turned down the lamp. She came back and sat next to me. I leaned my head into her lap. She patted my hair, saying in a slurred voice, "You're a good little one. A good one. Boy."

The last thing I remember before I fell asleep was the chicken crawled under my hand and I petted it. I murmured something. I don't even know if I was trying to make words. I felt so comfortable, all I wanted to do was hum.

CHAPTER 43

When I finished sleeping, I slid out from under Jabez's hands and stood up in the dark. The mammoth tooth was still hanging from my neck. Jabez snored softly. I didn't know the time, but judging by how rested I was, I must have been out for some hours. I felt in my pockets for my matches, lit a cigarette, and whispered, "Merry Christmas."

One of Jabez's eyes cracked open and then went shut again. I allowed her to pretend.

I untied the sock from my head and carefully peeled the pocket off my temple. By the light of my cigarette, I found my wool hat and my coat and the rest of my things. I wished the chicken good luck and then climbed out into Christmas day.

It was windy and it was snowing ice pellets. The sun was covered by clouds but the day was still bright enough that I had to squint. The snow must have just started, as the ground was still visible.

I whistled for the horse. She snorted at me from the bottom of the depression. I clapped my mittened hands, hoping she'd trot up to me. She didn't.

I jogged down toward the trees, the necklace bouncing against my sternum. The horse had her nose against the stall, talking to the cow.

I patted her neck, "You get cold last night?"

She did not reply. I said, "The responsibilities of my life are great. I can't keep everyone happy."

By the time we arrived back home, the sun had begun to show

itself behind spotty, low clouds. The snow kept sputtering, unable to lay down a blanket, unable to quit trying.

I released the dog from the house. She growled at me for leaving her alone all night, then sprinted out to bother the cattle. I busted up the ice in the stock tank, fed the critters. I went to the barn and I pulled my mittens off to milk the cow. I shook the mud from my hands. There wasn't a single blister.

In the shower, the cut on my head opened up. The water on the bottom of the tub turned pink. Once I dried off and dressed, I lay on my bed with a hankie tied around my head. It had been a long night. I intended to spend Christmas asleep.

The phone woke me in the afternoon. I was still dressed, lying atop the covers. The clock showed 3:18. Even though I knew I shouldn't answer, I got up and plucked it out of the cradle.

It was Kitch. "Merry Jesus Day!"

I said, "Merry Christmas to yourself."

"We just finished dinner. Mom cooked. I must say, it was tasty as hell. She's cleaning up the kitchen. Dad's asleep on the couch. It's like being home."

"It sounds more like home than home is."

Kitch's voice got quiet. "Can you do me a favor, J.R.?"

"Please don't call me J.R."

"I wouldn't do otherwise. I need Mom and Dad to clear out of here before eight. I'm hosting a party. It's going to be wild. I need you to convince them to stay in a hotel."

"Have you suggested this to them yourself?"

"They'll say it's ridiculous for them to stay in a fancy hotel when I have so much room at my place. I could insist, but that'd hurt their feelings, which would make me look like a jerk. You, on the other hand, are thousands of miles away and could therefore give a fuck what anyone thinks about you."

"How's Dad?"

"He hasn't hit anyone, if that's what you're asking. Actually, it seems like our parents are getting along pretty well. Mom's been thirsty, but what's new? Let me put her on with you."

I heard the phone move into the kitchen.

Mom spoke, "Your brother's got me working like a mule."

"Merry Christmas, Mom."

"It's snowing here. Did your brother tell you?"

"He sure did. Listen, Kitch is having some friends over tonight and he's hoping to have the house to himself. Do you think that you and Dad could stay in a hotel? Kitch will pay for it."

"We couldn't do that."

"I know. Can you put Kitch back on?"

I heard a hand cover the phone and then there was a sound of muffled voices. They got loud for a moment and then calmed down. And then Kitch came on. "Thanks, brother. I don't know how you do it."

"It's a mystery to me as well."

"Did you get any Christmas presents?"

"What do you think?"

"I know you have some reading material. Right? Some magazines? Those were from me. What else did you get?"

"I got a tooth. A big tooth."

"Who from?"

"The tooth fairy."

Kitch said, "Dad gave me a watch. A fob, old fashioned. It's covered with diamonds. Dad says they're just glass, but I'm going to tell everyone they're diamonds."

In the background, I heard mom say, "Don't do that, Kitch. Someone will try to steal it."

Kitch said, quietly, "That money you loaned me. I'll get it back to you, just like I promised. With interest. I've made some investments. You're a real brother. See you on New Year's Eve. Adios."

Before I could crawl back into bed, the phone rang again. I answered again.

"Johnny? It's Charlie."

"Hi there."

"You sound like you were asleep."

"I just got up from a nap."

"Would you like to come over?"

"To your house?"

"I know. It's Christmas and you're probably doing something else. But—" she cleared her throat. "Things didn't go well for me today and I'd like to visit with someone."

"I'll be right over."

I took a drink of whiskey, whistled for the dog, and put on my coat. As we walked out the door, the phone started ringing again. I let it go.

I parked in Charlie's driveway so I could see into her living room window. She was alone on her couch, picking her nails.

I tooted the horn. She looked up and saw my truck and her face got happy. I stepped out with the dog following behind.

The snow had continued from the morning, but slowly. The wind had stopped blowing, which allowed the flakes to fall straight down, exactly like they should on Christmas.

Charlie opened the door and I was inside a warm, nice place with the dog chasing about and making Charlie laugh.

She touched my eyebrow. "How'd you do that?"

"The horse. I was riding the horse and I stopped paying attention and she walked under a tree limb and it whacked me on the head."

Charlie said, "Were you drunk?"

"No. But the horse was."

"Are you drunk now?"

"Not particularly. Why?"

She ran to the kitchen and returned with a bottle of rum.

We sat on the couch and passed the bottle back and forth. In between swallows, Charlie told her woeful tale. The night of our date—the one she'd canceled—Mr. Goodland had come to town to make amends. After an evening of earnest apologies and promises of fidelity, which included hints of a possible marriage proposal, Charlie was sufficiently moved to allow Mr. G to spend the night. As he was leaving the next morning, Charlie invited him back in a week for Christmas dinner with her family.

But Mr. Goodland had failed to make his appearance. Charlie and her parents held up dinner for two hours, waiting. Maybe he'd suffered an accident, maybe he'd got caught in a blizzard.

Finally, after the food was cold and everybody was half worried and half disgusted, Charlie gave up and tried calling the bastard. He was dumb enough to answer the phone. He told her he'd decided not to make the drive to Keaton on account of he was in love with his new, trampy girlfriend, who may or may not be pregnant with his unfaithful seed.

"He had the gall to ask me to tell my parents Merry Christmas."

"Did you hang up on him?"

"He hung up on me. First, I started yelling at him. I don't even remember what all I said, but at one point, he told me to relax. I told him that I would relax tomorrow, after I burned down his house."

I said, "So we're going to Goodland tonight?"

She took the rum from me. "My parents stuck around for a while and we ate dinner and they tried to cheer me up. I pretended to be happy, otherwise they'd still be here. I didn't want them to have a crummy Christmas just because of my stupid ex-boyfriend."

"You're a thoughtful one, Charlie."

"No I'm not. I talk about myself all the time. How's your Christmas?"

"I've been asleep for most of it. You wouldn't have anything to eat would you?"

"Leftovers okay?"

"I'd eat sawdust if you put some pepper on it."

"Stay put."

She went to the kitchen. I squatted in front of her record console. There was an Elvis Christmas album on the turntable. I started it to playing at a low volume and returned to the couch.

Charlie came out with a plate of mashed taters and turkey, all covered with gravy. I scooped a forkful into my mouth. "It's good."

"Mom did the turkey. I did the mashed potatoes."

She sat next to me while I ate. Elvis sang about a white Christmas. Mr. Goodland was far, far away. It was just the two of us in a warm house.

I said, "Charlie, I want to say something. For the longest time, ever since Kitch went off to college, I've been half stupid. Disoriented, I guess. I'm not out of my mind; I know where I am and what I'm doing, but other than that. You ever see one of those birds that fakes a busted wing in order to trick you into chasing her away from her nest? And then, just as you're about to grab her, she takes off? For so long, my happiness has been that bird. Long enough that I don't even chase after it any more. But not today. This is a day worth chasing."

Charlie's eyes watered up. She passed me the rum bottle. I was grateful that she didn't pat me on the head.

When I cleared my plate, I brought it to the kitchen and started washing it in the sink. Charlie came behind me and put her hand on my arm. "Look out the window."

I did. It was snowing and the sun was dimming. The look of the world hit me. The whole day did. From waking up on Jabez's lap, to getting woke up by Kitch's phone call, to being right where I was.

Charlie put her arm around my waist and I held her wrist. Elvis was singing Silent Night. We stayed like that, looking out the window until the song finished.

I said, "I have to go home and look after the critters."

Charlie got up on her tiptoes and made like she wanted to whisper something at my ear. Then she darted around and kissed my mouth. It was quick, but lasted long enough for me to think that she had some real soft, wet lips. The rum made her tasty. I said, "Or I could stick around for a little while."

She poked me in the belly. "You'd best get home, mister."

I was confused.

She poked me again. "Take care of your critters before the snow gets too deep. Do it quick." She pecked me on the cheek. "And when you're done, come right back here. I'll watch the dog."

I couldn't hardly speak. I ran out that door and leapt in my truck. As I was turning the ignition, Charlie came outside, pulled open my door, and handed me the bottle of rum.

She said, "One for the road."

I took a good drink, then she took a drink and we kissed with the liquor seeping between our mouths.

I tore out of that driveway.

CHAPTER 44

There wasn't any traffic on Highway 36 so I allowed the truck to drift from lane to lane. Night had taken over and the snow was coming down hard. I stomped the brights on and off to see which worked best with my one headlight. Dim was slightly better than bright. Even so, the snowflakes danced in a most distracting fashion. I squinted and drove fast. The highway was flat and I was alone.

I put the radio on the rock station. In between the static, I heard, "City sidewalks, busy sidewalks. . . ." I joined in, with Charlie's rum kiss still warming my lips.

The heater on, the outside world a swirling mystery, Charlie waiting for me back at her place. I felt like I'd swum back into the womb and was ready to be birthed again.

When I got home, I jumped out of the truck without even turning the engine off. I sprinted straight to the stock tank. I axed the ice and threw the broken chunks on the ground. The cattle looked at me like I was a nut. Cattle with snow on their backs. Enjoy the water. I got two rum kisses and I'm going to get more. Then up to the loft to toss out hay. Down the ladder and a quick hello to the chickens. And then straight into the house, grab a bottle of whiskey, and sprint out the door and right back into the pickup all warm and ready for the road.

I drove just as fast as the weather allowed. I wedged the whiskey bottle between my thighs, unscrewed the lid, and drank, making sure to keep one eye on the snowflakes. The headlight was mostly worthless. I had ditches on either side. I didn't need to see where I was going.

"White Christmas" came on the radio. I sang, "I'm dreaming of a Charlie Christmas. We'll get fresh and fool around."

When my dirt road reached Highway 36, I took the corner like a stunt driver. I let the ass of the truck slip to the right and I turned the wheel to the right. As the truck whipped, I twirled the wheel with the heel of my palm and got her straightened out. Then I dropped into first gear and gave her what she had, straight from the hot rod textbook. The wheels spun with a whirl on the slickening road.

I pressed the throttle down and drank my whiskey. The road was mine, the night was mine. I'd be at Charlie's in less than ten minutes.

I worked into the center of the highway, a straight, frosted cake with powdered sugar falling from the sky. The radio station began to drift. I bent down to adjust the dial. Rudolph, save the day. Charlie, wait for me.

When I looked back up and out the windshield, a brightness overcame me. A hundred yards away, in the center of the road, a semi-truck in Christmas glory. Rows of red lights and head-lights headed flat-out in my direction. And me, driving with one worthless headlight.

With no other option, I veered to the right, straight into the ditch. I looked to my left just as the truck passed by. Between the falling snowflakes, I could see the driver's face, lit up by the glow of the lighter he was about to touch to his cigarette. He looked like a nice enough fellow.

And then I was right back in my pickup, shooting off the road. I'd taken a poor angle into the ditch. I heard the corner of the shoulder smack hard into the bottom of the pickup. I tried to steer back onto the road, but my momentum dictated otherwise. I let the truck take itself where it would, which was directly into a barbed wire fence.

When the shaking was over, I assayed my situation. Snow had sprayed up and covered the windshield. I had a bump on my forehead. The whiskey bottle had fallen sideways and was spill-ing on the floor.

I needed to get to Charlie's. I put the truck in reverse and pressed the accelerator. The engine revved, the truck stayed put, and a distressing clatter erupted below my feet.

I went out to investigate. My tire tracks were brown scars in the snow. My front bumper and the grill were dented against a fence post. I looked under the truck and discovered that the drive shaft had fallen off. I found it a few feet behind the truck. I would not be going to Charlie's or anywhere else.

I climbed back in and shut off the radio. The truck stank of whiskey. My guts stank of whiskey. I reached down and picked up the bottle. I drank the few drops that hadn't spilled. I shut off the ignition. I pulled on my mittens, covered my ears with my hat, and stepped outside. It was well below freezing. Icicles were already forming in the wheel wells. The wind maintained a gentle, swirling snow fall. A blurry half-moon glowed grey behind the clouds.

My house was a little over two miles straight north. I walked down the middle of the road, every step wishing Jabez would appear out of the dark and lead me onward. I'd walked in the dark before. I'd lived thru a blizzard, I would live thru Christmas. I stumbled and I stood back up. It was whiskey and rum that had done me in, turned the snowflakes into twins, made the cold feel distant. I would not be spending this evening with Charlie.

I ran north.

Run, fall, stand up. My body sweated. My lungs grew large. Into a rhythm, cross the intersection at the first mile, fingers and toes all full of feeling. You can smoke a cigarette when you get home. Another half mile and the yard light peeked at me, small, between the snowflakes. I ran steady, letting the light guide me. To the ranch, to the driveway, to the front steps. Inside.

I hadn't any choice but to call Charlie.

After several rings, she answered with a sleepy hello.

I said, "It's Johnny."

"Oh. I feel asleep, I think. Where are you?"

"I'm home. I'm okay. I can't come see you tonight. My truck's in the ditch."

"What happened?"

"I went into the ditch. Lost the drive shaft. I gotta—"

"I'll come get you."

"This weather's no good for driving."

"Hell, Johnny."

"I know. I'm sorry. Just go to bed. I'll call you tomorrow. Take care of the dog. You can feed her turkey bones."

She yawned. "You're okay?"

I said, "Just dandy."

"You sound sad."

"Merry Christmas, Charlie. I had fun tonight."

I dressed in my coveralls, put on two pairs of socks, and went outside. As lousy as I felt, I had to get my truck out of that ditch before daylight. I couldn't have the whole town knowing.

I own a tractor, a John Deere R. I use it to haul trailers, pull tree stumps, and tow my truck out of snow banks. It's a diesel, no cab, hates the cold.

I started the pony motor, engaged the diesel, and waited while the engine temperature crept upward. Once we were in the green, I flipped the compression lever and, thank my lucky stars, the diesel roared. I rumbled south toward Highway 36 at ten miles an hour, the snow hissing against the exhaust manifold.

When I got to the truck, I backed the tractor into the ditch and parked hitch to hitch. I tossed the drive shaft into the back of the truck, then chained the truck to the tractor and towed my mess home.

I went to bed without looking at Kitch's magazines and without touching any whiskey.

CHAPTER 45

In the morning, I stayed in bed, searching for a way to blame the accident on something other than the fact that I was a drunk. I was not successful. Charlie Morning had kissed me, and she would have kissed me more if only I'd had the common sense not to take my eyes off the road while driving in a snow storm. Getting piss drunk and driving like an idiot on an evening of such great significance, that's the kind of thing Kitch would do.

I didn't have a drink for breakfast, I did my chores without drinking, and I didn't have a drink as I dialed the telephone and called my neighbor to the south and asked if he could help me fix a busted drive shaft.

Some farmers, they'll act like you're the dumbest person in the world just because you don't own an arc welder. Emmett Williams wasn't like that. He was a good fellow, several years older than me and clever as hell. He lived just a few miles away.

A half hour after I hung up the phone, he drove into the yard and stepped out of his truck, followed by his kid, who was spinning the propeller on a handmade toy airplane.

Emmett pulled a tool box out of the back of his truck. He squatted and looked under my pickup. "Went off-roading, did you?"

"Involuntarily. Every time you turn around there's another blizzard."

Emmett said, "Good news. All you need is a u-joint."

"I don't suppose the Co-op would have one."

"They aren't open today. I might have one."

He pawed thru his tool box until he found the correct part, a metal cross with caps on each end. It fitted easily in his hand. "This ought to be copacetic. You'll need a hammer and a block of wood. Don't forget to put those snap rings on. When you get the u-joint in, poke the shaft into the transmission, then bolt it to the rear end, and you're done. Make sense?"

I nodded.

"I'd stick around, but the in-laws are in town."

"I understand."

Emmett heaved his toolbox back into his truck. "Be careful about those snap rings. They like to pop out."

"Roger that."

He put his hands around his mouth and hollered, "Shakes!" As the kid sprinted toward us, Emmett said to me, "Your hands are trembling."

"I'm working on that."

He was just a couple years older than me, but the look he gave me felt fatherly. Not like my father, like a real father.

He said, "Stay out of the ditches."

Then he got into his pickup, followed by his kid, and drove away.

I started wrestling with the drive shaft. It was cold and my hands wouldn't stay still. It took me fifty-six thousand tries to get those snap rings in place. But I did it and when I was done my truck worked.

For lunch, I ate a peanut butter sandwich and drank four glasses of water. Kitch called as I was washing my plate.

"They're making us play the night after Christmas. Can you believe that?"

"The bastards."

"I sense sarcasm. You don't understand. I haven't slept. I am fucked." There was a noise like a breaking glass. Away from the phone, he yelled, "The broom's next to the fridge!"

I said, "Good party?"

"Good question." Again, away from the phone, he shouted, "Chou-Chou, how was the party?" Back on the phone. "It was a success.

It's the next day and there's a naked French chick running around my house, smashing glasses and shaking her titties at me."

"Did Mom and Dad enjoy their hotel room?"

"Here's a fact. Sleep is overrated. According to Chou-Chou, Leonardo Da Vinci called sleep the little death, but he was a queer Italian so what the fuck does he know. The French, they call *orgasms* the little death." Off the phone. "Hey Chou-Chou! What's that word for orgasm? The little death?"

Back on the phone. "Yeah. It's 'pity-more.' God damn, I love being alive. We're playing the Nets tonight. I'm going to swat Dr. J like a raggedy doll. I'm trying to talk Chou-Chou into sneaking into his hotel room before the game and giving him a little death. And then, afterward, while he's taking his fuck-nap, she'll shave his afro. Get rid of the hair, get rid of the Doctor. Whaddaya think?"

I didn't have any thoughts on the matter.

Kitch said, "You still there? J.R.?" I remained silent. He muttered something about the crummy phone connection and hung up.

I smoked a cigarette. I missed my dog. I don't know what I'd do if I had a naked French woman in my house. I knew what the dog would do. She would ask the naked French woman to let her outside.

I gathered whiskey bottles from the cabinet, from the bedroom, and from the living room. I had more than I expected. Two of them were unopened. Five others were in various states of optimism. Some were a third full, others were three quarters empty. I left the two full bottles on the kitchen table and carried the other five outside, along with my twelve-gauge shotgun, and balanced them atop the fence posts behind the barn.

Water tricked down the icicles warming up in the sun. I breathed deep. I made my hands stop shaking. I fired five quick shots. The reports boomed across the plains. The cattle walked away from me. The twelve-gauge is a powerful gun. It can turn a jack rabbit into a splash of red paint. It turned those bottles into clouds.

I did my afternoon chores and then I took the phone off the

hook and went to bed without dinner. The sun was still up. With the blanket pulled over my face, I tried not to think overly much about the two bottles of whiskey that I'd left sitting on my kitchen table.

Sometime later, I fell asleep.

I was awakened by the sound of my front door opening, followed by quiet footsteps. It was dark now and I couldn't see the hands on my alarm clock. I lay in bed and waited. If my visitor wished to bring me to harm, I hadn't the strength nor the desire to fight back. A clattering set about upon the kitchen floor, then reached the living room carpet and changed to a patter. And then my dog sprinted into my bedroom, leapt onto my bed, and began licking my chin.

Charlie's voice sounded from the kitchen. "Johnny, you back there?"

She walked into my room and turned on the light. When she saw me, pity came into her eyes. Then she became bright again. She said, "You realize it's only seven o'clock. Hardly the time to go to bed."

"I believe I have a touch of the flu."

"I figured you'd be hungover, but a flu's even better. I'll fix you something to eat. I brought orange juice, cigarettes, and chicken noodle soup."

"I'm not hungry."

"You should eat. I'll be right back."

She went to the kitchen. I quickly reached under the mattress to make sure Kitch's dirty magazines were still in place and out of sight. They were. Then I grabbed an undershirt from the floor and pulled it on. I placed my pillow against the headboard and sat up. Ten minutes later, Charlie returned carrying a tray with a bowl of soup and a glass of orange juice. She put the tray on my lap. I dipped the spoon into the soup. As I brought it toward my mouth, my hand shook so that the soup spilled out.

Charlie said, "Where's your thermostat?"

"Next to the bathroom door."

She left and came back a minute later. "No wonder you're

shivering. You had it at sixty-two degrees. I turned it up to seventy. Also, your phone was off the hook, which explains why I got a busy signal when I called to tell you I was coming over."

The thermostat clicked and the furnace turned on.

I lifted the orange juice to my mouth without any major spills. Charlie started idly wandering around my room. She poked her toe thru piles of clothes. She stood on her tiptoes and regarded the one photo I had hanging from the wall: me and Kitch on a family trip to the mountains when we were kids. We're both dressed like little cowboys, in boots, hats, jeans, pearl button shirts. Kitch is trying to climb a boulder, I'm standing behind, ready to catch him. Mom and Dad are out of the frame.

Charlie said, "Cute kids," then migrated to my dresser. Atop it was my bowl of unsorted arrowheads. It was a pretty big bowl, more like a salad dish. Charlie was impressed. She ran her finger over the top, letting the arrowheads clatter against one another. "Did you find all these?"

"That's some of them."

"There's more?"

"Look in that top drawer."

It required some effort, but she got it open. She took a minute to appreciate what a drawer full of arrowheads looked like, then she said, "You found all these?"

I said, "Those are just the arrowheads, the good ones. There's more stuff in the other drawers."

She closed the top drawer and opened the next one down. It was only halfway full.

I said, "Those are the spear points. There aren't as many of those."

Charlie picked out a four-inch point, held it in front of her eyes. "Did somebody actually use this thing?"

"Probably. They didn't make it just so it could sit in my dresser."

"What did they use it for?"

"Tie it to a stick and throw it. Buffalo. Bears. People. Shoot, there might have been saber-tooth tigers out here. I've never studied this stuff. You can keep that if you want. I have plenty."

She fake-jabbed it toward me. "Are you sure? I'm deadly."

"It's your Christmas present."

"I didn't get you anything."

I spooned some soup into my mouth. "It all balances out. You brought me food and orange juice. That's plenty. You can look in the other drawers. They aren't as interesting."

She opened them up. One contained stone tools. Scrapers and hammers. The other was nothing but broken bits of arrowheads and spear points.

Charlie said, "How do you find them?"

"There's clues. Like, if there's wild gourds growing, that means Indians lived there. Mostly, though, I just look for a flat spot where the wind blows."

"You must do a lot of looking."

"I only go out when I'm in a bad mood. I get on my horse and ride and stare at the ground."

Her eyes watered for a minute. I wasn't trying to get her to pity me. She slid the spear point into her pocket and, with a grunt, she shoved the last of the drawers shut. "You must be an uncommonly unhappy person."

Charlie sat on the edge of my bed with the dog in her lap and watched me eat. When I swallowed the last of the soup, I moved the tray to my night stand.

Charlie said, "I noticed those two nice bottles of whiskey in the kitchen. Would you like me to fix you a drink?"

"I've decided to stay away from liquor for the time being."

She tilted her head at me. "I'm beginning to think that you don't have the flu."

"Affirmative."

"What's it like, this non-flu?"

"I'd say it's like a hangover, but a good deal worse."

"So, in plain words, you've decided to stop drinking because you drove your truck into the ditch last night."

"That is the case."

"It could have happened to anyone."

"If I hadn't been drunk, I would not have gone in the ditch. I'm going to make sure nothing like that ever happens again."

She scrunched her eyebrows together. "You ever done this before?"

"Stopped drinking? Never felt the need."

"I can stay here tonight. I mean, I'd sleep on the couch. I could bring you anything if you got to feeling bad. Water and blankets."

"I think I need to wait this out by myself."

"You shouldn't be alone."

"I'll be fine, Charlie. You don't have to worry about me. It just takes a few days. I appreciate you coming over."

She stood up and lifted the tray from my night stand. She said, "What are those?"

"Which?"

"Those tickets." She put the tray on the floor. The dog hurried over to slurp out of the soup bowl. Charlie picked up the tickets. "New Year's Eve? You're going to see your brother play on New Year's Eve and you didn't tell me?"

"I'm not going."

"Of course you are."

"I don't want to drive all the way to Denver just to watch Kitch play a stupid basketball game."

"It's not just a stupid game. It's a basketball game in McNichols Arena. And you have free tickets."

"Charlie, I don't feel too hot right now."

"I know, but—" The phone rang. She said, "You want me to get that?"

"Let it ring."

We stared at each other for a solid minute while the phone continued to sound. Eventually, she said, "I'm going to answer it." She walked out of the room. I heard her lift the receiver.

"Yes. . . . He's not available. Can I take a message. . . ? Who's calling. . . ? That's none of your bee's wax. . . . Yeah. Whatever. I'll tell him. . . . And you do the same."

She came back to my room. "He wouldn't tell me his name. He wanted me to ask you if you had any luck convincing Kitch of the seriousness of the situation. He sounded like an asshole. What's your brother got himself into?"

"I don't know. Something stupid."

"I'm serious, Johnny. What's going on?"

"I really don't know, Charlie. I think it might be gambling. That guy's called me a few times. He doesn't say anything except that I'm supposed to tell Kitch to keep his promises. It's just some dumb mess Kitch has got himself into and I'm not going to get sucked into it any more than I already have."

"So you're already sucked in?"

"I gave four hundred dollars to a couple of guys from Denver. Kitch said it was for a gambling debt. He says he'll pay me back if I go to the game next week."

"Then you ought to go to the game."

"There's no point. Kitch isn't going to pay me back. If he ever had the money, he's spent it already."

"That's all the more reason to go. You need to see what he's mixed up in."

"Whatever it is, he'll talk his way out of it. That's what Kitch Riles does."

"He's your brother, Johnny Riles. I don't care how much of a dope he is and I don't care how sick you are of everybody reminding you of how special he is, you need to go to that game. That guy on the phone sounded like he was in the mob or something. You were basically Kitch's father for a whole year and now you don't even care that he's got the mob after him?"

"What day is it? What's the date today?"

"Friday. The day after Christmas."

I counted on my fingers. "I'll make you a deal. If you promise to leave me be for just a few days while I get myself together, I promise I'll go to the game. And if you meet me here at noon on Wednesday—that's New Year's Eve, the day of the game—I'll bring you to the game with me."

"What about Charlotte?"

"Who's Charlotte?"

"Your dog. I named her last night. Turns out she likes having a name." She made a pouty face at the dog. "Don't you, Charlotte?" The dog wagged her tail.

"I don't generally name my animals."

"That's because you're weird, Johnny."

"I'd be grateful if you could take her home and look after her until Wednesday."

"I can do that. What about your chores?"

"The activity will be good for me."

"The whiskey bottles in the kitchen. Do you want me to get rid of them for you?"

"I want them to stay there."

"The cowboy way. Look temptation in the eye."

"Something like that."

"You're foolish, trying to do this on your own." She bent down and kissed me right on the lips. "But I'm proud of you."

I said, "You won't come by before Wednesday?"

"I won't come by. I won't call. I'll let you be all alone in your lonesomeness. Although, I would like to state for the record that I think you're being a dope."

She patted her pocket. "Thanks for the spearhead." Then she scooped up the dog and I was alone.

CHAPTER 46

The next morning, I lay in bed and listened to the water melting off the roof. My skin felt like it was no longer attached to my body. I could feel the air flowing over my muscles. My bones were shrinking. It had been two days, almost, since my last drink.

The phone rang and continued to ring as I got out of bed, put on my warm clothes, gathered up my whiskey bottles, did the chores, and saddled up the roan.

I took the horse and the two bottles of whiskey across the prairie and across Old Stinkum.

It was tedious, my life. The same things over and over again. I didn't want the same things over and over. I wanted Kitch to stop being Kitch. I wanted to live with someone who could drink coffee with me in the morning and tickle my chin at night. I wanted to stay between the ditches.

I removed the mitten from my left hand and gave an empty finger stump to the sky. It was a full moon night. Was it? It wasn't. There was no moon. It was still daytime.

My cold-hit, shrunken-bones body. My fever shakes. My need for pleasure. Pleasure was clanking against pleasure in the saddlebags.

The horse brought me to the hatch. I climbed down and kicked with my heel. I hollered out loud. There was no Jabez. I sat on the ground, looked at my thumbs, and waited.

I was struck on the cheek by a snowball. Jabez stood down the hill from me, blowing into her bare hands. She had on a long coat that fluttered in the wind. She walked straight to my horse and extracted a bottle of whiskey from one of the saddlebags. In a moment, the bottle was two inches emptier. She handed it to me. I placed it upon the ground in front of where I sat.

I said, "Would it be okay if I spent some time in your tunnels? I'm trying to give up the drink."

She put a hand on my shoulder and then used me as a support as she bent down to pick up the whiskey bottle. "More for me."

Jabez hadn't yet slaughtered her Christmas chicken. The bird followed her, clucking as Jabez situated me in the big room, the room with the paintings and the giant bones. In the center of the floor, she made me a nest out of some old, stiff blankets next to which she placed a lantern, a clay jug full of water, and a bucket for anything that might leak out of me.

I said, "This will do fine."

"Where's your dog?"

"She's with Charlie."

"The woman with a man's name. Please excuse me. I'm going to go have a drink."

I said, "If I'm not better by tomorrow morning, can you check on the ranch? All you have to do is feed the cattle and the chickens and make sure they have water. And gather the eggs."

"I've watched you do it plenty of times."

"You'll do it, then?"

"What if you should die while you're here?"

"Then the ranch is yours."

"I'll see to it that you don't die."

"I feel like I may."

"I hear that's part of the experience."

She left me, followed by the chicken. I lay on my back and stared at the bones buried in the walls and the paintings around them. I was glad to be here. It was easier in the caves than in my bedroom. I closed my eyes. My blood moved fast and then slow, like it was a little dog running alongside a horse. I heard the breath of the tunnels. I began moaning my favorite song. One line, I repeated over and over.

The ocean is a desert with its life underground.
The ocean is a desert with its life underground.
The ocean is a desert with its life underground.
The ocean is a desert with its life underground.
The ocean is a desert with its life underground.
The ocean is a desert with its life underground.
The ocean is a desert with its life underground.
The ocean is a desert with its life underground.
The ocean is a desert with its life underground.
The ocean is a desert with its life underground.
The ocean is a desert with its life underground.
The ocean is a desert with its life underground.
The ocean is a desert with its life underground.
The ocean is a desert with its life underground.
The ocean is a desert with its life underground.
The ocean is a desert with its life underground.
The ocean is a desert with its life underground.
The ocean is a desert with its life underground.
The ocean is a desert with its life underground.
The ocean is a desert with its life underground.
The ocean is a desert with its life underground.
The ocean is a desert with its life underground.
The ocean is a desert with its life underground.
The ocean is a desert with its life underground.
The ocean is a desert with its life underground.
The ocean is a desert with its life underground.
The ocean is a desert with its life underground.
The ocean is a desert with its life underground.
The ocean is a desert with its life underground.
The ocean is a desert with its life underground.
The ocean is a desert with its life underground.
The ocean is a desert with its life underground.
The ocean is a desert with its life underground.
The ocean is a desert with its life underground.
The ocean is a desert with its life underground.
The ocean is a desert with its life underground.
The ocean is a desert with its life underground.

CHAPTER 47

I awoke, dry throat, tongue crusted up. I reached for the jug and poured water at my mouth. Much of it ended up on my shirt. I stared about. In the lantern light, the walls became rubbery. The mammoth skull grew and shrunk. The elk slid up the wall. The paintings blistered and bubbled and dripped. I closed my eyes.

I woke to the sound of the cave's breath. The lantern had burned out. I needed to pee but I could not see to find my way to the piss-bucket. I spoke Jabez's name. I shouted her name. I screamed her name. She did not appear.

I slid out of the blankets, out of my underdrawers, and felt for the bucket. I crawled away from my bed. The room had expanded. Time had expanded. I held my breath for an hour. Stubble grew on my chin. The walls didn't exist. I tried to stand but grew wobbly and fell right back to my hands and knees. I peed that way, splattering on the floor, on my thighs. The urine flowed downhill around my hands and toward the center of the room, toward my bed.

I crawled for ages trying to find my bed again. I crawled straight ahead until the walls reappeared. The room had shrunk. The ceiling brushed against my shoulders. I crawled forward and down into the dark. I heard the mammoth and the elk murmuring behind me. They could not follow in this place.

Dim lights shone from the walls, like fireflies. They wandered along the stone, forming into shape of hands, always small. The room was a tunnel and I followed it, with these pricks of light glowing all around me, and piss drying on my leg hair.

The walls contracted and expanded like they were breathing. They squeezed me tight and then they let me go. When they allowed, I crawled forward. When they shrunk, I waited.

Then they opened up altogether and I was in a tiny, round room with glowing pin pricks in the walls, like a sky of stars. Before me, a dark figure sat up and shook itself. Long hair flapped. A blackness extended and pressed a wet kiss against my chest. It was a baby, this figure. The baby kissed me with its trunk. It was like being touched by an egg yolk. The saliva smelled of milk. The scent brought me to the day I found Excal under the rock and I ran home to show the rusted blade to Kitch. That day had been a proud one, as a big brother, as a boy who lifted rocks. The trunk withdrew and the pin lights dimmed.

I retreated, crawling backwards, past the breathing walls, into the expansion of the room, and still backwards until I found my blankets and fell into sleep.

I awoke to Jabez staring at me, lantern in hand.

I said, "Do you have whiskey?"

"The whiskey's mine. You drink this." She handed me her bowl. "It's soup. There's some rabbit in it."

The soup was salty and good, with bits of tendon floating. I drank the entire bowl and set it on the ground.

She said, "I filled your lamp with oil. And there's matches." She sniffed and wrinkled her nose. "I brought fresh bedding."

She shone the lamp toward a pile of blankets on the floor. I recognized them from my bed at home.

I said, "How long has it been?"

"A couple of days. Your cattle are fed and the chickens are happy. Get up. You can't sleep in your own pee."

I did as told. I was still undressed. Her eyes passed over me with a nurse's indifference. She scooped up the pissed-on blankets. "I might bring these to your house and wash them."

"Wash anything you want."

She left me alone.

I slept and awoke, staying near my nest, making sure to keep the piss bucket close. Jabez brought soup and carried my waste away in the bucket. I did not attempt to crawl any more. When I was awake and when the lamp was on, I stared about at the walls of the big room.

The elk was not popular with the other animals and so he was my favorite. He moved with pride, even as his antlers scraped against the walls of the cave. Better to be a clumsy elk than to be, for one second, a saber-tooth tiger. The tiger can barely open his mouth. But his teeth are knives so people respect him. Same with the mammoth, famous because of his teeth and his fur, and because he can shit a hundred pounds at a time.

I asked the elk about the baby hands, the prints in the tunnel. He gave me various answers. "They were small people." "You are inventing the baby hands." "They were made by the fastest man in the world."

I asked him about the baby mammoth. He said, "There is no baby mammoth." "There were once two baby mammoths."

I said, "Why is he in that room? Who put him there?"

"The mammoth is a female." "She was not put there; she lives there." "Ba-boom, ba-boom." "Who pulled the trigger?" "You ought to fuck somebody, Johnny Riles."

The elk was not helpful.

I slept and awoke and again Jabez brought soup. When I finished it, she said, "You're better," and then she left.

With this, I understood that she expected me to climb out of my nest and make something of myself. I stood, feeling weak, but tall. I peed one last time into the bucket. Then I told the elk goodbye. He didn't respond. I suppose that meant I was better.

When I walked into the main room, Jabez was sitting on her wooden chair with the chicken on her lap.

She said, "Morning."

"How long have I been down here?"

"Four nights."

I twisted my neck back and forth, stretched my arms wide. "Sun been up a while?"

"It's almost noon."

"I gotta get home."

"You got an appointment or something?"

"Sort of. I'm going to Denver tonight, to see my brother play a basketball game."

She stared at me. "You going to see your brother in Denver, just a few hours after pissing all over yourself in a cave full of dead animals."

"Correct."

"The brother you don't particularly care for."

"There's more to it than that."

She thought for a moment, then she said, "You're going on a date. You're bringing that girlfriend of yours."

"Charlie's not my girlfriend. But, yes, she's coming along."

"Then I expect you'll need someone to do your chores tonight and tomorrow."

I said, "We're coming back tonight."

"Get a hotel and have yourself a good look at that girl's nipples. I'll take care of the animals."

"Even though you think I shouldn't go at all."

Jabez said, "Johnny, I'm going to assume that you've never been with a woman before."

"I don't answer questions of that nature."

"It was more of an observation than a question. You've just gone four whole days without a drop of liquor for the first time in who knows when. You're feeling hale and hearty and more than a little horny. It's New Year's Eve and for once in your life you've got someone to kiss at the stroke of midnight. Stay in a hotel."

The chicken clucked softly.

I said to Jabez, "Are you ever going to eat that thing?"

"I don't think so."

"She'll give you good eggs for a long time."

"Just be smart, Johnny. What happened to you in there," Jabez pointed to the dark end of the cave, "it didn't turn you into a super hero, it didn't empty those animals out of that ark in your brain. All it did was help you not drink for four days."

I gave her a quick nod to let her know I'd heard what she said and then I started toward the exit.

When I was halfway up the tunnel, Jabez shouted after me, "Your bull has a blind eye."

I shouted back, "I know. It's from the pink."

Jabez said, "He walks circles, day and night."

PART III

SANDMAN

CHAPTER 48

Charlie was sitting at my front step when the roan carried me into the yard. The winter sun shone on her real nice, with her sunglasses and her big white teeth smiling from a lipstick mouth. A suitcase was balanced atop her knees.

She said, "You're looking well, Johnny. Been hunting arrowheads?"

"I figured I ought to try it when I'm in a good mood for once. Didn't find any. Don't care. Nothing clears my head like an hour on a horse."

"And how is your head?"

I said, "I'm ready for the world."

She patted her suitcase. "Me, too. And I don't have to work tomorrow."

"Neither do I. And I got someone to watch the animals while I'm away."

"Emmett Williams?"

"Good guess."

"Being as he's your neighbor." She slapped her knee and said, "Let's get cracking. Put your horse away, change your clothes, and let's go."

"May I bathe first?"

"Hurry."

Charlie gave a whistle and the dog sprinted out from the windbreak with a dead toad dangling from its jaws.

The first thing I did when I went into the house was to go to the kitchen, find my list of things to do, and cross off item number four:

~~No more whiskey.~~

I drove toward Denver with Charlie sitting next to me with the dog on her lap. The snowy plains stretched out to the horizon. The truck's heater sent straw-smelling air into the cab. I smoked cigarettes, ashing out the vent window. I felt more normal than I had in a long time. I very much wanted to tell Charlie where I'd been for the last few days, what I'd seen. I ached to tell her that the experience had cleaned up my mind and made me ready for anything we might encounter this evening. I kept my mouth shut; I wasn't sure that part was entirely true.

For no good reason, Charlie reached across the seat and kissed me on the cheek. The poodle, who had been asleep, looked up and then closed its eyes again.

Traffic picked up after 36 merged onto I-70. Charlie watched behind and told me when it was okay to change lanes. As we passed the dog food factory on the way into town, the poodle put her paws on the dashboard. She could smell the horsemeat.

At the mousetrap, we took I-25 south and McNichols Arena came into view. Home of the Nuggets, bigger than life, white and shiny and new in the midst of Denver's haze. Across the street from the arena there was a circular hotel, ten stories tall. At the very top was a sign: "Mile Sky Inn."

Charlie said, "I wonder if that top floor rotates."

I veered toward the exit. I said, "Let's find out."

Charlie said, "We can't stay there. It'll cost a million dollars."

I said, "Hell. It's New Year's Eve."

In the lobby, at the desk, the lady who checked us in saw my license and said, "Any relation to Kitch Riles?"

Charlie answered for me, "Yes, ma'am. This here is Kitch's brother."

On account of my famous sibling, we earned a twenty percent discount and a room on the second-to-top floor.

Two beds. No pets allowed. We sneaked the dog thru a side entrance. She whimpered as we rode the elevator. When we entered the room, Charlie put her on the floor. She sniffed around and then crawled under one of the beds.

Charlie said, "Somebody's not a fan of fancy hotels."

I opened the curtains and Charlie and I admired the city, the football stadium, and the mountains, snow-white and ready to crumble at any minute. I had traveled a great distance since waking up in a room full of dead animals. I recalled Jabez's lecture. Don't worry, you old tramp. I'm ready for whatever the night can show me.

I said, "I'm fond of you, Charlie Morning."

I hugged her shoulders, then I kissed her on the neck. She squirmed away, giggling. I caught up to her on the other side of the room, in front of the dressing mirror. We held hands and looked at ourselves. Two country folk in the nicest room in the roundest hotel in Denver.

Charlie said, "We're a hell of a couple."

"Couple of what?"

"I dunno, Johnny, but I'm hungry as hell."

According to a brochure next to the telephone, the floor above us was a restaurant and, naturally, that's where we decided to eat. The dog was still under the bed when we left the room.

We rode the elevator up to the restaurant, which didn't spin after all. We got a table near the window. As night took over, the city lit up. Skyscrapers, stoplights, headlights, and tail lights.

The waiter asked if we wanted wine. We ordered pop instead.

Charlie said, "For the game, do we have good seats?"

I reached into my shirt pocket and pulled out the tickets. We looked at them and pondered what the section, row, and seat numbers meant.

I said, "Do you think I'll actually get close enough to talk to him?"

"You just need to find someone in charge and tell 'em you're Kitch's brother." She looked at her watch. "Let's go. The game starts in half an hour."

"What's to hurry about? The food's good and I like talking to you."

Charlie smiled at this.

The restaurant had begun to fill up with people who all looked rich as hell. Women with sparkling dresses, men with silver medallions around their necks. They sat upright at their tables and drank wine. Charlie and I sat across from one another and drank our soda pops, me dressed in my pearl-button shirt and Sunday jeans, Charlie in a yellow blouse and a pair of polyester slacks.

We were two hicks in a fancy restaurant. Nobody noticed us.

After dinner, we went back to our room, took a few moments to pet the dog, and then headed out for the stadium.

I tried to keep a slow pace, but Charlie tugged my hand. She said, "If you don't hurry, we'll miss the whole game."

We walked down the sidewalk and crossed a couple of streets. On the corners were Mexicans selling burritos and blacks trying to scalp tickets. The arena grew larger and larger and then we were in a short line of fellow latecomers in front of the main doors. As we shuffled ahead, Charlie said, "Who do you want to win?"

I thought for a moment and said, "It don't matter. It's like cheering for the weather. It's gonna happen whether I want it to or not."

"You want the Colonels to win."

"I want my brother to be smart. That's all."

"Good enough."

The line drew us to a lady who tore our tickets in half and told us to enjoy the game.

Charlie took my hand and pulled me under an archway and into the main arena.

CHAPTER 49

Never in our lives had either one of us been in such an enormous room. I had trouble seeing across to the bleachers on the other side. The ceiling was so far away, it might as well have had clouds hovering.

Tomorrow would be 1976, and the folks at McNichols Arena intended for us to be aware of the bicentennial nature of things. They'd hung Old Glory from every rafter, on every wall. And, this being the Centennial State, there were Colorado flags hanging wherever the Stars and Stripes weren't. A surprising number of fans—men and women both—were dressed like Uncle Sam, with striped britches and cotton beards.

We stood at the edge of this great bowl, getting jostled as people squirreled around us. Dads and kids, grandpas and dads. More women than I expected. Lots of wild outfits. Bright plaid, bell bottoms, shoes with heels that looked like they'd break an ankle. The women had eye makeup. The men had paisley shirts. I'd seen pictures, but this was something else, a whole city dressed like clowns.

An usher asked for our tickets and pointed upwards.

Our seats were right at half court, at the very top row. As we stuffed our coats under our seats, Charlie said, "On the bright side, if one of us takes a tumble, there's plenty of people to cushion the fall."

The building shuddered with a burst of applause and, for the first time since we'd entered the arena, I directed my eyes to the action on the court, which was so far away it seemed almost incidental.

It took me a moment to spot Kitch. He was the second-tallest white man on the court. He had his hands on his hips and, from where I sat, it looked like he was breathing heavy.

The game was halfway thru the first quarter. The Nuggets led, twenty-one to fifteen.

Kitch's Colonels inbounded the ball and promptly missed a basket. The Nuggets rebounded and ran the ball to their end of the court. Bobby Flowers, the Nuggets' superstar rookie, faked a jump shot and then drove hard and fast. He leaped from just outside the key and Kitch followed, stretching his hand for a backside block. Ignoring Kitch, Bobby cradled the ball in his right arm and swung. At the point when a normal human would have fallen back to the floor, he just kept climbing. He hovered in midair for half a second and calmly threw the ball thru the hoop. He landed on the ground out of balance, dancing and pirouetting between the legs of the giants around him. The fans loved it. The man was one of the shortest people on the floor; he had no business jumping that high. The game ceased to be incidental.

The Colonels missed their next shot. Ray Eiffel, the Nuggets' lumbering sharpshooter caught the outlet pass and drove toward the lane and attempted a seven-footer. Kitch was waiting for him and slammed the ball into his forehead.

Foul. Eiffel sank the free throws.

And back and forth.

Every score, every turnover, every foul, made the crowd shout and stomp like hail on a zinc roof. The Nuggets sank shot after shot. The Colonels could not keep up.

Kitch earned his second foul on a reach-in and took a seat on the bench. The Colonels played better without him. On consecutive possessions, their guards fed Clovis Fletcher, their seven-two giant, for patented two-hand power slams, the second of them so menacing that the Denver crowd said, "Oooh!" in spite of themselves.

Charlie said to me, "I've never seen anything like this."

I agreed.

At the end of the first quarter, the Nuggets led thirty-eight to thirty-five. Kitch had two fouls and zero points.

The Nuggets put in their short players to start the second quarter. They allowed Bobby Flowers to jump center against Clovis. It looked ridiculous. Their skinny kid versus our Kentucky giant. Flowers flew straight up and tipped the ball to his point guard, who drove the lane and scooped in a layup.

The Nuggets' small lineup zipped around Clovis, making him look slow and confused. Hoping to match the Nuggets for size, the Colonels replaced Clovis with my brother. Kitch being Kitch, he shot the ball every time it touched his hands. He missed several but then he made one. And then another. He got fouled and made his free throws. He was solid for a few minutes, then he picked up a charging foul and went right back to the bench.

The Nuggets dominated the rest of the quarter. By the time the clock buzzed for the end of the half, the Colonels were getting creamed, sixty-seven to fifty-one. Kitch had thirteen points, but he'd missed twice as many baskets as he'd made.

As the players walked off the court, Kitch held his hands behind his head. Kitch Riles, the rising star of Strattford County, the darling of Dorsey. Sloppy and sucking air.

As the fans emptied the stands for halftime piss breaks and hot-dog runs, I said to Charlie, "I need a cigarette."

Charlie said, "I'll stay put if that's all right." She pointed to a man in a striped shirt who was selling popcorn several rows below. "I've had my eye on him ever since we sat down. Smoke your cigarette and when you come back I'll have some popcorn for you."

Walking down the stairway, I considered going straight to the locker room and telling Kitch to get off his ass and start playing like this game meant something. I abandoned that idea immediately once I reached the walking-around area, the hallway that wraps around the second level of the arena. Women in short skirts, drunk men with big bellies, kids with cotton candy stuck in their hair, everyone hooting, hollering, walking fast and without regard for common decency.

I saw a sign for a men's room and eased myself in that direction. Inside, the floor was covered with piss and everyone was miming Bobby Flowers' dunks with the way they tossed their paper towels in the trash can.

I did my business and got out of there.

Just outside the john, I saw a roped-off smoking section. A hundred people packed in like cattle, puffing and wheezing. I couldn't find the entrance so I ducked under the rope and lit up. Being packed into a pen like that with a mess of city people didn't exactly help me relax. I smoked quick and headed back toward Charlie.

By the time I arrived, a black woman had taken my seat. She was wearing the tightest, greenest dress I'd ever seen. It was squeezing hard to keep all her parts from flying out. Her sandals were golden lace-ups like a Roman would wear. She wore blue make-up on her eyes, her hair was fluffy, and she was sharing Charlie's popcorn.

When Charlie saw me she said, "He survived!" She put her hand on the shoulder of the black woman. "This here is Suzanne. She's the girl from the dog pound. She's where your poodle came from."

Suzanne smiled at me. "You look just like your brother."

I said, "He's taller."

Suzanne shook my hand. I'd never touched a colored person before. Her skin was soft.

She said, "Charlie tells me you and Prance are getting along."

I said, "Prance?"

Charlie said, "We call her Charlotte."

Suzanne laughed. "She? You're a cowboy, Johnny Riles. Can't you tell a boy from a girl?"

I said, "I can tell that she doesn't have any balls."

Suzanne said, "That's because they've been removed."

Charlie patted my back. "It's okay, Johnny. You can still love him even if he isn't a girl."

Suzanne slapped five with Charlie. They laughed the way women do when they're teasing a man.

The buzzer sounded on the game clock.

Suzanne stood, "I gotta head back to my seat. I'm sorry Kitch stuck you up here." She turned to me. "If it makes you feel any better, these are the same tickets he got your parents."

Charlie said, "Thanks for visiting."

Suzanne hugged Charlie. "See you at the party."

After Suzanne left, I said, "What party?"

"There's a party afterward, for both teams. Guess where?"

I shrugged. The idea of a New Year's party didn't appeal to me one bit.

Charlie said, "In our hotel. Same place we ate dinner. Can you believe it? You can see Kitch tonight without having to talk your way into the locker room."

"I don't know if I should be going to any parties."

"If you're not comfortable, you can always bring him back to our room for a quiet conversation."

Charlie really wanted to go, I could tell. Crowds didn't bug her like they do me. And she hadn't spent four days in a cave trying not to drink.

I said I'd think about it.

CHAPTER 50

Kitch started the second half as a whole different player. He had energy and smarts. On offense, he passed the ball to his teammates for easy baskets. On defense, he moved his feet and helped out rather than lunging at every pass and swinging for every shot. Coach Brown took him away from defending Bobby Flowers and put him on the Nuggets' small forward. Now Kitch could help out on Flowers or Eiffel without having to fight either of them one-on-one.

It worked. Flowers and Eiffel still earned most of the Nuggets points, but more often than before, they had to pass it back out and watch one of their teammates miss a jumper.

With four minutes to go in the third quarter, Kitch swished a baseline jumper that cut the lead to nine. After the basket, he pointed right at Charlie and me and tipped an imaginary cowboy hat. Charlie shouted Kitch's name.

I said, "He can't hear you." But I was proud.

At the end of the third quarter, the score was Nuggets ninety-nine, Colonels ninety-three. I clapped hard as the players gathered around their coaches for the quarter break.

Charlie squeezed up next to me.

I said, "Flowers is going to get tired. Nobody that small can jump that high for an entire game."

"How many points do you think Kitch has?"

"Twenty one. And eight rebounds and seven assists."

Charlie looked at me. "You're into this."

I smiled at her. A real, honest to ornery smile.

She said, "Johnny Riles is having a good time."

I said, "Charlie Morning is pretty as hell."

She gave me a kiss on the lips. She lingered there for a long moment.

On the first play of the fourth quarter, Kitch chased down a loose ball and stood dribbling in front of the Colonels' bench. He said something to his coach, who gave him a thumbs-up. Kitch dribbled between his legs and tore off. He zipped past four Nuggets and leapt right at their skinny forward. In mid-air, he presented the ball with his left hand. Before the Nuggets could knock it away, Kitch brought it down and, still sailing, switched the ball to his right hand and slipped in a finger roll right at the front of the rim. It was the prettiest play I'd ever seen in my life. I jumped out of my chair and whooped and hollered. Charlie was right with me. She stole my hat and waved it around.

Kitch sprinted down the floor and intercepted a pass from the Nuggets' backup point guard. Kitch spun on his heel and chucked the ball sixty feet to Clovis, who was all alone under the Colonels' basket. Clovis stuffed the ball so hard it practically tore the rim off the backboard.

We were within two. I jumped and stomped and pumped my arms. Charlie was screaming.

Kitch stole Denver's inbound pass just outside the three-point line. Bobby Flowers leapt at him. Kitch shot the ball over his fingertips. It circled the rim and slipped thru the net. Tie game.

I shouted, "That's my baby brother!" Charlie hugged me and we jumped and jumped. This was the ABA. This was wild, pure basketball. That was my brother.

As the final quarter progressed, Bobby Flowers jumped higher and dunked harder than ever, and Kitch kept right up with him. It seemed like nobody missed a shot for the next nine minutes. Dunks and three pointers. Alley oops. The lead jumped from one team to the next as the score ratcheted higher and higher.

Whenever there was a break, Kitch would put his hands on his knees and look like he was about to die. But when the game resumed, he went right back into it. He'd scored twenty-five points in the first ten minutes of the fourth quarter, putting him at forty-six for the game. It was the work of an All-Star.

With two minutes to go, Kitch dodged and weaved and sank a jump shot over Eiffel to put the Colonels up by two.

On the other end of the court, Bobby Flowers wove and drove for a lay-up. No dunks here. The ball went in, but it lacked the excitement of his earlier baskets. Bobby Flowers was finally getting tired.

The Colonels' point guard made a wide-open jumper to bring their lead back to two.

With the exception of Kitch, the players on both teams were now dragging. But they kept pushing the ball, refusing to walk as long as running was an option.

Eiffel hit a three-pointer, putting the Nuggets ahead by one. The crowd screamed in joy and demanded defense, defense, defense.

While the Nuggets celebrated the return of the lead, Kitch darted down the court to slam a dunk that passed thru the hoop, bounced off the floor, and collided against the bottom of the backboard. Kitch landed, pounding his chest, howling like a mighty beast. If I'd been counting right, my brother had scored fifty points in a professional basketball game. His team led 137 to 136 with forty-six seconds remaining.

On the Nuggets' inbound, Clovis tipped the ball straight to Kitch at the top of the key. Three Denver Nuggets ran at Kitch, leaving one of his teammates, Robin MacAlaster, unguarded behind the three-point line.

I could see Kitch hesitate. He was playing like a monster. He knew and I knew that he could attack those three Nuggets and probably score. But his teammate had a better shot.

Kitch made the pass.

MacAlaster caught the ball and sent it toward the basket. If it went in, we'd be up by four, 140 to 136. It was damned unlikely that the Nuggets would make up those four points in forty seconds.

The ball drew a perfect arc. The crowd silently begged it to miss. I knew it would go in.

It hesitated at its peak and then dove toward the hoop.

Down, down, and then a *thunk* and everything stopped.

The ball had neither made nor missed. It had wedged itself between the rim and the backboard. The players, the crowd, we all stared at it, as if it were a raindrop that had changed its mind right before it struck the earth.

In this game, where the pace had moved so quickly for so long, it was downright shocking. The refs and players blinked their eyes.

Clovis reached up and, with a little hop, plucked the ball out of its perch. He handed it to one of the officials. The refs had a brief conference and announced that there would be a jump ball. Clovis Fletcher and Bobby Flowers took their places on opposite sides of the free-throw line. But before the ref could toss the ball, the Colonels' coach waved Clovis away and motioned for Kitch to take the jump.

Clovis refused to move. The coach stomped his feet and shouted. Clovis, shaking his head, stepped aside for Kitch.

The ref tossed the ball up. There was a pause as both Kitch and Bobby waited for the perfect moment to leap. Kitch jumped first and he jumped higher than I thought possible. I could have walked underneath without smelling his feet. At the top of his leap, just as he was winding up to swat the ball, Bobby snuck in and gently tapped it to his teammate, Ray Eiffel. The big-legged beast crossed half-court, made sure his feet were behind the three-point line, and forced the ugliest line drive I'd ever seen. It clunked off the back of the rim, flew straight up and then dropped neatly thru the net, putting the Nuggets ahead 139 to 137.

The arena got so loud I had to put my hands over my ears.

With only twenty-two seconds left, the Colonels absolutely had to score. Rollie Petit fed Kitch on the wing for a wide-open jumper. Bobby Flowers sprinted at him with both arms raised. Once again, Kitch didn't take the shot. Instead, he passed it in toward Clovis. The ball didn't make it. The little bastard Eddie Renard stole it away and chucked it to Eiffel, who was streaking down the floor. He jumped to a stop and took one of his unmissable eighteen footers.

It missed.

Kitch shouldered his way toward the basket. If he caught the rebound, there was still a chance. But Bobby Flowers. Fucking Bobby Flowers grabbed the ball out of Kitch's hands and stuffed it thru. The end.

Final score: Denver Nuggets, 141, Kentucky Colonels, 137.

Charlie led me down the stairs and out the stadium amongst a mob of delighted Nuggets fans.

CHAPTER 51

We made it back to our hotel room just after nine o'clock. The post-game party wouldn't start for another hour. We sat on the bed, Charlie holding my hand.

She said, "You're upset."

"I wanted Kitch to win."

"He practically did."

I said, "That coach of theirs. He shouldn't of let Kitch jump that tip at the end of the game. Fletcher is the jumper. You don't ask a forward to jump for a tip ball when the game is so tight. And you sure as hell don't give the job to Kitch. Not when you have Clovis Fletcher."

"Johnny—"

"The only reason he did it was so Kitch could match up against Bobby Flowers. He wanted our rookie against their rookie. He wants Kitch to be the rookie of the year. Basketball is not about awards."

"Johnny!" Charlie stomped the floor. "I won't have you getting upset tonight. Your brother played incredible. His coach trusted him. Kitch earned that faith. Anyway, Clovis was tired and Kitch still had some gas in his tank. It's just bad luck that Flowers stole it from him."

"Dumb luck is more like it."

"If Kitch hadn't been playing so good—and so smart, may I add—the Colonels would have lost by forty points. His coach saw that and gave him a shot to win the game. But it didn't work out. It's not the coach's fault. It's not Kitch's fault. And I think you should stop calling your brother a dummy. He's just impulsive."

I said, "Really? He had a naked French woman in his house the day after Christmas."

Charlie started laughing. It was the kind of laughter that seems fake. Like she was making fun of me. She bent over and slapped her knee. "You'd have to be dumb to turn *down* the opportunity to have a naked French woman in your house, on any day. When you've got sex looking right at you, then shut up and do it." She flopped onto the bed next to me and said, "Jesus, Johnny."

I wasn't accustomed to her being mad at me. I said, "Charlie?"

"Yes, Johnny."

"Are you talking about me now?"

"I suppose I am."

"Is sex looking me in the eye right now?"

She propped her head up on the heel of her hand. She batted her lashes.

I reached toward her cheek.

She pushed my hand away. "Don't you know how this works? First we go to the party. Then you and Kitch have your little talk. Then you and I come back here and make love just after midnight on the first day of 1976."

I forgot all about jump balls and bad coaches and dumb brothers. I said, "To tell the truth, that's more or less what I was hoping would happen."

"But I'm the one who had to say it."

"I don't normally talk about that sort of thing."

"I usually like that about you." She grabbed my hand and dragged me upright. "Let's get moving. Cowboy Johnny and Cash Register Charlie are gonna crash a party."

The restaurant had been decorated with red, white, and blue crepe paper and Old Glory tablecloths. We were the first people to arrive. We sat at the same table we'd had before. We asked for a menu and the waiter said there would be no menu this evening. However, complimentary hors d'oeuvres would be served shortly and would we be interested in something to drink? He gestured toward the wine list that was sitting on our table.

I said to Charlie, "Go ahead and get something."

"Are you sure?"

"It's not a problem. I can handle a party."

Charlie said to the waiter, "I'd like a bottle of your second-cheapest red wine."

I said, "And some water, sir. In a pitcher or something."

The waiter agreed to this. He returned with wine, water, and glasses.

Charlie filled her wine glass and took a sip. "Really, this is okay? The drinking?"

I sipped some water. "That stuff doesn't even look good to me." A lie. The wine looked wonderful. But I didn't intend to drink and that was that.

People started to trickle in. I didn't recognize anybody. I didn't care. I toasted my water against Charlie's wine. "Here's to a straight-talking gal."

She toasted me, "Here's to a frustrating feller."

I toasted her, "Here's to a night on the town."

She said, "Here's to a new year."

I said, "You're pretty."

She said, "You only have one middle finger."

CHAPTER 52

The first basketball-type person to arrive was the Nuggets' assistant coach. Someone shouted, "Doug's here. The party has officially started!"

Assistant Coach Doug walked straight to the bar, ordered a drink, and then told a joke to the group of people standing nearby. Big laughs. He saw me staring and walked right up to our table, drink in hand.

"You gotta be related to Kitch Riles." He had a real thick New York accent.

Charlie said, "That's right, mister. This here is Kitch's big brother, Johnny."

He said, "Your little brother played a helluva game. I didn't know that goofy little bastard had it in him."

He clinked my glass and then went away.

I said to Charlie, "How does everybody know I'm Kitch's brother?"

"You look exactly alike. Nobody's ever told you that?"

"He's a foot taller than me."

"Maybe it's the way your mouth is always half-open."

Tall men, some white, most black, began to enter, some with women, most without. The Colonels' scrubs came first. People applauded, not because they cared about these men, but because they knew that somewhere behind them were the stars.

After the scrubs came the Colonels' starters. There were whoops and hollers when Clovis Fletcher arrived. He ducked his head to pass the threshold. People crowded around him. I expected Kitch to follow shortly. He didn't.

After a pause of appropriate length, the Nuggets commenced their entrance. Charlie sensed my distress. She said, "He's on his way."

Of the Nuggets' scrubs, Scooter Morris received the biggest applause. Everybody likes the short guy, sometimes.

The Nuggets starters entered. People shouted their first names as if they had all grown up together. Bobby! Chuck! Ralph! Eiffel got a full-on chant. Tower! Tower! Tower!

And then a long, long pause. They were waiting for one man. I was waiting for a different man. But we were all waiting. The pause lasted long enough for Charlie to pour herself another glass of wine and drink most of it.

The clock behind the bar declared that it was eleven o'clock. I wondered if Jabez was slaughtering my cattle one by one and hanging their meat on mammoth tusks.

There was a ruckus near the doors. People started hollering and clapping. A few women screamed. I don't know how they knew it, but everybody knew Bobby Flowers was on his way. He entered, walking side by side with Kitch. Two warriors dressed in shining suits. Kitch was a solid six inches taller than Flowers and he looked pale, bloated even. But he had a giant smile and he shouted, "Who's ready to party?!?"

Applause and general delight. Somebody shook a beer and thumbed the hole. Fizz squirted on Kitch and Bobby. They lapped it up. Champagne corks popped. It was like they'd won the world championship when all they'd really done was walk into a non-rotating restaurant on the top floor of a circular hotel.

A pair of women fell to the sides of Kitch and Bobby. Bobby Flowers' left arm went around Suzanne, wearing the same dress she'd had on earlier, but seeming tighter somehow. Kitch's right arm went around the most beautiful woman I'd ever seen. Black hair, bell bottoms, and a top that made my eyes sting.

Without looking at me, Charlie said, "Does she look French to you?"

I lifted up the wine bottle. It was almost empty. How could Charlie have finished it so fast? I gulped the rest of my water and then poured the last drops of wine into my glass. I held it to my nose and sniffed. It was better than the stuff Mom and Dad had brought for Thanksgiving.

Charlie said, "What are you doing?"

I drank it, quick. I didn't even let it swish in my mouth. Lift, pour, swallow.

Charlie stared at me.

I said, "It's just a sip." What a sip it was. My gut begged for more.

She shook her head.

"I swear, Charlie. I just wanted a taste."

She reached across the table and fondled one of my ears. "Since you finished my bottle, perhaps you could be a gentleman and order another."

I said, "We have plans for later, remember."

"I won't get sloppy, if you don't."

"Don't worry about me. I do not intend to screw this up."

I looked for our waiter but couldn't see him thru the crowd. Bobby and Kitch were slapping five. Double fives. Hi, lo, everywhere. Their girlfriends slapped fives. Then they all combined to slap twenties. Teammates and teammates' girlfriends joined to slap multiples of twenty. Pretty soon the entire restaurant was slapping hands.

I walked to the bar. I'd never spoken to a bartender in my life. I did not know how to address him. Her. She was a woman wearing a tuxedo shirt with the top buttons opened up to show the space between her bosoms. She asked me what I craved. I said I'd like a bottle of red wine.

"What kind?"

"Something cheap."

"Work with me, sweetie. Merlot? Noir? We have a pretty good house Chianti."

Kitch's arm reached around my shoulder. With his free hand, he pointed to a bottle on an upper shelf. "Laurie, this here is my brother, Johnny. Give him one of those, okay?"

Then he was gone and there was a bottle of joy in front of me. I didn't recognize the brand, but the burnt sunshine splashing inside looked plenty familiar. The bartender asked if I wanted ice. Silly question. The moment you put ice in your whiskey, it starts being water.

I said, "Can I have the whole bottle?"

"You're Kitch's brother, for reals?"

"I helped raise him."

She handed me the whiskey and slid me a glass. I strode toward our table. While I was gone, Charlie had managed to acquire two bottles of wine, one white, one red. And she'd also made a friend. She was sitting next to the beautiful, possibly French woman, about to clink glasses in a toast. They interrupted themselves as I approached.

Charlie said, "Johnny!"

I said, "Charlie!"

The beautiful woman said, "Bruhzer."

I raised my bottle. Charlie raised an eyebrow.

I winked at her and said, "It's New Year's."

She almost looked relieved. "Cheers to us."

The French woman lifted her dewy glass of white wine, Charlie raised her glass of red, and I raised my bottle of whiskey. We clinked hard, liquid splashing onto our wrists. We drank. I put my tongue over the neck of the bottle and only let a little whiskey in my mouth. Inside my belly, a dam began to crumble.

I made a face. The women laughed and we became bonded.

The beautiful French woman who had shaken her naked breasts at my brother while I spoke to him six fair days ago scooted her chair up close and said she was enchanted to know us.

Charlie and I slobbered. Both of us were empty of words. We had a private audience with someone who had a private audience.

The woman said, "Let us speak our names."

Charlie said, "Charlie!"

I said, "Johnny!"

The woman said, "Charlotte!"

Charlie and I exchanged telepathic snickers. The French woman had been named after our male poodle. She had the largest bell bottom britches I'd ever seen. Her top was notable in that it looked like it came from the bottom drawer of my father's dresser. Two handkerchiefs, one red and one blue, had been folded into tiny triangles. One over her right breast, the other over her left. They were knotted between her breasts and again between her shoulder blades. I stared quickly and then looked away into Charlie's eyes to let her know that I found it amusingly distasteful. Charlie's eyes agreed.

That little bit of whiskey changed things. The world gained a goodness that it had lacked a few moments ago. My nerves were replaced with snowflakes. I wondered why I had ever chosen to give up this life. The dam crumbled.

Charlotte said, "I am so happy to meet both of you." Her eyebrows were astonishing. They curved like inchworms, dividing her face between her round forehead and her brown speckled eyes. Charlie and I both reached up and felt our own eyebrows.

Charlotte said, "You may call me Chou-Chou. Like zee train. You are hungry?"

Charlie and I both nodded. We hadn't eaten since our dinner ever so long ago. It was a miracle we were still alive. Chou-Chou understood this because she was perfect.

With a gesture from one of her astonishing eyebrows, a waiter sprinted to our table carrying a silver plate burdened by glorious yum yums, all skewered with toothpicks. He placed the plate upon our table and spoke in Chou-Chou's ear. She nodded and he sprinted away. Charlie and I ate various species of meat, mushrooms, salty pink things. I poured myself a glass of whiskey.

Chou-Chou raised her arms the same way a preacher does at the beginning of church when he declares that this is truly a blessed day. She said, "I want you to ask me any questions you would like."

Charlie asked what had to be asked. "Are you from France?"

Chou-Chou made a poofing noise which briefly displaced her angus-black bangs. "Absolutely, yes. I am born in Paris. I grow up and then I come to the States immediately once my opportunity presents himself. I will never return home. It is free here. Not sexually, of course. But in other ways. The landscape, for example. The nature is so much more powerful. Especially here in the West. You are fortunate to live with the mountains in such a beautiful land. The States are full of the wonder." She pointed to her glass of wine. "I miss my France only for this. You cannot make it here like we make it there."

Charlie and I laughed because it was so, so true.

Chou-Chou touched the knot between her breasts. "But, please, I talk too much. You are the true strangers here. This is a room full of people of the city." She beckoned at the other humans with one perfect, naked arm, then nodded toward Charlie and I. "You are not of the city. Kitch says to me you come from a dying world. Tell me of it."

Charlie and I fought to speak. Charlie told of this. I told of that. Everything we said was met with a gentle brush of Chou-Chou's hand against ours. Charlie and I competed to make her touch us more fondly. I told her that at night you could see the stars fall down like rain. Charlie told her that men expect their wives to cook them dinner. I told her how to cut a young bull's nuts off. Charlie told her that she'd seen horses fuck donkeys. I told her that I'd taught Kitch how to play basketball but he grew tall so that's why he was famous and I was just a rancher. They both touched my hand for that one.

I kept going because I saw Chou-Chou look at my missing finger. I told her that I'd lost the finger because. I stopped. This was not appropriate.

I raised my bottle, we all raised our bottles, for the waiter had returned with bottles of everything we wanted as well as a bucket of ice and a plastic dish filled with olives, lemons, limes, and pickled onions.

I said, "We are all of the same world. Let us celebrate this!"

Charlie said, "Let us celebrate."

Music was playing, the funky kind. I knew what funk was and I didn't much care for it. In order to celebrate properly, we had to hear America. I needed to speak to the disc jockey, wherever he might be.

I excused myself.

Upon standing up, the need to urinate became greater than the need to hear Horse with No Name.

I had to see a man about a horse with no name.

My feet had difficulty finding the floor. I focused on keeping upright. It was slipping away: the Christmas ditch, four days in the big room, conversations with dead animals, Jabez's tenderness. I hoped a trip to the bathroom would help me focus. Or justify more drinking. In either case, it would bring clarity.

As I crossed the room, everyone was my friend. I brushed against sparkly clothes. My hat was lifted off my head. A hand placed a cigarette in my mouth. Another hand lit it. I said, "Where's the john?"

Hands pressed me forward and thru a door. Here, it was silent and clean with white tile. I said hello to the mirror. My hair was flat from my hat. I ruffled it up.

Voices from a stall. More voices than one would expect. Boys and girls. One of the boys said, "Don't be a pusshole!"

I recognized the voice. I opened the door.

Kitch was there with two women and a man, all bunched up around the toilet. The man was shorter than Kitch and black. This was Bobby Flowers, the best dunker in the world. One of the women was Suzanne, in her green dress. She nodded at me. The other woman had blonde hair. She was not Chou-Chou. I did not belong here.

I backed away.

Kitch said, "Don't you be a pusshole either."

Up close, in the light of the bathroom, Kitch did not look healthy. Swollen. Pale. He beckoned to me. Hands pulled me into the stall and shut the door. Five of us around the toilet, shoulders touching. Kitch reached into his jacket and handed me a small rectangle of glass.

"Hold that just so. Not above the shitter, please."

Then he reached into his britches pocket and removed a 30-30 cartridge, about the size and length of a woman's pinkie. With a twist, he pulled the bullet off the top. He tipped over the brass casing and tapped some white powder onto the glass. His other hand went into his pocket and extracted a gold credit card with which he divided the powder into three stripes. I held the glass level and steady. This was not easy in my current state.

The blonde woman leaned in. She sniffed one stripe and then another. She left the third one alone. Kitch said to her, "Three lines, feel fine!"

She did the third stripe. Kitch reloaded the glass and looked at Suzanne. She leaned in and did three sniffs, one after the other.

Kitch loaded the glass once more.

Bobby Flowers said to Suzanne, "What's it like?"

She didn't speak. She bobbed her head like a pigeon. The blonde bobbed as well. Their eyes were wide.

Kitch said, "Did you see me in that second half? *That's* what it feels like. This shit is good for fifty points a night. It'll add three inches to your vertical leap. And your prick."

The blonde giggled. Suzanne's eyes roamed the stall. Perfume and cologne mingled with piss and urinal cakes.

Bobby said, "It's bad for you."

Kitch said, "Maybe the shit in North Carolina is bad. But this is *good*, brother. It comes from Peru." He licked a finger and tapped one of the stripes. He showed us the powder. "It's pink and pure as the baby Jesus. I've tried the flour you've heard about. The second you come down off it, you need more. It makes you a sicko. But this shit. You use it, then you go on with your life. No hangover, no habit."

Suzanne said, "I must say, Bobby, I feel really, really, really, really, really, really—"

Bobby Flowers said, "Fifty points a game?"

Kitch said, "For you, seventy. I speak the truth."

Bobby Flowers sniffed a stripe of the powder. Then he did a second and third.

Kitch said to me. "Your turn, little brother."

I said, "Big brother, brother."

He arranged the powder into three more stripes. "Prove it."

Whether it was the liquor in my gut or the lure of hiding in a stall with the world's greatest professional basketball players and two pretty women on the top floor of a non-rotating circular hotel in the midst of a New Year's Eve which promised to conclude with lovemaking, or simply a desire to be equal to my brother, I leaned forward and proved it.

CHAPTER 53

Kitch checked our nostrils for powder and then we exited the bathroom in a tumble. We had passed beyond drunkenness. We had reached a moment of optimum existence. I inhaled air and exhaled the nectar of domination.

We migrated to a spot under a mirror ball and began dancing. The five of us were a squad of motion, sliding and pointing, powered by the funkiest funk in the land. We waved our arms to the sky. I *loved* funk music. I was no longer even a little bit drunk. Charlie and Chou-Chou joined us, both of them off their rockers with wine. Soon, the three of us were rubbing our asses together.

Charlie danced with Kitch. I danced with Suzanne. Suzanne danced with Charlie. The blonde woman danced with herself, running her hands up and down her body.

I danced with Chou-Chou. She spun around with one arm in the air, shimmying her rear end toward my crotch. We danced and danced and danced. Then the music stopped. The song wasn't even over.

Before I could be disappointed, everyone in the room began counting down. *Ten.* A cone was placed upon my head. *Nine.* Chou-Chou held my hand. *Eight.* A plastic glass of champagne was placed in my other hand. *Seven. Six. Fiveforthreetwoone.* Charlie leapt into my arms. I dropped the champagne and let loose of Chou-Chou. Charlie hugged me with her legs around my hips, her arms around my neck. Plastic horns tooted and all was tremendous. When we kissed, our teeth clattered against one another. I squeezed her close. I felt her bra beneath the back of her shirt. This was the city.

I said, "Happy cottonpickin' new year!"

Charlie said, "Is your nose bleeding?"

I excused myself and went directly to the bathroom. A voice from the stall said, "I see those boots. Get in here, Johnny."

I got in. Kitch was holding his square of glass and Bobby Flowers was sniffing from it. After he finished, Bobby looked up and said to me, "Brother!"

I said, "Brother!"

Kitch said, "Brothers!"

We hugged, the world's greatest basketball players and me.

Then Kitch said, "Bobby, I hate to be an asshole but I need a word with my little bro."

I said, "Big bro."

Bobby said, "Cool, bro." He exited.

It was just me and Kitch in a stall in that shiny white bathroom. There was still some powder on his square of glass. He held it under my nose. I sniffed. I grew taller. It was time for our talk. I was ready, ready, ready.

Kitch said, "I've got good news about your investment."

"Investment?"

"That money you loaned me."

"The money I dropped off in Last Chance."

"Yes. I used that money to purchase a little bit of cocaine, which is what we call the stuff you've been putting in your nose tonight. I sold most of that little bit and was able to double down and buy more. I sold most of that and then doubled down again."

He tore some toilet paper off the roll and handed it to me. "You've got some blood."

I dabbed around my nostrils.

Kitch said, "I'm selling to half the guys in the ABA. Why do you think this league is so exciting? Me and my product, that's why. And Bobby Flowers is my newest customer."

He grinned hard. "Here's where it gets good. I could pay you back your four hundred dollars right now along with an extra hundred dollars for your trouble. Or I could reinvest that money and buy a huge stash. Seriously huge. It'd be like doubling down three times. I'm eighting down. Do you see the opportunity here? By buying in bulk, I get a discount from my wholesaler. With that discount, my profit margin jumps thru the roof. And I need that profit. You might not know this, but I don't make that much money. Yes, I have a $200,000 contract, but most of it is back-paid. It's shit. With the exception of Dr. J, every single ABA contract is shit. They tell us we're making one, two, three hundred thousand. The truth is almost all our money goes into annuities that don't begin to pay off until we turn forty-fucking-years old. Forty years old. Who lives that long? Otherwise, it's a biweekly paycheck for a couple hundred dollars. I could make a better living at a carwash. The ABA is a disaster. There's no real money. We might be the best basketball players in the world, but that don't mean dick as long as the assholes in the NBA won't let us get on network TV. Without TV, we get no exposure, even though we put out a superior product, thanks to my superior product. The ABA won't last another year. After that, I'm broke until I'm forty. Assholes. This party tonight is going to cost me a couple grand, which I don't have. But wait. With our investment, we don't have to worry about assholes and I won't have to wait until I'm forty. I'll get my money now. I'll buy houses for you and mom and dad. It's a brighter future for everyone. Capeesh?"

"I lent you that four hundred dollars to cover a gambling debt."

"And now you know the truth. And you understand. You've tasted the product. People love cocaine. It's free money. Are you in? Before you answer, consider this: if you give me two thousand dollars, I could acquire even more product. You have to do this. You'd be an idiot not to. Sell the cattle if necessary. Sell the whole fucking ranch. You'll never get another finger bit off in your whole life. I'm telling you the truth here. Consider it. We're brothers. I owe you so much. We all owe you. You shot Dad. If you hadn't done that, Mom and him would still be on the ranch, hollering at each other, making life hell. Have you noticed how happy they've been since they got us out of their lives? It's beautiful."

I said, "We're their children and they don't like us. That's not really beautiful."

"It *is*, brother. Because they do like us. But they like us better when they don't have to see us all the time. I'm not going to dance around it. I'm a handful. And, no offense, but you can be a downer sometimes. But everything has worked out. You're on the home place, doing what you do best. Our parents are happy together in Saint Franny. And I'm a titan of basketball. I love you, Johnny. You practically raised me. You taught me basketball. You made our family happy. You're a man. I'm so god damned proud of you, I could punch a mirror."

Kitch's eyes were twitchy and shot with blood. I was sure mine were, too.

He said, "I'm so fucking glad you're here tonight."

He hugged me tight and patted my back. We both sniffed. Our talk was going wonderfully. I could sort out the details later. For now, only one thing mattered. We were brothers. Brothers stick together. Brothers tell the truth.

Still hugging, I said, "A cow didn't bite my finger off."

Kitch stepped back. "Huh?"

My mind was alive. Kitch told me the truth. I would tell him the truth. It's what brothers do.

I said, "When did you ever hear of a cow biting someone's finger off? My finger's gone because of a woman in a hole in the ground. She killed my horse and I almost froze to death."

In that bathroom stall, I started talking. I talked so fast my tongue could hardly keep up. I told Kitch how I had been jealous of him the night of his first ABA game and how I went into the blizzard after a horse with a tiger skull tied to its saddle. I told of the mystery of the horse-killer, how my toes had fallen off, how I'd discovered the tunnels. I told him about strange, old Jabez. I described the walls and the bones and how the place seemed completely unknowable and beautiful and how no one must ever, ever know that it exists.

Kitch said, "This is some wild stuff you're laying down."

Clip clop shoes and the stall door banged open. Kitch's blonde friend lurched in with her tongue roving around her lips. She brushed a finger against my ear.

Kitch leaned back against the wall next to the toilet. The blonde squatted and unzipped his britches. Kitch pushed me on the chest, out of the stall. He said, "If you see Chou-Chou, tell her I'm getting a spit shine."

CHAPTER 54

As I left the bathroom, I bumped into three men in dark suits. Two of them were big, one was small. Of the big men, one had sideburns, the other did not.

I said, "I know you fellas!"

The small man said, "No, you do not." He had a high voice.

I said, "I do. They like ice cream."

"Where's your brother, kid?"

"He's getting a spit shine." That seemed like a funny thing to say so I smiled.

The men marched past me and into the bathroom.

The party had gone up a couple of notches. Several people were dancing on tables, including three members of the Denver Nuggets. A man dressed as a woman handed me a cigarette. It smelled just like the stuff Kitch had smoked when he visited me on the ranch. I inhaled and passed it back. Mirror ball reflections glided over every surface as one funky song merged into another.

I swiped a bottle of wine from an unoccupied table and I drank until it ran red down my shirt. A pair of immaculate hands reached out and dabbed the wine with blue and red handkerchiefs. The hands belonged to Chou-Chou. The handkerchiefs had previously been over her breasts, which now I saw to be small and alert and free, as breasts such as hers should be. She plucked the party hat from my head and used it to cover one of her tiny boobs. The other boob stared. A wink. Chou-Chou plucked another hat off another head and made herself more or less decent. Someone poured a drink into her mouth. I walked away. I wished to find Charlie. I wished to leave this place.

I circled the room over and over and over and over and finally found her asleep in a corner, behind a plastic plant.

I petted her hair. "Hey, Charlie."

She opened her eyes and smiled at me. Then she went right back to sleep. I carried her to the bar and sat her upon it. The bartender brought me another bottle of whiskey. With Charlie in my arms and a bottle of whiskey in my hand, I walked toward the exit, dodging dancers and drunks and drugs.

Someone put my cowboy hat back on my head. It was Bobby Flowers. He had a cigarette in his mouth. His shirt was missing. Shirts were optional at this point in the evening. He said, "Your brother is a three-alarm fireplace."

Dressed only in her panties and a cape fashioned from one of the red, white, and blue tablecloths, Suzanne sprinted from across the room and leapt onto Bobby's back and shouted, "Giddyup, dunk-boy!"

I fled.

CHAPTER 55

JANUARY

On the first day of nineteen seventy-six, I awoke on a bed in a room in a circular hotel in Denver. The TV was on and a half-empty bottle of whiskey was balanced on my chest. I was still wearing my clothes, even my boots.

The Denver Nuggets had defeated the Kentucky Colonels 141 to 137. My brother was a degenerate. Marihuana cigarette. Chou-Chou had pale nipples. Powder on glass. Men in dark suits.

A rasping sound. Someone was breathing next to me. I removed the bottle from my chest and rolled over to have a look.

Charlie lay on her side with her back to me. Like me, she was on top of the blankets and, like me, she was wearing all her clothes.

We'd failed to make love. I was more relieved than disappointed. It would have been awful under those circumstances, both of us insane on things that don't merit repetition.

Repetition. Less than one day after I'd gotten healthy, I was once again a drunk. My flesh felt like a sponge left to dry on the hood of a car. My jaw ached. My lungs were clogged with cigarette ash. The whiskey had burned a hole in my throat. My brain was swollen, pushing my eyes out of their sockets. My finger stump ached.

I had spoken of Jabez to Kitch.

If I'd had a pistol, I would have put it in my mouth and pulled the trigger. No, I would not have done that. It would have woken Charlie.

I held my breath as long as possible, hoping to die. It didn't work.

I went to the bathroom and found Chou-Chou there, asleep in the tub. Bell bottom pants. Party hats still stuck on her breasts. I flicked the light on and off. With her eyes still shut, she said, "Your bruhzer is an asshole."

There were hotel robes in the closet. I tossed one to Chou-Chou. With her back to me, she popped off the hats and put on the robe. "Charlie is very nice. Tell her I am happy she permitted me to sleep here."

She walked out the door and down the hall.

I showered and then dressed. Charlie was still asleep. I pressed upon her shoulder. She opened her eyes, looked at the clock, and said, "Jesus, Johnny. It's only nine."

"We need to go."

"Checkout isn't until eleven."

"I know."

"Can't we sleep in? My head." She rubbed her face. "My face."

"I have to get out of Denver."

"What's the hurry? Did you kill somebody?"

"Maybe."

"Relax. We went to a party last night. We got drunk and danced and acted silly and now we're hungover. That's what happens on New Year's. Except this year we were in a crazy, crazy scene. There's a whole lot of people who should feel a lot more ashamed than you this morning."

I said, "I saw some wild things. I *said* some wild things."

I noticed my cowboy hat was halfway under the bed. I picked it up and put it on.

"Like what?"

"Nothing. I feel crummy is all. I'm hungover and I'm mad as hell at myself."

"For drinking?"

"Among other things."

"So am I. So's everybody. That's why New Year's Day is a holiday."

"But I *quit* drinking."

"It was one night. You'll be fine." She didn't say this like she was talking down. She said it like she had faith in me. "You're Johnny Riles. You can do it." She tilted her head. "You didn't cheat on me, did you?"

I was genuinely surprised that she asked me this. She saw the look on my face and kissed my cheek. "You're a good man. Let's go home."

In the pickup, with the city giving way to the prairie, Charlie helped me out of my mood. She talked about how much she'd enjoyed the basketball game. She laughed about how she'd convinced the basketball players to do a square dance to a Stevie Wonder song. She marveled at Chou-Chou's grace. She thanked me multiple times for carrying her back to the hotel room in one piece. Her conversation took me out of my head, away from the animals, away from the lopsided ark.

As we approached Last Chance, Charlie asked to stop at the Dairy King for a burger.

I said, "I'd rather not. I need to get home."

"I'm hungry."

"I told Emmett we'd be home by noon."

Charlie didn't persist. Instead, she said, "How did things go with Kitch?"

"Not like I'd hoped."

"But you talked to him, right? About the gambling?"

"We talked about a great number of things and managed to resolve none of them."

"That's how it is, sometimes. You talk and talk and sometimes you just have to stop talking and move on." She was remembering Mr. Goodland, I could tell. "For what it's worth, your brother seemed all right to me. The guy throws a good party. And he's a hell of a ball player."

When we got to my place, I helped Charlie load her suitcase into her car. She sat in her driver's seat with the door open and said, "Thanks for bringing me, Johnny. Even if you didn't have any fun."

I said, "I'm glad you came."

She tilted her head. "Speaking of which, what are you doing tonight?"

"I hadn't thought about it."

Charlie leaned forward and gave me a kiss on the lips. "It's still the first day of 1976. I'll call you tonight."

She pulled her door shut and drove away.

Home was the prettiest place on Earth. The scrubby trees and the sandblasted barn. The land, patchy with old snow. The cottontails chasing each other around the windbreak. I would never leave this place again.

I checked on the animals. The cattle were healthy, the horse was happy, the cow was milked, and the chickens clucked. Jabez had done well.

It wasn't until I walked in the house that I realized that we'd forgotten about the poodle.

CHAPTER 56

I telephoned Charlie.

"The dog."

"Oh, Jesus." said Charlie.

"She wasn't in the hotel room this morning."

"Definitely. She was not in the room. We would have noticed."

Charlie said, "Maybe, while we were at the party, she started barking and someone with the hotel heard her and confiscated her because of the no-pets policy."

"They would have left a note. Or said something when we checked out, don't you think?"

Charlie said, "Maybe we accidentally let her out when we got home from the party."

"Maybe Chou-Chou let her out."

"Chou-Chou?"

"She slept in our bathtub. She said you let her in."

"Is that so?"

"She told me to thank you." I didn't mention the party hats. I said, "We have to call the hotel."

"Do you own a Denver phone book? 'Cause I sure don't. Oh, Johnny, we loused this up."

"We sure did."

Charlie said, "She'll be okay."

"She's a boy, remember?"

As soon as I hung up, the phone rang again. I picked it up, expecting it to be Charlie. Perhaps she'd found the dog hiding in her suitcase.

It was not Charlie.

Kitch said, "Crazy night, huh?" His voice sounded criminal, and I felt like his accomplice.

I said, "Yes, it was crazy."

"Get any sleep?"

I said, "Not enough."

"I hope you and your country girl left a mess on those sheets."

I didn't reply.

"I'll take your silence as an affirmation. Say, have you given any thought to my proposition? Sorry we didn't have a chance to come to terms. Distractions."

"Terms about what?"

"About you loaning me money for a guaranteed bonanza of profit."

I said, "I feel horrible today. I woke up feeling horrible and I still feel horrible. That stuff is bad. I don't think you should be selling it or using it."

"Too late for that. I'm hooked. To selling and using, both."

"I'm not interested."

"You seemed plenty interested last night. At least in the using."

"That was a mistake."

"Mistakes are a myth."

I said, "I told you a wild story last night."

"Refresh me."

"About my finger."

"The thing with the mammoths? It seemed a little on the fantastical side, frankly."

"This is exactly what I'm talking about. That powder makes a person tell tall tales."

"Don't call it 'powder' or 'stuff.' It's cocaine and it's going to make us rich. Give me some money so we can get rich. As soon as possible."

"I don't think so."

"I'm committed. My supplier shipped a large quantity of the stuff, direct from Lima. I'm a good customer. I had a long talk with him last night. He knows I'm good for the money. I'm going to earn a bonus for making the All-Star team."

"You made the All-Star team?"

"The results haven't been released yet. Or tallied. But you saw me. Fuck. I'm lifting up the entire league with my work. They should—"

"I'm not loaning you any more money."

"I need a commitment. My flight leaves for Louisville this evening."

"No."

"Would you be more inclined to help if I told you I had your dog?"

God damn Kitch.

I said, "You're still at the hotel? I'll be there in two hours."

"You don't need to be here. I'm practically there."

"Where?"

"Where you are. I'm in Last Chance. At the Dairy King. The folks here have kindly permitted me to make a long distance phone call. Warm some coffee. I'll be right over."

I called Charlie.

I said, "The dog has been located."

"Thank Christ. Is she okay?"

"Kitch has her. He just telephoned from Last Chance. He's on his way."

"To your house?"

"He wants me to give him money so he can invest in a large quantity of cocaine, which he plans to sell to his fellow basketball players."

"Johnny Riles."

"Yes?"

"What in the fuck are you talking about?"

"That was the conversation last night. Kitch got me goofed up and tried to talk me into some business deal he's into. I mean, it might not be drugs. It didn't entirely make sense. He might need the money so he can pay off gambling debts. He's been saying lots of different things. What's really important is that he's on his way and he has the dog."

"Jesus."

"I know."

"I'm going to call Chester."

Chester was the Sherriff's deputy. At the moment, he was probably in his trailer, warming up some popcorn for the Rose Bowl.

"I can handle Kitch."

"He kidnapped your dog."

"That's not for certain."

"I'm going to call Chester and then I'm coming over."

"Don't you dare call Chester. If he gets involved, Kitch will go straight to jail."

"Sounds like that's what he needs."

"It's not what I need. Let me talk to him first. He's my brother."

She waited a moment, then said, "I won't call Chester. But I'm coming over, and if you don't let me, I'm canceling our date tonight."

"You may come. But wait an hour. I want to talk to him brother to brother and I don't want to scare him off."

"Half an hour."

"An hour. It'll take him at least forty minutes to get here. That'll leave us twenty minutes to talk."

"An hour, not a moment longer."

"When you get here, if I'm gone, use the phone in the kitchen to call Emmett Williams. You can call Chester, too, if you want."

"I thought there was nothing to worry about."

"There isn't. But just in case. And if we're not here, I expect we'll be at a place north of the river. It's straight north of my house. It's a rough drive but you can get there in your car, I suspect. But it'd be better to take Emmett's truck."

"What are you talking about?" She sounded a little panicky.

"I'll figure out a way to let you know where I am. If we're not here, we'll be there. Don't come over right away. If there's a problem, get Emmett. Between the two of you, I'm sure you can handle anything. And Chester. You call him, too, if you get nervous. But there won't be a problem. I'll calm things down."

"This is silly."

"I think you're something else, Charlie."

"Promise you won't let your brother talk you into anything horrible."

CHAPTER 57

Less than twenty minutes later, a Corvette skidded into the driveway.

I stood on the front step with my elbow resting on the railing. I wanted to look approachable, but also potentially violent. To that end, the four-ten shotgun was leaning against the door behind me, and Excal was in my hip holster.

Kitch climbed out of the car, dressed in his Kentucky Colonels uniform. Shorts, tank top, gym shoes. One of his eyes was swollen shut. There was dried blood on his temple. And he was more bloated than ever. His calves swole out over his tube socks. His cheeks and his shoulders were puffy.

He slapped the hood of the car. "This is a fast god damned automobile. How long did that take? Fifteen minutes?"

I said, "You're dressed awful warm for such a chilly day."

"I don't even feel temperature anymore."

"Where's my dog?"

"In the trunk. Don't make that face. She's a miniature poodle. A trunk is a mansion to her. Fuck. I haven't pissed in a week."

He dropped his shorts, pulled out his pizzle, and grunted. Nothing came out.

"See?"

He hitched his shorts back up, letting the elastic snap against his waist. I noticed that the middle finger of his left hand was crooked. He saw me looking and held it up for me. The finger was bent backward at the second knuckle.

He said, "What do you think? Is it broken?"

He was awful bloated, like what happens to a steer when a

person runs a water hose into its mouth to get it up to weight the morning before an auction.

I said, "What happened to you?"

"I blame our father."

I said, "You could use some sleep."

"That's funny. It's true, but funny. The last time I slept was the last time I pissed, which was the day after Christmas."

"I didn't know that was possible, going that long without sleep. Or pissing."

He took a step toward me. "Reality and I have come to an arrangement of sorts. I have abandoned her and she has abandoned me. Take, for instance, the concept of brotherly love. I love you like a brother because we are, in reality, brothers. But I need you to understand that I'm in dire fucking straits at the moment." He wagged his left hand so his injured finger flopped around. "I suspect that you have, in the house and on your person, no more than two or three hundred dollars. A goodly sum, but not enough to satisfy my creditors. Or debtors. I'm not sure which is the appropriate term. Whatever you call them, they've stepped things up a notch and now require payment posthaste. Very posthaste. Very, very, very posthaste. Like right now. Obviously, you cannot sell your cattle today, or withdraw any cash from the bank, what with the holiday. So I'm here to appeal to your sense of brotherly love and seek alternative means of raising the funds."

I said, "You're talking funny."

"How so?"

"You're talking smart."

He said, "That's because I am more cultured that you."

"I don't like it. You aren't yourself. You haven't been for a while."

"Whoever I am offers his most sincere of apologies."

"I'm not going to help you buy drugs."

"Certainly not! Except under extraordinary circumstances, which I shall now explain. It's a simple story, but it's long. Were I to tell it in full, the dog would likely die of asphyxiation before I finished. Also, certain details are murky. For the most part, it's as I described it last evening. I owe a large quantity of money to a large, underworld organization for a large-volume drug transaction. The transaction was to be paid for by the winnings from a wager I made on the outcome of last night's basketball game. Alas, the wager failed to pay dividends because certain point spread-related requirements were not met, in spite of my best efforts. Or because of them. I was on fire. It seemed worth it at the time. We were supposed to lose by no less than five points and instead we lost by four. Blame, as it were, could be applied to many individuals, but I choose to lay it squarely at the toes of everybody but myself." He swatted his good hand in the direction of an imaginary foe. "Whatever. It's all trolls under the bridge, as they say."

Kitch walked to the foot of the steps and put his left hand on the railing. "I was delivered a message last night." He rubbed his broken finger against his swollen eye. "The message was simple. Failure to promptly remonstrate the money will result in further punishment for the leading contender for the ABA rookie of the year. That's me. Your expression betrays your loyalties, you Bobby Flowers fetishist bastard. Don't be sad. I'm not insulting you. I'm describing you."

He tucked his shirt into his shorts. "Subject at hand. Punishment could range from a severe rebuke, which is unlikely, to the removal of a digit, which is clearly not out of the question, to the extraction of one or more testicles, which terrifies me. This latter possibility grew a great deal more likely when my supplier discovered his lady friend suckling my goose in a bathroom stall eleven hours ago, which, incidentally was the event that precipitated my current state of dishevelment."

He reached into the front of his shorts and pulled out the 30-30 cartridge and removed the bullet. From the casing, he tapped powder on the back of his left hand and snorted.

"I believe this brings us to our present situation. Our present *solution*, if you will. Once I acquire sufficient capital, I'll return to Denver, pay off my creditors or debtors, hop on the plane, go to my lovely home, fuck my sexy French girlfriend on my marble kitchen counter, eat some goofballs and enjoy a dozen hours of gol' darned sleep. Also, at some point I intend to piss out the ten gallons of urine that is poisoning my beautiful, athletic body."

He placed a foot on the first step. "I see you have a gun. You're obviously trying to tell me something. You could have brought out the twelve-gauge, a weapon of far greater heft, better suited for both self-defense and intimidation."

He climbed to the next step. "Instead you choose to display that pea-shooter of a four-ten. Still potentially lethal, but far less so than the twelve-gauge."

He climbed another step. "Isn't that the gun you shot Dad with? Perhaps you're trying to say, 'I shot one man with this gun and I'm not afraid to shoot another.' The poetic choice. Speaking of choices, I know you shot him on purpose. Be proud. You killed a bird and crippled a man with a single tug of your trigger. It was the best shot I ever saw. With the possible exception of that final three-pointer I made last night."

"The one that didn't win the game?"

"Sometimes your language lacks romance."

I said, "At least I talk real. Let me see my dog."

He climbed toward me. "I'm going to step inside first. Splash some water on my face."

I put my hand on Excal. "You're not going into that house."

He said, "Aw, Johnny."

Then he came at me, faster than a bloated, six-foot-nine insomniac had any right to move. Before I could put my hand on my knife, Kitch had slapped me on the side of my head, shoved me aside, and snatched up the shotgun.

He pointed the gun pointed at my chest and backed me down the steps.

"Gimme the knife."

I tossed it at his feet. He put it in the elastic of his shorts. He said, "I wish these things had pockets."

Keeping the gun on me, he walked to the Corvette, leaned in the open window, and removed the keys from the ignition. He walked around behind and put a hand on the trunk.

He said, "I know you don't have a mattress full of money. I checked the last time I was out here."

I said, "What do you want me to do? Rob the bank?"

"Too risky. What I want is much simpler. I want to meet your shell-shocked, horse-eating nurse. I want you to put a saber-tooth tiger skull in my hands."

Of course.

I said, "I have a dresser filled with arrowheads. Take those instead."

"Nobody pays money for rocks, Johnny."

Kitch opened the trunk. A barking erupted from within. With his left hand, he scooped up the dog. With his right hand, he held the shotgun and pointed the barrel at the dog's head.

"Take me to your fossils or I turn the bitch into soup."

I said, "His name is Charlotte."

The cattle watched us from the pasture.

CHAPTER 58

A cloud slid in front of the sun. It was a little cloud, trailed by big clouds. A south wind picked up. It was January first, maybe thirty-five degrees. Nothing to worry about.

Kitch said, "Let's take the 'vette."

"No."

"You're intimidated because it looks like a penis."

My brother was standing before me with a shotgun pointed at the head of a poodle, thinking that we could drive a sports car across the riverbed.

I said, "We have to cross Old Stinkum. Horses would be ideal, but I only have the one and she can't carry both of us. We'll take the pickup."

"What you lack in romance, you make up for in practicality."

I thought hard, looking for a way to end this. I said, "Do you mind if I bring along some hay? I don't know if I mentioned it last night, but there's a cow down there and she'd appreciate the gesture."

"I recall everything. Yes. Get your hay. But hurry. I'm on a deadline."

I said, "I'm glad to see that you still understand the concept of rancherly obligation."

As I pulled the truck up to the barn, I said, "Lend a hand?"

Kitch said, "I'd love to get a little hay under my fingernails. But if I help you, I'll have to let go of both the gun and the dog, which would seriously compromise my position as a negotiator."

Kitch sat in the cab with the poodle on his lap and watched

as I pitched four bales into the bed of the truck. While I worked, the horse came to the fence, ready to be saddled up. I said, "Be lucky you're not coming along on this one, girl."

No sign of Charlie. It hadn't yet been an hour.

I drove us north, slowly. Kitch scratched the poodle's ears. The dog tolerated it.

Lonesome snowflakes began to drift out of the sky.

I cracked the window and reached into my shirt pocket. "Cigarette?"

"Thank you."

We crossed the lumpy land, smoking.

Kitch said, "I miss my old horse."

"You never had a horse."

"That grey mare the hermit ate? She was a birthday present from Dad to me."

I said, "She was mine."

Kitch snorted. "Who's delusional now?" He rolled down the window and spit. A line of phlegm stuck to his chin. "I was never meant for this country. I require trees, buildings, action, pussy. I need life. All this nothingness. It'll drain your brain. And the people. Ignorant, dumb, and racist. Not my type. I can only thrive in a free society."

I said, "Those ignorant people are also your biggest fans."

Kitch said, "My appeal is universal."

After we crossed the riverbed, the snowflakes grew more numerous, dropping silently upon the windshield and landing white upon the winter-dead grass all around.

Kitch said, "You been getting much snow?"

I pitched my cigarette out the window and lit another.

"More than normal. We'll get a big storm and then it warms up for two weeks and then we get another."

He said, "You know what they say about the weather in Colorado."

Old joke. Keep him happy. "Tell me."

"If you don't like it, go fuck yourself."

I tried to laugh an old laugh.

We crossed the wasteland where I'd collected my arrowheads and then we passed by the spot where I'd staked Polly and Eleanor.

I finished my cigarette, pitched it out the window.

Kitch said, "It doesn't snow like this in Kentucky. I can't stand this shit."

I lit another cigarette. I didn't particularly care for the snow either, not at this moment. I'd hoped to start a prairie fire with my cigarettes, hoped to draw Charlie out this way. But wet grass doesn't burn.

The snow fell harder.

We crested the edge of the depression. The cottonwood patch at the bottom was barely visible thru the falling snow. Mist floated upward from the water seep. I eased the truck next to Jabez's hatch and shut off the engine.

Kitch said, "Wake her up."

I nodded down toward the cottonwood patch. "We should feed the cow first."

"Afterwards."

I got out of the truck and kicked my heel on the door. A moment later, Jabez swung it up, wearing one of my dress shirts. She leaned out and smiled at me. Then Kitch stepped out of the truck in his Kentucky Colonels uniform, bloated, beat up, and shiny, with the dog in his arm and the shotgun in his hand.

Jabez shook her head at me. All she said was, "Come on, then." She disappeared down the hole.

Watching her, Kitch grinned like his face had been cleaved by an axe.

I took a final drag on my cigarette and pitched it into the back of the pickup so it landed just under the edge of one of the hay bales, protected from the snow. It was a good toss.

I started for the hole but Kitch pushed me aside. "Professional basketball players first."

Still holding the dog and the gun, he rushed to the hole and climbed in, head first. I could have shut the hatch, parked the pickup on top, and walked home. Instead, I followed after Kitch.

When I emerged into the main room, he was pointing his gun at Jabez, who was pointing her bow and arrow at his chest.

The chicken was asleep on Jabez's bed. The dog saw the bird and began barking and thrashing in the grip of Kitch's left hand. The chicken awoke and sprinted into the darkness at the end of the room. Even as her clucking grew faint, the dog continued to bark.

Kitch screamed, "Shut up!" The dog whimpered and became silent. To Jabez, Kitch said, "Lady, put the Indian popper on the floor or I will shoot you. You *could* get silly and try to sink that arrow into my heart, but judging from the way your hands are shaking, you're going to miss and then my sense of self-preservation will force me to shoot you and the dog, kick the shit out of my brother, eat your chicken, and take all your goodies. Bear in mind that I do not wish to commit any of these acts, with the exception of taking your goodies. And I don't want all of them. Just enough."

Jabez pulled the arrow back tighter.

Kitch was a giant. I'd known he was tall, but I'd never appreciated what this meant. His head came close to the top of the cave. The shotgun looked like a toy in his meaty hand. His shoes, his teeth, his moustache, the beads of sweat on his shoulders. Every bit of him was half again larger than necessary.

Puny Jabez stared up at him, pointing her wavering arrow.

I stepped between them. "Put it down, Jabez. Put your gun away, Kitch. You know what you want. Get it and leave."

I tried to look apologetic to Jabez.

She said to me, "This is because I killed your horse."

"No. It's because I did cocaine."

Kitch thought that was the absolute brand-new funniest thing anyone had ever said.

Without taking her eyes off Kitch, Jabez hung the bow on the wall and then scooped some milk into a bowl and set it on the floor.

Kitch said, "What's she doing?"

I said, "The dog just spent two hours in the trunk of a car. Can you stop being a prick long enough to let it drink some milk?"

Kitch said, "If you think I'm incapable of affection for my dumb brethren, you are mistaken. I am a rancher, after all."

He kissed the poodle on the head and lowered it to the floor. The dog approached the milk and began lapping.

Kitch said, "So where's this tiger skull I've been hearing so much about?"

Jabez looked at me. "What does he need a tiger skull for?"

Kitch said, "J.R. can apprise you of the details later, certain of which may strain plausibility. The only thing that should matter to you is this. If I don't gain access to your treasures, I lose my testicles."

Jabez showed him her teeth.

Kitch said, "You think I'm an asshole, justifiably so. I'm normally very agreeable, but I have been altered by life and all its glorious temptations." He gazed around the room. "This place is outtasite."

Jabez said, "Go away."

Kitch said, "Not an option. Can I please have your itty bitty saber-tooth tiger skull?"

I said, "Give it to him, Jabez. Technically, it's mine. I found it first."

"See?" said Kitch. "J.R. wants me to have it."

I said, "He'll go away if you give it to him."

"If you don't. . . ." Kitch pointed the shotgun at Jabez, then at me, and then at the dog.

She nodded toward her bed. "It's underneath there. Get it and proceed to your next foolish decision."

Keeping an eye on Jabez, Kitch reached under the bed and pulled forth the skull. He held it aloft, examining its black mass closely in the lantern light.

Kitch said, "That's one big pussy." He dropped it on the mattress and said to Jabez, "You're a nurse." He showed her his cockeyed finger. "How about you fix this?"

Jabez said to me, "He's going to promise he'll leave if I do just this one more thing for him."

"If you straighten up my finger, hell yes. I'll take my skull and venture forth to meet my fate."

I said, "Why don't we all go outside so she can look at your finger in better light?"

Jabez said, "Because he's lying." She grabbed hold of the bad finger. She tugged gently and then gave a quick yank. There was a clicking sound as the joint went back into place. Jabez stepped away. Kitch waggled his fingers and said, "Didn't hurt a bit."

Jabez said, "Now leave."

"Don't I get a tour first? I'm a very curious person. I mean, the things J.R. told me. The place sounds fantastic."

Jabez took a backward step. Her Bowie knife was laying on the shelf behind her. With a quick motion, Kitch darted around and plucked the knife off the shelf. He leaned toward Jabez and held the blade so it reflected the lantern light into her eyes.

Kitch said, "Show me the room with all the bones in it. Johnny said it was a, quote, magical and elegant place, endquote." He looked at me, "You don't remember saying that, do you? I worry about you, Johnny. The way you were putting away the whiskey last night, I think you might have a drinking problem."

I glared at him.

He continued, "And you're so damned moody." He slid the Bowie knife into his shorts right next to Excal. "I have the weapons. We do as I please."

Jabez said, "You bastards."

Kitch rolled his eyes. "You didn't tell me she was one of those man-hating types."

Jabez said, "Let's go." She lifted the lantern from the floor and walked to the dark end of the room. Kitch shooed me to follow. The poodle sat next to the milk bowl and watched.

Jabez led us quickly thru the first vent room and then into the big room.

This was where I'd pissed in a bucket, where I'd talked to animal bones, and where I'd gotten, briefly, sober. Even with my brother there, the place held its dignity.

Kitch took the lantern from Jabez. He limped around the room, muttering expletives of astonishment.

He sniffed the horse jerky hanging from the bear's ribs, he licked a finger and tried to rub paint off the Elk. He reached up and tapped one of its antlers. He stopped at the mammoth with its tusk poking out of the wall. He pressed his cheek against it. "Ivory. What do you think I could get for this thing? Five thousand dollars?"

There was a sound from the other end of the room. Kitch pointed the lantern toward it. Jabez's chicken was walking in circles, still panicked from seeing the dog.

With Kitch watching, I crossed the room, picked up the bird and came back to stand next to Jabez. She petted the chicken's head with a tenderness I'd never seen from her.

Kitch shook his head at us, like we were pathetic. Then he set the lantern on the floor and hooked his arm over the mammoth tusk. He bounced up and down. It started to loosen. Dust slid from the wall.

Jabez walked directly up to Kitch and spit on his chest, right above the curve of his tank top.

Kitch let loose of the tusk. He picked up the lantern and held it up right in front of Jabez's face. "I don't know why my brother likes you. You're not pretty and you're not smart. And you eat horses."

He pressed the gun against her left breast. He pressed hard enough that she backed into the wall, right against the painting of the elk. The barrel made a deep dent in her shirt. Jabez stared up at him.

I said, "Knock it off, Kitch."

"Or?"

I said, "Or I will kill you, you god damned prick."

CHAPTER 59

Kitch looked disappointed. "You're my brother."

"Sometimes brothers kill each other."

Kitch stepped toward me and held the lantern in my face. "It's usually the brother with the gun who does the killing."

I threw the chicken at him. It was not the act of courage I had envisioned. But my brother had a gun and two knives and he was being cruel to Jabez so I threw a chicken at him.

It went as one would expect. The bird careened into his face, flapping madly. Kitch swung at it with the shotgun and knocked it to the ground. Before the bird could gather herself, Kitch pulled Excal out of his shorts and drove the blade into its back. The bird squawked and went still.

Kitch stood up, staggering. Blood was running down his forehead.

Jabez took a step toward him. Her arms were at her sides and she looked calm. I suspected she wasn't.

She took another step. Kitch gave her a quizzical look. She took another step. She was still ten feet away from him.

Kitch said, "The chicken started it." He pressed two fingers against his forehead and showed her the blood.

This was the woman who had slugged my temple when I didn't recognize a mammoth-tooth necklace, who had pinned me to the ground and threatened to roast my balls the first time I met her. She had been to war, she had walked across a hundred barbed wire fences to find this place, she was not going to let Kitch destroy her home.

Kitch scooted back. He had a gun in his hand and a Bowie knife in the elastic of his shorts and he wasn't a bit scared.

He said, "Lady, I will—"

Jabez walked three more steps and stood before him, her face directly in front the numbers on his jersey. Kitch's fingers twitched on the stock of the shotgun.

Jabez made a fist and slowly brought her arm back.

Kitch said, "Careful, now."

Jabez swung hard, right for Kitch's belly.

Even in his bloated, pathetic state, Kitch remained quick. He turned sideways so Jabez's fist glanced his jersey. She had stepped into the punch and her momentum carried her forward. As she went past him, Kitch lifted one of his size-sixteen high-tops and kicked her in the ass.

She skidded belly-first against the floor. Kitch squared his feet and pointed the gun at her. Jabez remained on her stomach, arms splayed, breathing heavy.

Kitch shouted, "I'm the enforcer!" He approached her and kicked her in the ribs so hard her whole body moved. She curled up, wheezing.

I waited. A time would come.

After a moment, Jabez pressed herself up and scooted backward until she came to the wall, against the painted legs of an upright bear. Blood seeped out of her cheek from where it had collided with the floor.

She pointed at Kitch and said in a shallow voice, "You are a stupid boy."

Kitch squatted to speak to her directly. "You should have seen me last night, Bertha. Fifty points. Twelve rebounds. Eighteen thousand people screaming at me. I am an athletic miracle."

He ran to the center of the room and ran laps around the murdered chicken, swinging the lantern, flinging shadows all about. He stumbled and regained himself and stumbled again. Around and around and finally he wound down and came to a stop, chest heaving. "Boy, I'm pooped." He pointed at me. "Be a gentleman. Help her up."

I offered Jabez my hand, she pushed it away. She got up on her own and we stood side by side under the skull of the giant bear.

Kitch set the gun at his feet, then pulled out his cocaine cartridge and tapped the remaining powder onto the mammoth tusk. As he snorted, he seemed to grow more bloated, more shiny, more taut. He put all his weight upon the tusk. He bounced up and down and parts of the wall flaked off.

Excal was just fifteen feet from us, lodged in the back of the dead chicken. Neither Jabez nor myself made a move for it. If she was thinking like me, she was waiting for the animals in the walls to come alive and stomp Kitch to a pulp.

This did not happen.

Kitch bounced on the tusk until, with a frightening *crack*, it split all along its length and clattered to the floor in two perfect pieces.

Surely, Charlie had made it to my house by now. Surely, she was headed north. Surely, the hay in my truck had caught fire, beckoning her.

Kitch wiped his hands on his shorts. "This is going to end happy. I'll bring the tiger skull and the tusk to my guy and he'll let me keep my balls, assuming he realizes just how valuable this stuff is, which he will because he's reasonable. We're in the clear. But first, I wanna see that baby mammoth. J.R. said it was the most sacred thing he'd ever laid eyes on. Show me the mammoth, I skedaddle. Deal? Let's do this. Go Colonels!"

CHAPTER 60

I led us into the crawling tunnel. Jabez followed and Kitch went behind her. The crawl was quiet. The way was dark, but not as difficult as when I'd been here before. I knew where we were going.

In the tunnel, I fell back to October, chasing my horse thru the blizzard, blind, with snow pecking at my eyes. Further back, the feel of arrowheads in my pocket and the thud of a basketball on the ground and the slap of a palm against my face. I remembered our first sip of whiskey, me at fifteen, Kitch at seven, Mom asleep, and Dad off to Strattford.

I held Kitch when he was still birth-wet. His first word was my name, "'Onny." And he stood up and chased wasps and he tore open Christmas presents. He prayed before dinner. He always knew the top forty songs in America, but he couldn't remember who sang my favorite song. He grew and ran fast and leapt over fences and yucca plants and the corpses of cattle. I taught him basketball. When he played well, he was the bird who dragged her wing to distract you from her children. He distracted us from what mattered. And what mattered?

Thanksgiving, hunting pheasants, all in a line. My four-ten fires tight. The pellets wouldn't spread out enough to strike the bird and Dad both. There were two sounds when I pulled the trigger. Two reports. *Ba-boom.* There's no echo on the plains. The second sound came from Kitch's gun.

He shot Dad. I shot the bird. Mom and Dad ran away and fell in love. Kitch got spit shines in bathroom stalls. I only had enough fingers and toes to count to seventeen. Everybody wins but Johnny.

I continued forward, a worm leading worms in a tube painted by babies.

I wondered if Kitch was afraid. Or if he felt anything at all. If he knew what he'd done, what he was doing. Likely not. His watch spring was wound too tight. And he wouldn't allow it to spin-out. Instead, he just kept cranking on it, click by click. Eventually, it'd be too tight to move any more. He was exhausted and, I suspected, growing weak. The time was coming. The first chance I had, I would kill him.

I reached the final, tight collar of the tunnel and I squeezed out into the room. It was dark as anything, no glowing lights this time. I sensed the roundness of the place, the smoothness of the walls. The scent of sage remained. I inhaled deep but the thin air didn't fill my lungs.

Jabez slipped thru after. I heard her sit opposite me. We were on either side of the entrance. I pressed my back against the wall, against the ledge shelf. I found one of the stick figures there and gripped it tightly, wishing it could tell me something useful.

Now came the sound of Kitch. He'd moved more slowly than Jabez and I. The crawl must have been difficult, him being so big. He huffed and puffed and then I heard him right in front of me in the dark. A breath. I felt his face emerge from the hole.

I slugged him just as hard as I could. I'm not a weak man.

It was a direct pop, even in the dark. Right on the temple. I felt Kitch's hair against my knuckles. He gave the grunt of a man struck. The stick figure shattered in my fist.

I reached forward and found Kitch's face. I grabbed him by the hair and lifted his head up. I felt for his mouth, put my ear close, and listened.

Jabez said, "Did you kill him?"

"I don't know. I don't think he's breathing."

"There's only one way to be sure."

I said, "I don't want to be sure. Let's drag him out of the tunnel and leave him here and then get ourselves outside. You got any candles?"

"I left them in the other room."

"I wish we could see."

Jabez said, "Candles would just take up air."

"I could light a match."

"Two seconds, but then you put it out."

I struck a match and held it aloft. Kitch's head was slumped out of the hole. Blood dripped from the chicken wound on his forehead. One arm was dangling. The other arm remained inside the crawling tube. No gun. His mouth hung open. I looked at Jabez. Her face was grim. I shook the match dead.

Jabez said, "Help me pull him out."

Groping in the dark, we grabbed hold of Kitch's free arm. Jabez took the wrist, I held on just below the elbow. She said, "Ready?"

"Ready."

We yanked as hard as we could. He slid forward a few inches and then stopped.

"He's a fucking cork," said Jabez.

"Try again."

Kitch's arm flexed. He spoke. "Try to suck my balls."

I screamed. Jabez screamed. Kitch howled with laughter.

"I learned that from a chick I banged in Indiana. Bio-fucking-feedback is what it's called. You slow your heart to nothing. Or, in the common parlance, you hold your breath. Like you'd know anything about Zen. My melancholy brother and his mole monkey. Is it getting tighter in here? I'm finding it difficult to breathe."

His arm reached for me. His fingers felt my face. I backed away.

I said, "Where's the shotgun?"

Kitch said, "At the moment, it's in my other hand, pointing the wrong way, and rather hard to maneuver. Otherwise, I'd shoot the both of you."

I said, "Jabez, go ahead and hit him if you want."

I heard a hand strike flesh. Kitch cried out.

Jabez said to me, "Your brother smells like a whore."

Kitch shifted around. "This is French cologne, you unbathed toad."

Jabez slapped him again. Kitch cried out again. He shifted some. "Say, assholes. I think I might be stuck."

CHAPTER 61

"I'm serious," said Kitch. "Help."

Jabez slapped him once more. She said, "Apologize."

Kitch said, "My ribs. It's hard to breathe. I think the tunnel is shrinking."

Then Jabez slapped me. "*You* apologize, for telling him about this place."

I said, "I'm sorry as hell, Jabez."

"And for getting my chicken killed."

"I'm sorry."

"You're a prick."

"Yes, I am."

"Good. Now help me tug your brother out of that hole."

We pulled Kitch's arm until he screamed. Then we pushed on the flesh on his shoulders. He didn't budge, forward or backward.

Jabez said, "Everyone stop moving. We're breathing too much. Johnny Riles, do you have a pocket knife?"

Kitch said, "What do you want a knife for?" He was worried.

Jabez said, "So we can slit your throat and then, after you've died, cut you apart and take you out one piece at a time."

Kitch said, "One piece at a time. Johnny Cash. Good song. Please don't do that."

I said, "I only have one knife, Jabez, and it's stuck in the back of your chicken."

"Then," said Jabez, "we are going to die."

Kitch said, "I won't lie. This situation frightens me."

Jabez slapped him again, but I could tell from the sound that her heart was no longer in it. And that upset me. We were trapped in an unventilated hole by my idiot brother's giant, bloated ass. Fine. We were going to die. Fine. I wasn't going to get to screw Charlie on New Year's Day, 1976. Damned disappointing and yet, due to the fact that I was accustomed to not screwing Charlie, fine.

But for my brother to take the heart from Jabez, who had been treated so bad and survived so much and who had earned the right to live unmolested in this wonderful place, that was very god damned not fine. In fact, it was complete horseshit.

I said, "Kitch, you are an asshole. You stumble along, being cute, tossing a ball thru a hoop. You charm people until they let you dance on their bellies. You get everything. And all because you grew thirteen inches taller than me. That's all you have, Kitch. Thirteen inches. And what'd that get you? You climbed into a hole that didn't fit and now you don't know what to do because you've never had to work or think or struggle for anything, ever. Your whole life has been a stupid, lucky waste of spit. This pain you feel, you deserve every bit of it. Me and you both. We both deserve this. We're both idiots. Me for leading you here, you for dragging us here. But Jabez is an innocent woman and you are killing her. You greedy, stupid bastard. Apologize to her right now."

Jabez said, "He needn't apologize to me."

I said, "Shut up. You're the most courageous person I've ever known. You've survived in ways I couldn't imagine. You've helped me out in ways I can't explain. I think you're wonderful. And Kitch, you've been a complete, insane prick to her. Apologize."

In a childish voice, Kitch said, "There ain't some other way out of here?"

Jabez said, "Nope."

Kitch said, "Somebody should have told me how small this tunnel was."

I grabbed his ear and twisted it. "Say you're sorry."

"Lemme alone!"

Jabez shouted, "Stop acting like children!"

Silence. I had to breathe twice to fill one lung.

I said, "I'll say it, then. I'm sorry, Jabez. You helped me get better. Not just the drinking, but everything. You saved me, I think, from killing myself. And then I opened my mouth and killed all of us."

Jabez said, "You've already apologized. Now you're just wasting air."

Kitch said, "Yeah. Stop wasting air."

I said, "You shot Dad, Kitch. I know it. You're a coward. You let me take the blame. You let me live all this time thinking I'd done it. I should have figured it out before, but I couldn't. I wanted you to be good, I guess. But you aren't good. You gave me up. And as much a coward as you are, I'm twice the fool. Drinking myself stupid, paying your goons, using your drugs, blabbing to you about this place. I brought you here, Kitch, and you've clogged the tunnel and the woman who saved my life is going to die because you're a pathetic, lazy, stupid, fat, pig's pecker of a man. And if the next words out of your mouth aren't, 'Please forgive me,' I will grab your head and twist it until it pops off your neck."

Kitch said, "You don't know for a fact that I shot him."

I said, "Of course you did, dummy. I got the bird. You got Dad."

"The bird came up out of the grass. We fired at the same time. One of us got the bird, the other of us got Dad. Ain't no telling who got what."

It was a valid point, but I clung to the law. I said, "The bird was in my zone. You had no business firing your gun. You stupid fuck. And don't tell me, 'Everything worked out in the end.' This is the end. How are things working out? You lucky prick. You're the only one Dad never bothered to hit. Because what would be the fucking point in hitting someone like you?"

I expected him to say something smart. Instead, he began to sob. Tears plopped onto the floor. Kitch was not the kind of person who could pretend to cry. The sound of his sadness shocked me and I treasured it. I was winning.

Kitch continued to weep as we sat in the dark. Three people mulling the prospect of death.

Kitch swallowed hard and said, "I'd like to see it. Can I see the baby mammoth? Just for a moment? Gimme some light, Johnny."

Jabez said, "Let him see it."

I struck a match, then I gathered the broken pieces of the stick figure. I set them on the floor and lit them into tiny shivering flames. The room filled with a scent of long-dead wood. I watched Kitch's beat-up face. His gaze lingered at one spot, at the altar, at the mammoth. Bloody snot dangled from his nose.

He said, "It's looking at me."

I said, "It's dead."

"You can hear it."

"I can't hear anything, Kitch."

He said, "We'll be okay. They're coming for us."

I looked at Jabez. She shook her head.

Kitch said, "It's touching me with its nose. It smells like milk."

The mammoth lay dead on the altar.

The dry sticks burned quickly. The last flame flickered and vanished and the room went dark.

Kitch screamed. In a voice high and hoarse he shouted, "Jesus God fuck all! It's got me!"

There was a gun shot, muffled, but violent. Kitch howled once and then commenced to sobbing. On the other side of his body, we heard a barking. *Yip, yip, yip.*

I said, "What just happened?"

He didn't answer.

Jabez said, "I'll tell you what happened. Your poodle came looking for us. And she took a bite out of your brother. Because he's pathetic. And then your brother pulled the trigger on that gun of his and put a load of shot into his own leg. Because he's a fool. Ain't that right?"

Kitch said, "It hurts so bad. Oh, Christ. This place is crushing me."

I struck two matches at once. Across the flame, Kitch looked at me with his good eye, his mouth roiling in pain. I'd never thought a person could be so miserable. I suddenly felt as sorry for him as I'd ever felt for anyone. I wasn't winning anymore.

I set another of the stick figures afire. Long-term survival was no longer a concern.

Kitch panicked now. He wiggled his body, pounded his free hand against the wall of the cave, did everything he could to climb out of the hole. For a long moment, he wheezed, grunted, thrashed, grimaced. His effort was remarkable and utterly unsuccessful.

Then, exhausted, he went limp. Eyes closed, he wept in a private contemplation of death.

Jabez and I watched, wishing. I placed another of the stick figures on the fire.

Kitch opened his eyes, ringed with blood.

He said, "Tell Mom." His lips twitched and I saw that one of his eye teeth was missing. His voice was faint. "Tell Mom."

I leaned close.

He said, "Tell her I scored fifty points."

He slammed his head up and into the ceiling of the cave. He banged it again and again and again. Blood matted his hair and dripped down his cheeks.

He kept banging, harder and harder, longer than I thought possible.

Jabez reached over patted down the fire until the room went dark again. The thumping continued. The smell of Kitch's cologne mixed with the smell of his blood and the burned wood. It couldn't go on like this.

CHAPTER 62

Eventually, all that remained was the sound of drip, drips and the faint barking of the dog on the other side of Kitch's body.

Jabez scooted over and hugged me.

I curled into her arms. She rubbed my back and my ears. I said, "My head's going light."

"It won't hurt, Johnny."

"Charlie's coming for us. I told her to come north. I tossed out cigarettes on the way over here. They'll make fires, as long as the weather's not too bad. No matter what, the hay bales in the pickup should be burning. I pitched a cigarette right where it'd be safe from the snow. Charlie will follow the smoke and come down here and she'll bring Emmett and Chester. The dog will lead them to us. Emmett's a genius. They'll rescue us and we'll go back to the ranch and feed the cattle and ride the horse."

Jabez patted my head. "Yes."

"We'll be okay?"

"We're going to fall asleep soon."

She put her hand in my shirt and rubbed my heart. I kissed her neck. She kissed my mouth. I touched her back and the upside-down heart of her bottom. My fingers squeezed her flesh. She removed my shirt. I removed her shirt. Soon, we had removed our garments. We gripped each other tightly. She showed me where to put my hands.

After all, after all this. I won't say it was worth it, but it was far from not.

Acknowledgements

Maureen, as always, for reading early drafts and insisting that this was worth finishing. Early readers: Brett Duesing, Eric Allen, Marrion Irons, Paul Handley, Tony Parella, Lucas Richards, Erin Harper, Steve DeJong, Dale Oliver, and my mom, Judy Hill. I'm sure I forgot some folks. I'll get you next time.

More thanks: Tim Sears, this thing started several years ago when you told me the story of your horse that got spooked by the cow skull; Tom Hearty, you taught me all about frostbite and pinkies and toes; Brennan Peterson, you may not remember suggesting I set my Strattford books in progressively earlier times, but you did, and I liked the idea; Matt Shupe, for the artwork; Lisa and the rest of the gang at Leapfrog Press for being humans of extraordinary humanity; Mike Lindstrom for the hand-built guitars, upon which I strummed America songs whenever I needed a look into Johnny's cranium; Bruno the dog, for being small; everyone back home for putting up with all this; and huzzahs to the Hills and Williams and Heartys for your constant encouragement.

I'm incredibly grateful to the Boulder County Artist in Residence Program, where I was afforded the perfect setting to complete a large portion of this book.

There are three new bands to acknowledge: The Spider Kings (may they rest in peace), The Super Phoenixes (may they rise in glory), and The Tiger Beats (may they annoy everybody). And the Stables Boys are right on the horizon.

About the Author

Gregory Hill lives, writes, and makes odd music on the Colorado High Plains. His previous book, *East of Denver*, won the 2013 Colorado Book Award for Literary Fiction.

Visit his web site at www.gregoryhillauthor.com

Visit Leapfrog Press at:

www.leapfrogpress.com

and on Facebook at

https://www.facebook.com/pages/Leap-
frog-Press/222784181103418

and the author at

www.gregoryhillauthor.com

About the Type

This book was set in ITC New Baskerville, a typeface based on the types of John Baskerville (1706-1775), an accomplished writing master and printer from Birmingham, England. He was the designer of several types, punchcut by John Handy, which are the basis for the fonts that bear the name Baskerville today. The excellent quality of his printing influenced such famous printers as Didot in France and Bodoni in Italy. His fellow Englishmen imitated his types, and in 1768, Isaac Moore punchcut a version of Baskerville's letterforms for the Fry Foundry. Baskerville produced a masterpiece folio Bible for Cambridge University, and today, his types are considered to be fine representations of eighteenth century rationalism and neoclassicism. This ITC New Baskerville was designed by Matthew Carter and John Quaranda in 1978.

Composed at JTC Imagineering, Santa Maria, CA
Designed by John Taylor-Convery